THE WOMAN WHO RAN AWAY
FROM EVERYTHING

Fiona was born in a youth hotel in Yorkshire. She started working on teen magazine *Jackie* at age seventeen, then went on to join *Just Seventeen* and *more!* Fiona has three grown-up children, writes for many newspapers and magazines and lives in Glasgow with her husband Jimmy.

For more info visit www.fionagibson.com. You can follow Fiona on Instagram @fiona_gib.

FIONA GIBSON

The
WOMAN
WHO RAN AWAY
From
EVERYTHING

avon.

Published by AVON
A division of HarperCollins*Publishers*
1 London Bridge Street
London SE1 9GF

www.harpercollins.co.uk

HarperCollins*Publishers*
Macken House 39/40 Mayor Street Upper
Dublin 1 D01 C9W8

A Paperback Original 2024

3

First published in Great Britain by HarperCollins*Publishers* 2024

A catalogue copy of this book is available from the British Library.

ISBN: 978-0-00-849444-5

Set in Sabon LT Std by HarperCollins*Publishers* India

Printed and bound in UK using 100% Renewable Electricity
by CPI Group (UK) Ltd

For Helen Fisher, with love

PROLOGUE

Kate

Before I realise what's happening I've hoisted myself up onto the bathroom windowsill.

The window is already open. Gratefully, I take in a huge breath of damp evening air. The windowsill is an especially wide and sturdy one. But it's still quite a manoeuvre to push my straight navy-blue work skirt up over my ample hips without toppling off. Now my knickers – the ones my husband refers to as 'those massive drawers' – are visible through my sheer tights. I couldn't care less. The bathroom door is locked and there's no one in here but me. Slowly and steadily, I feed a leg through the open window.

Briefly, I glance down at my white blouse, the kind my boss at the hotel insists on as part of our uniform, and wonder what she'd think if she could see me now. If she'd reckon I'm 'projecting professionalism' as I find myself stuck with one leg in and the other dangling outside. The 'window straddle', I think you'd call it in yoga – attempted only by the drunk or insane.

Pull yourself back in before you rupture something you idiot! I tell myself.

Right leg in, or left leg out to join it? I picture me and George, my little brother, doing the hokey-cokey around our living room back in Glasgow, singing and laughing then stopping abruptly when the front door flew open, signifying that Daddy was home.

The dancing stopped then. We scurried, quietly, to our rooms.

Now I glance back, my gaze skimming our bathroom fittings. The bath, washbasin and loo are the precise, lurid shade of a blackcurrant Starburst sweet. 'How about we change them?' I suggested recently. 'The colour's getting to me a bit.'

'They're kitsch,' Vince insisted. 'I love them.'

My mother does too. She loves everything here – my husband especially. 'Oh, you're so lucky to have a man like Vince,' she's gushed more times than I can count. 'You really landed on your feet there, Kate!'

My name is Kate Weaver, and I'm forty-nine years old and not so sure that I have. Yes, I've landed *here*, in this quiet cul-de-sac – by default. But it feels like I am flailing in space. Which I am, kind of. At least, flailing on a windowsill in a 1960s bungalow. I look out at our garden and all the other, virtually identical bungalows surrounding us in the fading evening light.

The final straw, they call it. The thing that made

her snap. And suddenly, this leg in/leg out dilemma feels enormous, and it's crucial that I make the right choice.

It feels like the most important decision of my life.

CHAPTER ONE

Two days earlier

Being married to a comedian is no joke.

You might think it would be. Maybe you imagine life being hilarious all the time. Undoubtably, Vince's material *is* funny – but living with him is not. If our marriage were a comedy show I'd regret even buying a ticket.

If that sounds harsh, here's what happens as I lift a tray of gnarly brown lumps from the fridge.

'What the hell are they?' he asks in surprise.

'Easter nests,' I reply.

'But it's not Easter, is it? Unless they've shifted things around this year? It does get me,' he rattles on, smirking, 'that Easter's this moveable feast. Imagine if Christmas was like that. How would turkey farmers manage it? You'd have fattened birds in February—'

'Vince,' I cut in. 'I do know it's not Easter, okay? So I'm renaming them Chocolate Clusters.'

'Genius,' he enthuses. 'Because they don't look like nests. More like the deposits of a medium-sized dog with digestive issues—'

'Yes, *okay*. Thank you.' He's right, though. I'd chosen to make them because they didn't need any cooking. (They're just melted chocolate, butter and bashed-up Shredded Wheat.) But I didn't have the chance to buy any mini eggs to fill them with, and they look pretty gross.

Vince pats my shoulder. 'Never mind, Kate. People will buy any old crap at a bake sale just to shut up their kids.'

'Thanks!' I exclaim. 'That's *really* supportive . . .'

'Aw, stop making a fuss. It's not a competition, is it? It's the taking part that counts . . .' What does Vince know about these fundraising events? He's never 'taken part' in one in his life.

'I just don't want to let them down,' I mutter. In fact it's not simply a matter of producing something that people will pay good money for. It's also about fitting in. I've been to every drinks do and coffee morning going since we left London nine months ago. Now it seems I'm trying to woo myself some new friends with offerings that could have been made by an unsupervised five-year-old.

'What are you doing for the bake sale?' For weeks now the question has reverberated around this genteel Buckinghamshire town. It's a well-established feature of Shugbury's book festival, and initially – thinking it would get me off the hook – I volunteered to be a general helper. But one bright afternoon, when my guard was down: 'You'll be able to knock up something, won't you, Kate?' Chief organiser Deborah swooped on me in the street.

'Yes, of course,' I replied cheerfully. Naturally, being a man, Vince wasn't expected to involve himself with it.

My friends back in London would think I'm crazy, worrying about my substandard nests. 'Just buy something on the way there!' Tash would say with a honking laugh. She wouldn't understand that that simply isn't the done thing. So, with Vince still chuckling and making disparaging remarks, I set off with my Tupperware box.

*

At least I'm contributing, I tell myself as I arrive at the park on this bright June morning. Shugbury's book festival is the highlight of the year around here. In the distance, next to the face-painting stall, the bake sale table shimmers like a terrible mirage.

Closer now, I can see that it's *not* the taking part that matters. And it most definitely *is* a competition. For here we have:

Exhibit A. Deborah Spragg's red velvet cake. Triple layered and topped with creamy swirls, it rightfully commands centre stage.

Exhibit B. Agata Kemp's pastel-hued macarons. So pretty are they, they could have come from a fancy

French patisserie. Whereas my shabby offerings appear to have tumbled from the bowels of the unwell.

Tightening my grip on my box, I start to sweat. I can't do this. I can't foist them on our town's well-heeled inhabitants. No one will thank me or even think, *At least she brought something.*

It would be like trying to offload your rank old knickers at a charity shop. 'I'm not sure we can sell these, thank you.' Meaning: *Please take them away.*

I eye the towering cake, the beautiful macarons, the plumptious muffins and perfect custard tarts. The bake sale raises funds for the festival. But more importantly it's a test of one's domestic talents – because here in Shugbury it's forever 1957.

Thankfully, the stall is being manned by a woman I don't recognise, and so far no one I know has spotted me. At least, I hope they haven't. Feigning casualness, I glide away.

Vince would love the fact that I'm too ashamed to hand over my contributions. Luckily – albeit not surprisingly – he has yet to show up. He'll probably be lying on the sofa, being pestered by Jarvis for a walk. That's Jarvis as in Cocker – as in spaniel – who belongs to Edie, my stepdaughter. We're looking after him while she works in the States.

In a quiet corner of the park, I peel the lid off my box, take one last look at my misshapen creations and wonder what to do next. At just gone nine-thirty people are arriving already, checking out the stalls and chatting in groups. A marquee has been erected for the weekend of author events. Vince's was the first to sell out (as well as working the stand-up comedy circuit he has also written a book of humorous observations on everyday life). So we have that to come later. But first, what to do with my offerings? As I came here on foot, without a bag or anything to hide them in, my only option is to bin them – Tupperware and all. Then I can get on with my duties as general helper and think no more about it.

Spotting a litter bin by the park's entrance I head, missile-like, towards it. My plan is to casually sling my box into it as I stride past – like a thief disposing of a stolen handbag. I quicken my pace, focusing hard on the solid metallic receptacle that'll save me from mockery from the likes of Deborah and Agata – those properly functioning kitchen doyennes with their piping bags and silicone moulds in every conceivable shape.

Deborah lives at the end of our road and pops out, like a cuckoo, whenever she spots Vince strolling by. I once made the mistake of calling her Debbie and was sharply corrected. Here she comes now, an Amazonian six-footer in a billowing maxi dress, waving as she sweeps towards me. I march onwards, my gaze fixed determinedly ahead.

'Kate,' she calls out. 'Hey, Kate!'

Keep walking. Pretend you haven't heard and for God's sake don't look back—

'KATE! HEY! WAIT!'

I stop and turn, feigning surprise. 'Deborah, hi!'

'*You* seem in a hurry,' she remarks with a frown. Her coppery hair shimmers in the sunshine and her puff-sleeved dress is the precise green of a well-fed lawn.

'Just nipping to the shop,' I fib.

Her expression softens. 'Doesn't everything look *great*? And aren't we lucky with this weather?'

'We are, yes!'

She beams, exposing sturdy white teeth that could crack through a roof tile. 'Can't wait for Vince's event,' she enthuses. 'It'll be the highlight of the festival. Oh, is that something for the bake sale?' Her gaze drops to the box in my clammy grip.

'It's nothing,' I say quickly. 'I was just going to—'

'Let's have it then.'

I wince and step away. 'It just looked like there was so much stuff on the stall already . . .' Stuff? Deborah's red velvet creation isn't 'stuff'.

'The more the merrier,' she insists, going to grab at the box which causes me, instinctively, to tighten my grip. But Deborah is a mighty woman with a will of steel, and she wrangles the thing off me in a move so sudden and violent, the ill-fitting lid springs off (we have something like 625 Tupperware boxes yet not one possesses a properly fitting lid) and the sorry contents spill out onto the ground.

'I'm so sorry,' she exclaims.

'It doesn't matter. It's absolutely fine,' I insist. 'They didn't actually turn out too well . . .'

She grimaces and peers down. 'What *are* they?'

'Um, nests. I mean clusters. Chocolate clusters . . .'

'Oh.' Her sleeves, which until a second ago were as puffed up as airbags, seem to have deflated a little. Then someone calls her name and she brightens. 'Scuse me, Kate. I think I'm needed,' she announces, and swishes away across the park.

I turn back, about to gather up the sorry items so I can bin them and pretend this never happened. But already a terse-looking woman has grabbed the hand of a little boy.

'Don't stand in that, Casper,' she barks at him. Then, seemingly to no one in particular: 'On festival day too, with *children* here. How hard is it to pick up after your dog?'

CHAPTER TWO

It wasn't always like this with Vince and me. We met when I'd just turned twenty-four and I fell completely head-over-heels in love.

Tash and I had gone along to an open mic comedy night. We'd endured a succession of braying male comedians all projecting rock-solid self-belief. It was like being shouted at by one man after another, and we were on the verge of going home when this skinny guy with a shock of dark reddish hair shambled onto the stage. Immediately I knew he was different. In black corduroys and a maroon crew-necked sweater, he looked like a probationary geography teacher.

If he had been a teacher, his class would have sensed weakness in him and made his lesson hell. And indeed, the audience soon identified his nervousness.

'Get off, mate!' someone yelled.

Vince struggled on gamely. However, I caught the haunted look in his eyes that reminded me of my little brother, when he'd come home from school at twelve years old with a bruised face and his smart leather music case gone. A bunch of boys had attacked him, stolen his case and burned his piano music with a cigarette lighter.

I'd never been so angry in my life.

And now, in this scruffy basement club, I wondered if this Vince Weaver who was up there, dying on stage, had been bullied as a kid. Because there was definitely a vulnerability there – even though his material was original and very funny. And I wondered, is that why he's doing this? As a way of telling his bullies to fuck off?

'Enough, mate! You're shit!' yelled the man next to us.

Incensed, I swung around and snapped, 'Would you shut the hell up?'

'What's it to you?' he shot back.

'You're being a jerk, all right? That's what it is to me. Give the guy a break.' I turned back to the stage and caught the comedian's eye.

For a moment, he held on to my gaze like a lifeline as I tried to project a message: *You're good. You can do this. Ignore the twats.* He had lovely eyes, I noticed: deep brown, kind of intense. And a great smile too, because now he *was* smiling, and as he carried on with his act he seemed to grow in stature and belief in himself. The heckling had stopped and he was owning it, as people say now. But a quarter of a century ago it was just, 'He's actually pretty good! Don't you think?' That was from the girlfriend of the heckling guy. She caught my eye and smiled.

After the gig, Vince found Tash and me by the bar,

12

and insisted on buying us drinks – not to be flash but because he wanted to thank us, he said.

He didn't say what for. But I knew.

*

We met again the next night, and the one after that. Just the two of us, obviously. No Tash. At twenty-nine Vince was five years older than me, and I liked that, after dating guys my own age. He just seemed a bit more worldly, and on our third date he told me that he was the father of a little girl. 'That's amazing!' I said. 'Why didn't you say before?'

'Didn't want to put you off,' he replied with a shrug.

'It wouldn't have put me off,' I told him. 'Now I know you must have a responsible side buried somewhere in there too.' I grinned at him and he laughed.

'Don't know about that.'

It was true, though. I was thrilled by this new information because I loved babies and kids. As soon as I'd been old enough I'd been expected to play a part in taking care of George, because Mum worked all hours and simply couldn't do it all herself. I was delighted to meet my new boyfriend's daughter, and hoped I'd be able to get to know her – because I was crazy about Vince. He was such fun, and so handsome with those conker-brown eyes that hinted at adventure and naughtiness.

After we'd been together for a few months he'd kind of grown into himself, and his confidence had blossomed. I loved being with him, kissing him deeply as we wrapped ourselves around each other. He made me feel *complete*. And gradually I got to know his daughter, Edie – an adorable toddler who saw her dad on the weekends. The rest of the time she lived with her mum, Roxanne, a former model and still a dedicated party girl, by all accounts.

A year after we'd met, Vince decided that Edie would have a more stable life with us, just for the time being. Roxanne didn't put up any resistance, and for Edie, moving from her mum's ramshackle farm in Kent to a flat in London seemed like a wonderful adventure.

Did I mind? I absolutely didn't because Edie was an adorable girl who needed to feel settled and safe, just as I had. The fact that Vince cared so deeply about her made me love him even more.

Of course, 'just for the time being' turned out to be a permanent arrangement as Edie started nursery, and made friends, and we found a fantastic childminder (actually, *I* found Fatima) and we became a proper little family. Vince was gigging as much as he could, as well as doing shifts in our local pub. My clerical work was hardly scintillating but it paid reasonably well and we managed to get by. We moved to a bigger flat, and Edie started school and had her dance classes and drama club and Brownies. I took her to all of those and got to know the other mums, even though they were all so much older than me.

My friends had stopped saying, 'You're so young to be a stepmum!' because they could see how happy the three of us were. Vince was nudging his way up on the comedy circuit, and I'd accepted my lot as an office worker – until fate led me in a new direction.

As Vince was often away doing gigs, Edie and I would head to our local museum where there were activities for parents and kids. We did brass rubbings and made Viking hats with papier-mâché horns, becoming such regulars that we got to know the staff. I was tipped off about a job vacancy on the front desk. After landing that, I worked my way up to be an assistant curator – 'asscure' as Vince delighted in calling it – of the childhood section: the historical toys, doll's houses and the like.

'She's a world expert on skipping ropes,' Vince would announce at parties.

I didn't mind the teasing because I loved my work, and I was proud of getting where I was, without a degree or any training apart from what I'd learnt on the job. I really believed I had a charmed life.

When Vince proposed I was over the moon. We crammed a community hall with our friends and families, and I couldn't help noticing how queasy his parents looked, and that they made no attempt to hide it. I just wasn't posh enough for them. However, my mum glowed with pride. 'You're *such* a lucky girl,' she kept telling me.

I was delighted that he'd charmed her, saying things like, 'Honestly, Joyce, you and Kate could pass for sisters!' She'd blush and giggle. (I hadn't even known Mum was capable of giggling until then.) Meanwhile his parents had left our wedding reception early, seemingly 'in a hurry to get back'.

'D'you think you'll ever want to move back to Shugbury?' I asked him on our Cornish honeymoon. Really, I wanted reassurance that nothing would change now we were married.

'God, no,' he exclaimed. 'I'd rather die.'

'Why?' I asked, relieved.

''Cause it's full of posh wankers,' he said.

It wasn't that he'd lied. But people change, I discovered. As the years roll by, they change more than you could have ever imagined.

Or maybe they weren't who you thought they were after all.

We became more distant from one another. When he wasn't away gigging, Vince would be installed at his desk, working on material, locked in a world of his own. He was still a good dad, in that he celebrated Edie's every achievement and was always affectionate and sweet with her. I mean, he loves her. That's never been in doubt. However, he became less inclined to involve himself in the practicalities of our lives. If I felt put upon and resentful sometimes, I reckoned that was just part of being together when the sparkle had dimmed.

Meanwhile Edie grew up, went off to Manchester University and returned to live with friends in Brixton. She'd landed a job doing social media for an animal charity, and announced that she had adopted Jarvis, a nervous spaniel, when it hadn't worked out with his adoptive family. A dog in a young people's house share? I wasn't sure it was the best idea but she insisted it would be fine. She'd always loved animals and nature. Her favourite part of the museum had been the natural history section. Then last year she announced that she'd been offered a paid internship at a marine research centre on the north-east coast of the United Sates, and would be living in Maine for six months. We hadn't even known she'd applied.

She was thrilled and we were delighted for her, although we missed her terribly. Meanwhile, as Edie's young life was opening up in thrilling ways, mine had hit a kind of dead end. I still loved my job and my colleagues; they weren't the problem. The issue was at home. With Edie gone, there was no diluting of the Vince effect. It was just me and him and the glaring fact that he now did virtually nothing around the flat.

Working full-time, I'd come home to plunge into cooking, cleaning and picking things up off the floor. I wasn't a pushover. I'd try to discuss it and reason with him, and sometimes I'd boil over with rage.

How had this happened? I'd been brought up by a single mum who'd had the guts to leave a violent man, and tolerated no crap from anyone. Something had to change, I decided – or I'd combust. And then it did. And after decades of slogging away in crummy clubs, being heckled and pelted with boiled sweets on occasion, my husband's fortune changed.

Just shy of his fiftieth birthday, Vince became famous.

CHAPTER THREE

Being Shugbury Book Festival's main attraction, Vince's author talk is the last event of the day. The marquee is packed, the audience poised in rapt attention. While he's up there on stage, being interviewed by Deborah, I man the book stand, ready to take care of sales.

'I know you were amazingly successful before,' she gushes, 'but things really took off for you with the Scotland series, didn't they?'

'Well, kind of.' Vince smiles self-deprecatingly. 'It was an amazing experience, facing the elements with the guys. I'd always fancied doing something like that.'

Hmm, that's not *quite* the true picture. Along with a bunch of fellow jobbing comedians, Vince had been invited to take part in a week-long Highland hike.

'Fuck, no,' he said initially, even though it would be filmed for TV. Scotland was freezing, he moaned to me. 'And they want us to stay in these little shepherds' huts. They don't have any heating! Or places to plug things in! I'll be found frozen to death, savaged by – what do they have up there?'

Mainly rabbits, deer and squirrels, I told him. (Having spent my early childhood in Glasgow, I'd been taken by Mum on several camping trips to the wilds of Perthshire.) And what would he need to plug in? Hair straighteners? 'A phone charger might come in handy,' he muttered.

Vince grudgingly agreed to take part, and the show turned out to be a surprise hit.

'Did your life change after that?' Deborah asks now.

'Not at all,' Vince says firmly. 'For me, everything revolves around my family. And no way would they let me get above myself . . .' They both chuckle, while I wonder if I've heard correctly.

'So you're very much hands on?' she prompts him.

'God, yeah. Ask my wife . . .' There's a collective ripple of laughter and a few people glance round and beam at me, unaware of how things really panned out after the show. There were more TV appearances and gigs in bigger, grander venues. Vince's 'thing' on the Scottish trek had been his endearing inability to read a map, light a fire or in fact do anything useful at all. Pretty soon he'd gained a publishing deal and dashed out a book about the things he can't do that men are supposed to excel at. Stuff like changing a tyre, using power tools without suffering personal injury, and investigating scary noises in the night. 'Being crap at manly stuff' had become Vince's brand. Not only that, but as something of a celebrity now, he was not only avoiding *all* domestic

19

matters at home – but also expecting me to wait on him, like a maid.

'When's dinner happening?' he'd shout from Edie's old room in our London flat, which we'd turned into his study.

'I'm just in from work,' I'd call back. 'I don't know what it's going to be, let alone when it's *happening*.' Did he expect me to pull a perfectly roasted chicken from inside my coat? Very occasionally he'd put a wash on – but if I didn't unload it the damp laundry would've been left in there for eternity, reeking of rotten cabbages.

'And now, luckily for us, you've moved back to Shugbury where you grew up,' Deborah enthuses.

'Yeah.' He grins. 'It seemed like the right thing to leave London when we did. And we love it here. The peace, the beauty, the *people* of course . . .' She simpers and touches his knee, and again several people look round at me, unaware of how Vince had once described Shugbury's residents.

As an only child, he knew he'd inherit the house when first his dad, then his mum passed away a couple of years ago. But I'd assumed he'd sell it or let it out. I still loved London, where my beloved museum job, my mum and brother and all my friends were. Our flat was rented but our landlord had barely raised the rent in fifteen years. However, Vince had decided that we should move to his parents' place – that we'd be 'crazy not to'.

Hang on! Hold those horses! Hadn't he said he'd never move back?

'It'll be a fresh start for us,' he insisted when I voiced my objections. 'We'll have a home that's properly ours, with a garden.'

What did he want a garden for? Vince wouldn't know a hoe if it smacked him on the forehead. I suggested that, if he wanted to buy a place, then we could think about that – IN LONDON. We certainly weren't rich, but thanks to his book deal there would have been enough for a deposit. 'But you're sick of London,' he retorted.

'When have I ever said that?' I asked, genuinely baffled.

'Just the other day. You were complaining about that mattress in the road . . .'

'That doesn't mean I want to leave my job,' I protested, 'and all my friends and family—'

'You took a photo of it and sent it to me.'

As we argued I could sense the ground shifting beneath my feet. It wasn't the comforting rumble from the Central Line. It was more ominous than that. 'Only to be funny,' I muttered. 'Only because they'd left a dirty sheet on it.'

'Well, think how nice it'll be, being able to go for country walks and never see anything disgusting,' he retorted.

'When have *you* ever enjoyed walking?' I asked, reminding him of the fuss he'd made about 'traversing a mountain range on foot', as he'd put it – when the Scotland trek had been carefully plotted to avoid the tiniest hill. He wouldn't even walk his daughter's dog.

I felt trapped. Next thing he'd told Gareth, our kindly old hippie of a landlord, that we were giving notice on our tenancy. I knew then that I couldn't win. At least, not without Vince and me breaking up, and what kind of 'win' would that be?

However bad things were, I still loved Vince and didn't want us to split up. I was also worried about his mental health. He was bereaved – of course I sympathised – and now he yearned to return to his 'roots', as he put it.

So I gave my notice at the museum where I'd worked, happily, for nearly twenty years. Vince had often teased me that I'd become one of the exhibits and should have a label attached to my chest: *Kate. Homo sapiens, female, Gen X era. Stepmother. Wife.*

Was that it? I couldn't help thinking. The whole of me could be summed up on a tiny printed card?

The day was wet and grey as Vince and I drove away from our Bethnal Green flat for the very last time. A silence hovered between us and I realised my hands were bunched into fists. 'You said it was all posh wankers in Shugbury,' I reminded him.

He frowned, looking shocked. 'No, I didn't. I never said that. Some of them are *really nice*.'

Now, as Deborah winds up the interview and the audience erupts into applause, I remind myself that I agreed to move here for the sake of our marriage. Yes, Vince was persuasive, but he didn't force me. He didn't drag me into the car and bind me with gaffer tape to the seat. So I'm going to make the very best of it, I decide,

22

fixing on a bright smile as Vince joins me at the table and starts to sign copies of his new book.

He's so good at this, I reflect as, swamped with fans, he jokes and laughs with each person in turn as I deal with the sales. If he's pretty well known nationally, here in Shugbury he is something of a local hero.

Once the books are all sold, Deborah, Vince and I make our way out to the baking stall. She has organised for another batch of goodies to arrive first thing tomorrow, for the second and final day of the festival.

'You were so great today, Vince,' she enthuses, biting into the last remaining custard tart.

'No, *you* were great, organising it all,' he says.

She shrugs in an it-was-nothing kind of way, and turns to me. 'I hate to laugh, Kate, but that *was* pretty funny about someone bagging up your chocolate thingies as if they were poos . . .'

'Oh, yes.' My laughter spills out in jagged shards. 'You heard about that, did you?'

'Yes, Agata saw you on your hands and knees, gathering them up . . .' Agata of the perfect macarons, she means. 'But we shouldn't go on about it, should we?' She cracks a sly grin at Vince. 'At least you brought *something* . . .'

Vince smirks, perching on the sole chair at the stall. 'Baking isn't exactly in your skill set. Is it, darling?'

'Apparently not,' I reply.

'But she has her talents,' he adds, clearly unaware that I'm having to restrain myself from wrestling him

23

to the ground.

'I'm sure she does.' Deborah beams at me. 'Kate, would you mind checking the state of the Portaloos?'

I suspect I'm being exiled, leaving the coast clear for her to fawn some more over my husband. Perhaps she'll hoick up her maxi dress and straddle him on that plastic chair. She can do what she wants, I decide furiously as I stomp away.

In a Portaloo I snap on disposable blue rubber gloves and violently squirt the loo seat with powerful disinfectant. Tomorrow Vince will be back here to do a second event (such was the demand for tickets, he agreed to a repeat performance). Meanwhile I'll be safely occupied at the far end of town, on reception at Shugbury Spa Hotel. I don't normally do weekends but they asked me to cover holiday leave. Now, I'm extremely glad I said yes.

It's come to something, I realise as I give the toilet seat another vicious squirt, when spending my Sunday clopping about in excruciating high heels sounds like a treat.

CHAPTER FOUR

A brief account of my attempt to fit in in an affluent country town.

1. **Never, ever describe where we live as an 'estate'.** Residents of Shugbury Old Town are snobbish about The Glade, a collection of 1960s bungalows plonked a little way out into the countryside. From visits to Vince's parents I realised that this has fuelled a rabid neighbourhood pride, and the place has the eerie sheen of a too-perfect neighbourhood in a sci-fi movie.

2. **Accept that, for entertainment, The Glade's residents flit in and out of each other's houses, commenting on neighbourhood goings-on.** *I saw Maureen had a new sofa delivered . . . Yes, the van blocked our driveway and the man stood there smoking for ten minutes . . . Did you see the Watsons are having a conservatory built? . . . Oh, really? How do the Bennetts feel about having their view blocked?*

3. **Join a yoga class.** Immediately, it was apparent that this wasn't the gentle yoga I'd gone to with Tash in Bethnal Green. No, this was extreme stuff, requiring excruciating poses to be held for *weeks*, it felt like. 'Maybe this isn't the class for you,' the instructor remarked, after I'd put my back out and had to be dragged up off the floor.

4. **Get a job.** I suspect some people assume that, because Vince is a little bit famous now, we are loaded. This is absolutely not the case. I need regular work – it's feast or famine with Vince's job – and had to find something pretty quickly. As there are no similar jobs to my ass-cure role around here, I found a part-time position at the sleekly modern Shugbury Spa Hotel.

5. **Be insulted in a shoe shop.** The hotel's female reception staff are required to wear heels. It seemed incredible that I'd be required to attach such bizarre contraptions to the ends of my legs in this day and age, in order to 'project professionalism' as my boss, Wilma, put it. Yes, the heel enforcer is a woman. She might as well make me wear a corset.

'You're a very, *very* broad fitting,' barked the terse young assistant at Soled Out as she glowered at my feet. I'd known they were a little wide, yes, but never thought I needed specialist footwear which, this girl announced, 'We keep in the back.' Isn't everything 'in the back' in a shoe shop? Why was she making me feel like a freak? I wasn't used to such scrutiny in the anonymous high street stores of London. Off she bustled – to the famous 'back' – returning with the only heeled shoes she reckoned I'd be able to cram my colossal hooves into.

'We recommend these for bunions,' she announced. I don't have bunions. But I might as well have, I thought grimly as I tapped out my PIN.

When I showed them to Vince, I detected a rare glimmer of interest as he exclaimed, 'Ooh, heels!'

'Like them?' I asked.

'I do actually. With you being so short, they give you a bit of height.'

*

At least the hotel guests' demands go some way to taking my mind off the torture devices attached to my feet. All slate floors, glass walls and cedar relaxation pods dotted around the grounds, it really is the height of luxury. Today a group of glossy women are appalled that I can't magically arrange for them to all have their massages at the same time. Plus, one of them wanted macadamia nut oil (which we don't stock), the jacuzzi jets aren't hot enough *and* some kind of insect has landed on the surface of the outdoor pool. My shift whips by, and before I know it I'm swapping my heels for trainers ready for my walk home.

Along the way, Edie and I message back and forth, as we tend to do on weekends when she's not rushing to work. Her internship led to a permanent position on a whale research project, and at twenty-six she has a kind of easy confidence I've never possessed.

How's the job? she asks. *Still making you wear those stupid heels?*

Yep. That's not going to change unfortunately.

There must be a law against that! Edie wears T-shirts, dungarees and sneakers – she's already saying 'sneakers' – to work.

Employment laws don't apply at Shug Spa, darling.

You should look for something else. So how was the festival? Dad a raving success?

Of course! They loved him.

All that adulation. Don't let it go to his head! She loves to rib her dad about his relatively new-found fame.

Too late for that!

We catch up on her news, then sign off with kisses. I smile, grateful that I'm kept in the loop with what's going on in her life. More than her dad is, actually. Vince is always taken aback when I mention Edie's friends, flatmates and colleagues by name. 'D'you keep a file on her?' he often teases. He doesn't seem to have a yearning for all the details in the way I do.

Leaving the old town now, I follow the long, straight pathway that leads out of town. Clouds are starting to gather on this warm June evening. Vince will probably be home from the festival by now. I hope he's taken Jarvis out for a walk. He's more settled in the evening if he's had some proper exercise.

As I reach The Glade I perform a mental run-through of what's in our fridge, and what might be pulled together for dinner. There's some chicken pie left over from last night, and oven chips in the freezer. It's hardly Ottolenghi but it'll have to do. My feet are still pinching as I spot Dr Kemp and his wife Agata – she of the perfect macarons – digging out moss from between their patio slabs. They wave in greeting and I wave back. I can't think of Dr Kemp as Lenny as, humiliatingly, I'd had to see him about my terrible bloating shortly after we'd moved here. At least, back in London, the GPs had been interchangeable and wholly anonymous. Here, the very man who described 'the build-up of gas in your gastrointestinal tract' had been at our door the previous evening with a welcome bottle of wine.

As I turn into Sycamore Grove I'm figuring that I need to throw a work outfit into the wash, as I have another hotel shift tomorrow, and also clean the bathroom as it was looking a bit grotty this morning and Vince won't have troubled himself with it. Obviously, person-with-penis is exempt from cleaning the loo and the zone around it. And now I'm remembering that I'll also have to finish the final chapter of Vince's book from the notes he's given me. Zoe, his editor, is expecting it tomorrow. The whole book, that is – done and dusted. So as well as working tonight I plan to set a 5 a.m. alarm in order to give it a final check-through.

When I'm not at the hotel I work for Vince ('Not *for* me,' he insisted, when he first suggested the arrangement.

'I mean, *with* me. It's not like I'll be your boss. It's just, there's so much to do now with everything taking off.') As well as managing Vince's diary, social media and sundry admin – plus fielding the trolls and crazies and anyone else he can't be bothered to deal with – I also help to write his books.

'You mean you actually *write* them,' Tash said, laughing, when we spoke about it recently – which I guess is true. What I do is gather together the various thoughts and brain meanderings he's jotted down on the backs of envelopes and Post-it notes. Then I knock it all into some kind of order, so people other than Vince can understand it.

Of course, Vince is meant to do this. 'But you're so much better at detailed stuff,' he reckons. 'I'm more of a broad-strokes person.'

The only aspects I don't manage are Vince's comedy bookings and TV appearances. He has an agent for that. You could call me his PA – but he prefers 'back end'. As in, 'Speak to Kate about that. She takes care of the back end.'

Now I'm aware of the sound of chatter and laughter coming from one of the back gardens in our street. Sounds like a jolly gathering is happening. Next door, perhaps, at Gail and Mehmet's? I imagine we'll be invited – perhaps Vince is there already? – and try to ready myself for switching into a sociable mood. Recently, I vowed to myself that I'd say yes to everything in my effort to make friends. Contribute to the bake sale? Clean a Portaloo with my tongue? I can do that! Then, as the noise grows louder, it becomes apparent that it's *our* back garden it's coming from.

Vince's voice cuts through the hubbub and there's a gale of laughter in response.

'Oh, Vince, you kill me!' someone shrieks.

I inhale deeply, ready to pin on a big, wide smile – because it seems we have a party going on.

*

I find everyone chattering high-spiritedly and clustering around my husband on our patio. 'You had them eating out of your hand, Vince,' Deborah announces.

'That's sweet of you,' he says. 'They were a very kind audience . . .'

'No, you *charmed* them,' insists Colin, a short and wiry recently divorced PE teacher who lives across the road. 'Y'know, I never read books normally. But yours was a laugh.'

'Glad you enjoyed it.' Vince's grin sets a little.

'It's the kind you read in the loo when you're going to be in there for a while.' He sips his beer and smirks.

'Good to know, Colin. Good to know.' Despite his abundant charm, Vince hasn't managed to hide his disdain for this man. 'And if you run out of paper,' Vince adds, 'you can always rip out a few pages . . .'

Laughter erupts and Deborah glances round, spotting me. 'Here's Kate,' she announces in the kind of flattened tone she might use to say, 'Here's our taxi'

31

at the end of a fun night. I greet everyone with as much enthusiasm as I can muster. Judging by the wine and beer bottles cluttering the garden table, it looks like an impressive quantity has been downed already. Which is fine, of course. They're celebrating a successful book festival, and I must join in and knock back a few drinks myself. It strikes me now how at home Vince looks here in his parents' garden (it still feels like their garden) surrounded by people who love him.

'Kate?' he starts. 'We should do some food.'

'Oh, yes, of course. There's plenty of crisps and Wotsits . . .'

'Wotsits?' Looking startled, he beckons me down to the bottom of the garden by his dad's shed.

'What's wrong?' I ask, frowning.

'*We can't give them Wotsits*,' he hisses.

'Why not?' I only buy them at his request. He thinks they're funny and ironic.

'We need something more substantial than that.'

'Do we?' Next to the shed looms my late father-in-law's unfinished water feature: two huge fibreglass orbs, like giant testicles resting in a shallow dish.

'Well, yeah,' he says, 'or everyone's going to be smashed, aren't they?'

'But I'm just back from work,' I remind him. 'Literally just this minute. I didn't know people were coming round, or that I'd be expected to cater—'

'It doesn't have to be anything major,' he insists.

'Oh, doesn't it?'

32

Up on the patio Colin guffaws loudly at something Deborah has said. It's obvious he fancies her – she, too, is divorced – but it's equally clear that his feelings aren't reciprocated. Meanwhile formidable Sue Stone, who grows freakily large radishes, keeps glancing our way, perhaps picking up on the tension.

'Well,' I tell Vince, 'there's that chicken pie in the fridge . . .'

'We can't give them old pie,' he exclaims.

'It's not *old* pie. It's only yesterday's—'

'Isn't there anything else?'

'I don't know,' I snap. '*Is* there?'

He looks at me with exasperation as if – just like with the bake sale – I'm making way too much fuss. 'Couldn't you just knock up a buffet?' he says. Then, before I can answer, and with catering matters seemingly settled, he trots back up the garden and gets back to the business of entertaining 'our' guests.

CHAPTER FIVE

In the kitchen I lean against the fridge and try to quell my burning fury. Jarvis has trotted in to join me. Judging by the hopeful tail-wagging he hasn't been fed either. I administer the premium lamb casserole with vegetables and herbs that the Shugbury vet insisted we buy: 'If we're going to trim him down he needs around six hundred calories a day,' he instructed, 'so *please* stick to the portion sizes, Kate.' Although the food whiffs a bit – Vince won't involve himself with it – it's a sight easier to dish up than a buffet, comprising numerous dishes that must somehow work beautifully together.

What any sensible woman would do now is think *fuck it* and pour herself a massive glass of wine. Crisp, chilled Sauvignon, surging like an alcoholic river down my throat. That'd improve things. Thus fortified, mythical sensible woman would then glide back out to the garden and suggest, 'How about we order in some pizzas?' Sometime later, she might initiate A Big Talk with her husband and eventually, if things still didn't improve, walk out and never set eyes on him again. But I'm clearly not a woman of good sense, because rather than threatening Vince with divorce proceedings I now intend to assault him with an extensive party spread.

'*I'll* give him a buffet,' I announce to a startled-looking Jarvis. 'I'll give him a buffet like he's never had in his life!' I'm aware of how mad I'm sounding, and that if I were to substitute the word 'buffet' for 'hammering', then Vince would be right to be alarmed. As it is, I aim to 'show him' by means of the array of dishes I'm planning to conjure up. *Then he'll be bloody sorry!*

Through the kitchen window I spot Colin Carse trying to chivvy everyone to stand close together so he can take a group photo. Only Deborah is complying, as she's virtually clamped onto Vince. I bang various serving plates onto the worktop and microwave several pouches of ready-cooked rice. Ripping them open, I tip the steaming contents into a dish, and fling in olives, peppers from a jar and – controversially – raisins, then snip over some kind of fresh (well, fresh-*ish*) herb that Agata brought round from her garden.

What else? There's still time to dig out the take-away pizza menu from the drawer. But instead, sensing something rising in me – fury, or perhaps bile? – I pour myself a big glass of wine and gulp it greedily. Now, with booze flooding my veins, I remember a book about trailblazing women I'd bought Edie when she was a little girl. A book to ignite a feminist spark, I suppose. I'd wanted her to grow up believing she could be anything she wanted to be. She'd become obsessed with it for a time, poring over Boudicca and Catherine the Great: warrior women who feared no one. What would she think of me now, throwing together all this food in a feeble attempt to be liked? Yet I can imagine what our neighbours would say, if I didn't make the effort. *You know Kate, Vince's wife, with the massively wide feet? We went round for drinks and all she offered was crisps!*

Now I'm chopping a cucumber with unnecessary force, considering it's something like 99.99 per cent water, into crudités for the dip I've found lurking at the back of the fridge. I'm not saying Vince won't appreciate my efforts. He praises me occasionally, although I doubt if Marie Curie was ever described as 'good at that stuff that nobody ever notices but is actually pretty important'. Stuff like emptying the kitchen bin before it becomes a tightly packed cylinder of rotting filth. And finishing his book! Christ, that needs doing tonight!

Panicking now, I batter on with the crudités, stopping only when there's nothing left in the kitchen that can be chopped up into little sticks. Then I whack up the oven to max heat and load in frozen quiches, garlic bread, sausage rolls and literally anything else that might come under the banner of party food. Soon the kitchen fills with the aroma of browning pastry and saturated fat.

Pausing for breath, I figure that, while I'm not Amy Johnson, the first woman to fly solo halfway around the globe – Edie's favourite from the book – I'm possibly the *only* woman to have concocted what I'm terming 'couscous surprise', by sloshing boiling water onto grains that I seem to remember buying when we still lived in London, and adding kidney beans, bashed-up pistachios of indeterminate vintage and, yes, more raisins, and more of that mysterious garden herb that Agata brought over.

Quaffing more wine, I glimpse Deborah standing on our garden table. Unlike Colin, she commands attention and everyone shuffles into position obediently as she takes a group photo from above. Her long black pleated skirt is billowing, giving her the gravitas of a statue – the kind that gets toppled these days because it's offensive.

You *can* pull this off, I reflect, tipping the rest of my wine down my throat. Yes, Vince has acted like a knob tonight but I'm pulling out all the stops now. I'm an unstoppable force like Boudicca, on a roll – on a Lidl sausage roll – as out of the oven comes a tray of glistening pastry snacks. With a flourish, I sprinkle more of Agata's herbs over everything, including Jarvis, who's standing a little too close, and the crisps I've tipped into bowls. I'm wishing now that Vince would walk in – because although I'm tempted to chop *him* into batons I'm immensely proud that I've managed to pull together an extensive feast with zero notice.

You've done it, I tell myself, blotting my sweaty face with a tea towel. *You're a marvel, Kate Weaver, and this is going to be great.*

*

'Wow, you've been busy!' Agata has wandered into the kitchen.

'It was pretty easy,' I fib.

Doe-eyed and dainty, she runs a hand over her elfin crop. 'Oh, is that a *bought* dip?'

'Um, yes.' I curse myself for plonking the tub on the table instead of decanting it into a bowl.

'D'you never make your own?' She blinks at me. 'There are lots of recipes online . . .' As if I might be unfamiliar with this mysterious concept called the internet. 'You just give some feta a light whipping,' she adds, picking up a sausage roll and taking a tiny bite. Wincing, she sets it back on the table.

'Oh, are they plant-based sausage rolls?' trills Gail, who's just marched in.

'I don't *think* so,' Agata announces. As they share a smirk I wonder privately how the pair of them would respond to a light whipping.

It's not healthy, I realise, to have such violent urges. I never used to be like this, fantasising about lashing out at guests and flinging Wotsits in my husband's face.

Now light rain is falling, and everyone starts to drift indoors. They seem hungry, and actually grateful for the 'spread', as Mum would term it. After a couple of large wines I'm tipsy already, and decide that I've overreacted and everything's going to be *fine*. A silver-haired man whose name I've forgotten announces, 'This looks fantastic, Kate. You needn't have gone to all this trouble for us.'

38

'It was nothing, really . . .' There *are* some perfectly nice people around here, I decide. Then I catch Radish Sue peering at my couscous and muttering, 'I'm not sure about sultanas in anything that's not a cake.'

I bite savagely into a sausage roll.

'Same here,' Colin agrees. 'And what's that stuff you've sprinkled on everything, Kate? It's like an explosion in a potpourri factory!' He guffaws at his own joke.

'It's a garden herb that Agata brought round,' I reply brightly.

Agata turns to me, carrot baton brandished in mid-air. 'Oh, is that my lemon balm?'

'Yes. Looks good, doesn't it?' I beam at her, relieved that I rescued it from our salad drawer before it tipped over into the realm of inedible mush.

She smiles tightly. 'I was thinking more that you'd use it for tisanes.'

I blink at her. 'Tisanes?'

'Kate, do we have any more beers?' Vince calls out above the chatter.

'Yes, in the cupboard where they usually are,' I reply.

'You know, *tisanes*,' Agata clarifies. 'Herbal teas. Lemon balm's great for anxiety and stress.'

'Oh, is it really?' Perhaps I should stop self-medicating with cheap Sauvignon and brew myself some right now.

'What flavour crisps are these?' Colin barks, as if it matters.

Boiled testicle, I want to say, *with an arsehole tang.* 'Ready-salted,' I reply.

39

'Aw, d'you have any of those black pepper ones?'

'But they won't be chilled,' Vince announces, appearing at my shoulder.

'What?' I spin around and glare at him.

'The beers. They'll be room temperature.' In terms of a national emergency this ranks alongside a lack of macadamia massage oil at the spa.

'Put ice in them then,' I suggest.

'It's not really a sprinkling over salad sort of herb,' Agata says, frowning.

'Oh, isn't it?'

'Ice?' Vince barks. 'In beer?'

'Yes, why not?' He never used to be this fussy. Shortly after we first met, I watched him straining a bottle of 'bitty' wine through the gusset of his flatmate's tights stretched over a bucket. He didn't demand buffets back then. He didn't bleat about booze not being at the correct temperature.

My attention is caught now by Gail, who's just offered an excitable Jarvis a piece of bacon quiche. My mind flashes back to the vet's instructions about his feeding regime – 'No table scraps!' – but too late. He's chomped it down. I hand out insufficiently chilled beers and do a sweep of abandoned plates as Deborah brags that her new fire pit 'only' cost £750.

'You should get one, Vince,' she announces.

'We should,' Vince enthuses. 'I've always wanted one.' Has he really? I suspect that, if Deborah were to suggest, 'You should get a trough of steaming manure'

40

Vince would reply, 'We should!'

'Kate?' He waves over to me.

'Yes?'

'Gail and Mehmet fancy a coffee.'

A third glass of wine has rushed to my head. But instead of making me feel more buzzy I'm now overcome with exhaustion. Everyone's shouting over each other and asking if there are any clean glasses and accidentally stepping on Jarvis's tail. Couscous is scattered across the worktop, and there's a spillage of unacceptable bought dip on the floor. I rush to wipe it up before Jarvis can get to it.

A knock on the door signifies more neighbours arriving, and I find Carl and Mia clutching a bottle of champagne and a lavish multicoloured bouquet. 'Thank you,' I say, reaching out to accept them. But Mia tightens her grip and says, 'They're for Vince actually, after his wonderful talk today!' And she virtually mows me down in her eagerness to get to him.

'Kate?' Vince says when I return to the kitchen. 'These beers are really warm and there isn't any ice.' Should I have nipped home at lunchtime to pop them in the fridge? Or start firing ice cubes out of my arse?

'Put them in the freezer,' I snap.

'Last time she did that they exploded,' he tells Dr Kemp. 'The beer expanded, forcing the cap off and spurting out—'

'Really!' our genial GP says. I hope it's not reminding him about my gastric troubles.

Vince turns to me. 'Do we have more red wine?'

Although I suspect that Boudicca would have thrown the virtually untouched rice-and-lemon-balm salad at him, I find myself saying yes, there's some *in the cupboard where we keep wine*. Aware that my fury is building to unbearable levels, I scoot off to the bathroom and bolt the door.

Sitting on the closed toilet lid, I inhale deeply and try to tune out the noise. Just a few moments; that's all I need.

The chatter goes on, and then another sound becomes apparent. It's Jarvis retching – in the hallway by the sound of it. It's certainly very close.

'What's he doing?' Mia, the newcomer, asks.

'Just his dry-heaving thing,' Vince explains.

'Does he often do that?'

Only when he's fed scraps, I want to shout. *Only when he's given cheap quiche when he lives on specially prepared lamb from Rover's Kitchen.*

'Yeah, he's fine,' Vince says blithely. The chit-chat, which had dampened down momentarily, builds up again. I'm thinking I really need to get out of here and rejoin the others. For one thing, our bungalow only has the one bathroom and pretty soon someone will need the loo. So I get up and check my bleak, shiny face in the mirror. The day's make-up is long worn off, apart from my mascara, which has streaked beneath my left eye. I wipe it away with loo roll, willing myself to lighten up and be happy and fun—

An indescribable sound causes the chatter to cease immediately. There's a stunned pause, then Deborah exclaims, 'Vince, Jarvis has been sick. Should we do something?'

'Nah, don't worry,' Vince says dismissively. 'Kate'll sort that.'

And that's it. That's when I know I can't do it anymore – be 'obliging Kate', that is. I'm going mad, I think, but there's only one thing for it. And there's no going back.

CHAPTER SIX

Before I know it I'm up on the bathroom windowsill with one leg dangling out of the window.

Soft rain is still falling and a cool waft brushes my face. I breathe it in and glance at our garden table that's littered with bottles and glasses. A blackbird lands on it. I watch him for a moment, trying to will myself to clamber back down, vacate the bathroom and apologise to anyone who's been waiting patiently.

Sorry, just felt a bit weird. The wine must've gone to my head . . .

There are voices in the hallway. 'Um, I don't mean to be funny,' Colin starts, 'but shouldn't we clear it up?'

'Where's Kate?' someone else asks. Then seemingly the vomit is forgotten and the music's cranked up.

My hand goes to my pocket and my fingers fold around my phone case. I pull it out and open the case, my heart lifting as I see my debit card there in its slot.

Phone and card. Two everyday items that represent freedom – from feeling like a colossal idiot because I hadn't known that Agata's herb was for tisanes. From being barked at for even *considering* offering Wotsits to our guests.

Of course it's not just about tonight. It's been building up for a very long time, this sense of losing the very core of who I am.

You're good at that stuff that nobody ever notices but is actually pretty important.

Well, fuck that. Tonight is where it stops.

The seams of my skirt strain as, with difficulty, I manoeuvre my other leg out of the window. I perch there for a moment, bum on the window ledge with both legs dangling outside. Good job we're in a bungalow after all. Because it's not far to jump.

And that's what I do, landing in an ungainly heap on the damp grass. Scrambling up, I tug my skirt back down over my hips.

What now?

Briefly, I glance back at the bungalow and hear Deborah laughing raucously. Then the party sounds fade as I hurry across the garden and through our side gate, and stride away down Sycamore Grove.

I speed-walk until I come to the last of the pebble-dashed bungalows, their shrubbery primped, not so much as a nugget of gravel out of place. The pathway that leads into town is long and straight with flat fields on either side.

The first houses in Shugbury proper are low-slung cottages adorned with climbing roses and honeysuckle.

45

Then the town centre starts with its tearooms and antique emporiums, and its gift boutiques selling expensive candles and cashmere scarves. There's none of your rowdy small-town crowd here. No teenagers littering the town square with fast food cartons and 'copulating in the graveyard', as was reported on our local news site about an incident at a music festival at a nearby, less salubrious town.

Locals dismayed by youths' outlandish behaviour.

That would never happen in Shugbury. *Locals dismayed that Kate Weaver's dip is shop-bought* is as bad as things get around here. And teenagers generally don't come here. You see the odd one being dragged around the antique shops by their parents, looking as if they might impale themselves on the memorial gardens' railings if they're forced to look at one more grandfather clock. But they don't show up with their own tribe, for fun. And the only copulating in the bungalow I've just left has been taking place every couple of months at the very most, in recent times. Vince seems to regard it as a chore that's best done swiftly, with minimum fuss – like trimming his nasal hair or bleeding a radiator (not that he's ever bled a radiator). Last time we were doing it he didn't even finish the job. He gave up halfway through and rolled off me. 'Bit tired, Kate,' he announced, yawning for effect. He never looks tired when Deborah is fluttering around him. He's alert then, like a fox, primed for action.

Passing the library now, I shiver and rub at my chilled

upper arms. My work blouse is clinging damply to my body, and I'm aware of a hollow feeling in my stomach. *Go home, you raving bloody lunatic!* I tell myself. But I can't.

The bus station has come into view now: a graceful red-brick curve with planters of pansies at regular intervals. At nearly 8.30 p.m. the kiosk is closed with its shutter pulled down. Just one bus is sitting there with its lights off.

Across the road from the station, I perch on a damp bench. My plan is to compose myself, then head back home and quietly slip back into the house.

My phone rings, sounding far louder than it does normally. I grab it from my pocket. Of course it's Vince. It stops finally, and there's a brief pause before it starts trilling again. I stare at the bus station, feeling panicked now as my phone rings and rings.

Pushing my hair from my eyes, I watch a man with a rucksack checking his phone by the parked bus. An elderly couple are consulting the timetable on the wall, and the yellowy streetlights are giving the concourse a sulphuric glow.

Then the bus's lights flick on. A driver has climbed in, and now the engine has been turned on too. Its destination sign illuminates, displaying a single word.

The elderly couple are about to board. Gallantly, the man steps aside to allow his wife on first. The way he touches her arm as she does so seems to squeeze my heart. Now the bearded guy gets on too. At the sound of

47

feet hitting the pavement I turn to see a young woman with long dark brown hair racing towards me. Pausing to check for traffic, she sprints across the road towards the bus station. Even from this distance I sense her relief as she jumps onto the bus. She laughs with the driver then flops down onto a seat.

The driver seems to be checking something on a clipboard. Then the bus door closes.

Again my phone starts to ring. This time I don't take it out of my skirt pocket – because now my attention is on the bus.

It's pulling out of the stance. It's going to London. And all of a sudden I'm propelled right back to a rainy day in Glasgow, forty years ago.

'Where are we going, Mum?' I asked. She'd bundled my little brother George and me, plus a few bags of possessions, into a taxi.

'On a trip,' she replied.

'A trip? Where to?'

Mum was too busy dealing with George, who was three, to answer me as we set off. 'Just forget about them,' she murmured, kissing the top of his head.

'But I want them! I want my slippers!' he roared. In our rush to leave they'd been left behind.

'I'll get you another pair,' she promised.

'I want those ones. Can't we go back and get them?' George wailed as we left our familiar neighbourhood behind.

'Sorry, love. We just can't.' Mum doted on George

and would have asked the taxi driver to turn back if it had been possible. That in itself told me that we'd had to leave when we did. That it was more important than those furry brown slippers with claws – bear-feet slippers – that George loved so much he sometimes wore them to bed. At nine years old I understood that I had to be brave, even though Mum had let me grab only three of my Famous Five books and not my complete library of twenty-one.

She's a proper little grown-up, that one, my aunties used to say. George, meanwhile, had 'the face of an angel', whereas I would surely 'grow into' my looks. While that didn't happen, I'd later be praised for being a grafter at school, slogging to pass the exams I found far from easy. Meanwhile George, who'd turn out to be a musical prodigy, would gain straight-A grades, seemingly without effort.

On that wet afternoon all of that had yet to happen, and he wiped away his tears and looked up at Mum. 'Why didn't we get the bus?' he sniffed.

'Because a taxi's quicker,' Mum replied.

'*We* don't go in taxis,' he muttered, and he was right. Taxis were for posh people like our dad's mum, Granny Fleming, who lived in a smarter Glasgow suburb, where there were restaurants and expensive boutiques instead of off-licences and betting shops. She kept sherry in a crystal carafe, and reckoned our dad, Derek, was a perfect husband and father and the most wonderful man in the whole of Scotland.

On the outside he seemed it. The *outside* Derek Fleming was a respected surveyor who played golf and went fishing and had a favourite Italian restaurant where there was a trolley laden with puddings.

Outside Derek Fleming knew lots about whisky and wine – in company he'd make a great show of swirling his glass around and sniffing it – and adored our mum, Joyce, and his two children. But *inside* Derek Fleming was different. This Derek was convinced our mum was having an affair with the quiet man in our local corner shop, all because he'd given her a box of Terry's All Gold at Christmas.

Dad hadn't believed that the chocolates were for all of us. *Take these, Joyce. Share them out with the kiddies.* A big flat golden box with drawings of the different chocolate varieties on the inside of the lid.

Sometime after Christmas I'd found a Rum Truffle gummed to the base of the standard lamp and a Chartreuse Cream (what *was* Chartreuse? It sounded impossibly glamorous!) squished into the rug after our nice, respectable, golf-playing dad had booted the box across the room.

You're saying he gave you those chocolates for nothing?

This baffled me. What had Dad meant? What kind of exchange could have taken place?

Our house was a scary place in the evenings he was home. He'd chain-smoke and drink red wine from a giant bottle at the kitchen table – no glass swirling there

50

– meaning we couldn't go in. We'd have tinned spaghetti and macaroni cheese – stuff that could be microwaved quickly and cleared away before he came in from work.

Once, late at night, I heard him yelling and Mum crying and screaming at him. Next morning I found a broken chair, a big dent in the living room wall and Mum's favourite horse ornament lying on the carpet in pieces.

And now the three of us were in a taxi, without him. We'd left without warning – like the Famous Five in *Five Run Away Together*. Was this an adventure? Or something else?

The taxi pulled up at Buchanan Street bus station in the middle of town. 'Are we going on holiday?' George asked.

'Kind of,' Mum said distractedly. She handed me some of the bags and chivvied us through the station where there was a big board with all the departures on it.

'Will there be donkeys?' George perked up now. He remembered our holiday in Blackpool, where Dad had gone 'for a pint' and not returned to our B&B until the following day.

'Let me think for a minute, son,' Mum said.

'What about Dad?' I asked.

'Never mind Dad, Kate. It's just us now.'

'What's our plan, then?' I was an organised child who enjoyed timetables and lists. I kept my light brown hair clipped back from my earnest face, and my pencils ferociously sharpened.

'You and your plans,' Mum murmured, frowning at the departures board. There was no plan, I realised. She was making it up as she went along. 'You two wait here,' she added, then rushed off to the ticket office.

'Where are we *going*?' I asked when she reappeared.

'London,' she replied.

'*What?*' All I knew about London were the photographs in a school library book. Big Ben, Buckingham Palace, the Post Office Tower, which apparently spun round and round while you were eating your dinner in the restaurant at the top.

'I've bought our tickets,' she announced. 'C'mon, it's leaving in a minute . . .'

'Why are we going to London?' George exclaimed.

I grabbed his hand. 'For an adventure.'

'Will the queen be there?' His eyes widened. 'Can we see the crown jewels?'

'Let's just get on the bus,' I told him as the three of us hurried across the concourse. It *was* an adventure, I'd decided. People in London probably ate Chartreuse Creams every day.

On the bus Mum grabbed a seat for her and George and told me to sit across the aisle.

'We're going on a really long trip, Kate,' my brother announced.

'Yeah, we are, George.' I nodded.

'Will there be slippers there, like my ones?'

''Course there will be.' I reached across the aisle to squeeze his hand and tried not to think about leaving my best friend Tash, and my Famous Five books lined up neatly on my shelf.

'How d'you know?' George asked.

'London has *everything*,' I told him firmly.

It turned out that I'd been right. George's slippers were soon replaced by even better ones with more luxurious fur, and Mum built new lives for the three of us. I grew up and met Vince and somehow agreed to live in his parents' house, and be his back end – and here I am now in the middle of Shugbury watching the bus pull away. The driver stops, indicating, waiting for a car to pass by. And something clicks in me as I jump up and start waving frantically. 'Wait!' I yell. 'Please wait!'

At first, the driver doesn't seem to spot me. His focus is fixed on the road. Then he turns and his gaze catches mine, and there's a nod of acknowledgement in my direction – and I run.

CHAPTER SEVEN

Vince

'Vince, d'you have a minute?' Deborah has swept into the kitchen, looking tense.

'Yeah, sure! Everything okay?' Vince jabs his phone back into his trouser pocket and snaps to attention. He's been trying to get hold of Kate, who seems to have disappeared. She's been in a weird mood from the minute she walked in. Vince has searched the house for her; the garden too, in case she'd let Jarvis out for a pee. So where *is* she?

Deborah grimaces and beckons Vince into the hallway. Obediently, he follows. If truth be known he'd follow Deborah into a swamp filled with leeches, or even a packed TK Maxx on a Saturday afternoon – such is the allure of her magnificent body and lustrous copper hair that reminds him of . . . well, the only coppery thing he can think of are heating pipes, so not that. But something anyway. Something shimmery and seductive.

She indicates the bathroom door. 'I really need the loo, Vince. Someone's been in there for ages . . .'

'That's weird.' Frowning, he gives the door a sharp rap. 'Hello?'

No response. He raps harder. 'Anyone in there?' They both wait, exchanging exasperated looks that Vince savours like the first sip of a delicious cocktail; the one that rushes straight to your head. There's a whole lot more he'd love to exchange with Deborah. The situation right now is less than ideal, with someone hogging the bathroom – have they fallen asleep in there or what? – and a small pile of dog vomit slowly setting like porridge in the corner of the hall. Even so, he's grateful that they are alone together for once.

Vince knew Deborah way back in secondary school here in Shugbury. The kind of alpha girl who was good at everything, she'd run with a far cooler crowd than he did and always seemed to have some good-looking bastard on her arm. With his scrawny build and volatile complexion, Vince didn't get a look-in.

When he'd first mooted to Kate that they should move to Shugbury he'd been aware of the obvious benefits. Mainly, they'd own a home outright, and no longer be paying rent to that dopey pothead pixie. Vince was sick of their Bethnal Green flat and the way Kate was always out, either working at the museum or with her many friends. Even when she was home there was always some mate of hers popping in and hanging out in the kitchen, like Ingrid ('Ingo') from the museum, Julian and Shawn from upstairs ('Jules, Shawny') and her oldest friend Tash, all of them sipping endless coffees or wine depending on the time of day. Thankfully, as Kate seems to prefer nipping back to London to see friends, rather than inviting them here, that doesn't happen anymore.

But one entirely unexpected bonus of moving here is that Deborah turned out to be living at the end of their street. Incredibly, she is now his friend. Vince should be cool with that. Yet somehow, whenever she's around, that acne-prone thirteen-year-old rears up in him and he's desperate to impress. Tonight she's wearing a snug-fitting deep green top that shines like wet ivy and a long black pleated skirt that flows elegantly as she jiggles about. He's imagined – many, many times – that she'd be firm and powerful in bed, possibly smacking him around a bit and certainly leading the way. It would be like shagging the figurehead of a ship.

'Vince?' Her voice snaps him back to reality. 'I'm sorry but I *really* need to use your bathroom . . .' Of course, that's why she's jiggling.

He bangs on the door again and shouts, 'Can you hurry up please? Other people need to use the facilities!' They wait a few more moments. 'I don't think there's anyone in there,' he surmises. 'The door must've jammed. It's happened before—'

'Oh, God. What a pain,' she exclaims.

No, no, Vince thinks. *This is actually brilliant.* He suspects Deborah knows he gets flustered around her – enjoys it, even, and encourages him by flirting. That time when she'd brought round a home-made Christmas pudding, having gathered that Kate never bothered to make her own: 'I make mine early then feed it with brandy over a few weeks,' she'd explained. 'That way, the flavours can deepen and penetrate.' He'd had to grab onto the kitchen radiator for support, and knocked off Kate's vest that had been drying there. When had his wife started wearing thermal undergarments?

However, Vince suspects Deborah only likes him because he's funny. And deep down, he wants her to see him not just as this hilarious guy who has audiences falling about with his self-deprecating repartee about being a useless fuckwit. He wants her to understand that that's just his public persona, his brand. And that actually, underneath all that, he's a capable man who owns a spirit level – at least he thinks there's one somewhere – and one of those metal tape measures that shoots back into the silver casing. He even changed a tyre once. At least, he watched the AA guy do it. But it was so straightforward he could've done it himself.

Vince bangs on the bathroom door one more time and looks at Deborah, baker of three-tier cakes made of velvet when his wife can barely heat up a Lidl sausage roll. *Yes,* he thinks, *it's actually great that it's jammed itself shut.* Vince can tackle a bathroom emergency and show her the kind of man he really is.

Only now Colin seems to have caught a whiff of the drama, and has barrelled through to the hallway to 'help'. 'You can't just break the door down,' he announces.

'I'll have to,' Vince says coolly. 'No other way of getting in.'

'Seems a bit rash, mate. That's all I'm saying.'

He glares at Colin, willing him to go away and dance in his appalling fashion to the Bowie track that's currently playing. The minute he discovered that his neighbour is a PE teacher, Vince took against him. At school Colin is known as Mr Carse. Vince imagines the fun the kids have with that.

Serves him right, Vince reckons. What an awful breed those gym guys are, humiliating the non-sporty kids who can't vault over that horse thing that's not even a horse; it's just this massive wooden structure that small children are expected to—

'I'll have to go home,' Deborah announces, cutting into his thoughts. 'I'm bursting, Vince—'

'No!' he shouts, more forcefully than he intended. 'Don't worry. I'll sort it.' He's conscious now of puffing out his chest, of readying himself to slam his bodyweight into that door. He'll probably hurt his shoulder, but it'll be worth it. In his fantasies he's imagined doing something heroic, like scrambling onto a garage roof to rescue a mewling kitten – and Deborah just happens to be strolling by. Obviously, he's enjoyed fantasies far naughtier than that, involving velvet cake topping and penetrating her Christmas pudding – no, no, not her pudding, the other thing; it's a soupy swirl of rampant desire now. He's drunk, Vince realises. He's sweating too, which must be unattractive. Somehow he manages to drag his focus back to the matter in hand.

'You don't wanna break it,' Colin reiterates.

'What would *you* do then?' When is the sporty elf ever going to fuck off?

Colin plants his hands on his weirdly skinny hips. 'I'd ease out the hinge pins and then gently lift the door at the knob end—' Vince sniggers but catches Deborah giving him a sharp look '—while supporting the other side of the door and separating the hinges and sliding a pry bar under the door to take some of the weight . . .'

Vince gawps at him, uncomprehending, as if Colin is speaking in Russian.

'D'you have a flat-head screwdriver?' Colin asks.

If there's such an item in the house Vince has no idea where it might be because DIY is Kate's domain. He might as well have asked, 'Where's your stopcock?' – another thing men like Colin are obsessed with, along with creosoting fences and poking about inside fuse boxes: stuff Vince has zero interest in. 'I don't need a screwdriver,' he retorts.

'No, we do,' Colin insists. '*And* a pry bar, if you have one. It's a kind of little crowbar,' he adds, in a silly patronising voice, as if Vince were a child. Does he speak like this to the kids at school? If so, it's a wonder he hasn't been assaulted. He wouldn't blame them for that. 'This way we won't damage the door or the frame,' he explains.

What's with all the 'we'-speak? Vince thinks irritably. Oh, he knows what Colin's up to, trying to show off to Deborah while the poor woman tries not to wet herself. He's seen the way his neighbour goes all giggly and flushed around her, like a fourteen-year-old when the person they fancy has sat next to them on the bus. As both he and Deborah are divorced and single, Colin seems to think he's in with a chance.

However, Vince has no time for approaching things carefully. After the frankly substandard buffet, the dog throwing up and now this bathroom emergency, all Vince really cares about is allowing Deborah access to the loo.

'Stand back,' he commands. With his chin up and back rod-straight, he turns sideways to the door.

'Don't! You'll break it!' Colin shrieks, as if Vince were about perform a cataract operation with a Black+Decker drill. 'I can nip home for my tools,' he insists.

'I don't need your tools.'

'But, Vince—'

'Can you shut up for a minute?' he shouts, with a fury that would suggest it's not Colin Carse who's standing in his hallway, wittering on about hinge pins, but that malevolent PE teacher from Vince's school, who'd guffawed when he'd flopped like a pancake on top of the horse, and made him do it again and again until everyone was laughing and he'd loped off to the showers with tears coursing down his face.

'Vince-the-Vault,' his classmates had called him after that.

'Cry-baby Vincent, can't mount a wooden horse!'

60

'Take it from behind, Vince. It's easier that way!'

School was a nightmare then. Although there were only two PE sessions per week they seemed to inhabit around ninety per cent of his brain space – pulsing on his crumpled timetable like appointments with death.

His neighbour triggers him, that's the thing. Vince feels guilty even thinking this, when some of his classmates joined the army and saw active service in the Gulf War – but Colin Carse gives him PTSD. Vince glares at him, thinking it's no wonder his wife left him for her driving instructor, which might have explained why she'd racked up 275 lessons before sitting her test. Local folklore has it that she was ready after ten.

'I'm only trying to help,' Colin crows, and Vince sees him trying to exchange an eye-roll with Deborah.

Fuck you, Vince thinks furiously, picturing himself careering not towards a cheap 1960s bathroom door but that terrible contraption in the gym hall, his nemesis all through secondary school and the cause of all those humiliating horse sex jokes – as his upper body meets it with an almighty crash.

CHAPTER EIGHT

Kate

It's when the bus stops at the big roundabout that a terrible thought hits me: that Stilton and broccoli quiche. It was taking longer to cook than the other stuff and I never took it out of the oven.

Will Vince have done it? Probably not. What if it's in there all night, burning and filling the house with fumes and smoke? Instinctively, my hand folds around my phone. I must call Vince and alert him!

It's a quiche in the oven, I tell myself sternly, *not impending nuclear attack*.

Outside the window, the shops have made way for neat red-brick terraces with Farrow & Ball front doors; then it's the wide, flat expanse of the park where the book festival took place. The marquee is still up, bunting flapping damply. We pass the bowling green and then the less picturesque retail park where there's a Lidl. Deborah boasts about shopping there, but only in a middle-class way. *Their Parmesan's excellent and they actually have avocados!*

Now we're leaving the town and joining the dual carriageway. Someone's bound to be waiting outside our locked bathroom by now, growing more and more desperate. I picture Dr Kemp giving the door a polite tap: 'Hello? Hello?' Then he'll call Vince and say, 'I think there's someone in there. They've been an awfully long time.' And eventually Vince will gather, simply by elimination, that it must be me.

Maybe he'll think I've fainted after all that frantic buffet activity? Or died right there on the toilet, like Elvis? Then he'll realise he should have appreciated me more – but too late now! Because I'm not dead on the toilet. I'm sitting here with a single ticket to Victoria coach station and that quiche is probably a charred disc by now and I don't care.

It hardly seems real, what I've just done. My heart is thumping hard, adrenaline still coursing through me as we reach the motorway. Then gradually, the fuggy warmth of the bus starts to calm me. I snooze a little, realising when I come to with a jolt that we're already in London, and that my phone is ringing again. Still dozy, and without thinking properly, I answer it this time.

'Christ, Kate, I've been calling you,' Vince announces. 'Where are you?'

'Just, uh, up the road,' I start, blinking out at the city lights.

'Up the road? What d'you mean? We have a party

going on—'

'I know, I just—'

'What's wrong with you tonight?' he cuts in. 'You were in a right mood when you came in.'

'No I wasn't!' Why does he say this? Why do women have a monopoly on 'moods'?

'Did you know Jarvis has been sick?' In the background there's a babble of voices and a thumping beat.

'Has he?' I ask innocently.

'*And* the bathroom door jammed shut,' Vince goes on. 'No idea how that happened . . .'

'It did that before, remember?'

'Yeah, well, anyway, I've been having to deal with *all* of this . . .' There's a female voice now, jabbering urgently, clearly very close to Vince. 'Erm, are you anywhere near the garage?' he asks.

'What?'

'The garage. Are you near it?'

The bus is crawling past a vast office block – all glass and steel, its signage a swoosh of blue neon. 'No. Not really,' I reply.

'Can you swing by, though?'

'What *for*?'

'Just wondered if you could pick up some oat milk?'

I catch my breath. No, *Can you just come home now? I'm worried about you, darling. Is something wrong?*

'Uh, unsweetened, Gail says,' he adds, dropping his voice to a hiss. 'You know what she's like. If you can't

64

get that, she says almond's fine but not soya – *definitely* not soya – and if there's only sweetened oat . . .' the shrill voice pipes up again '. . . she'd rather have unsweetened almond than sweetened oat,' Vince clarifies. 'But if they only have sweetened almond then get pea milk—'

'Pea milk?' I repeat.

'Yeah.' A scathing laugh. 'Who knew it existed? I mean, what's that all about—'

'Vince, I'm nowhere near the garage.'

'—For feeding little baby peas?' He snorts. 'There's potato milk too, apparently. For baby potatoes. Anyway, just get whatever you can. I'm sure she won't keel over dead if it's the wrong kind—' And that's all I hear because I end the call.

'Pea milk,' I mutter out loud, realising we're pulling into the station and I haven't a clue as to what to do next. It had seemed like the right – no, the *only* – thing to do; to run away like Mum with George and me. But now, as I leave the coach station on this drizzly night, I'm hit with a wave of panic.

A hotel! That's what I'll do. I'll check into a cheap place, get my head together and figure out what to do in the morning. If Vince calls back I'll just ignore him, I decide, fury bubbling up inside me now. Maybe *he* can go out and get the fucking pea milk!

Using my phone, I find the nearest chain hotel. It's a grim slab of stained grey concrete, chequered with tiny windows. The automatic glass doors slide open and I glimpse the bar, which seems to be entirely empty and dominated by an enormous TV.

Of course the place looks bleak. It's a wet Sunday night at 10:15 p.m. Wishing now that I'd at least brought a jacket, I huddle under the canopy at the entrance, where I'm soon joined by a very thin young man. He smiles broadly, sidles towards me and bites into a dripping kebab. 'Like some?' he asks.

'No thanks.' I stride away, the feeling of panic rising in me again.

'Bitch!' he yells after me. All those years I lived in this city I always felt fine and unafraid, because I belonged here. But tonight I've found myself alone in the rain, having an unwanted kebab thrust at me – and now an angry driver toots his horn as I step into the road without thinking. Has London turned against me?

So far I've held off calling anyone. I didn't want to alarm my friends, or have them thinking I've gone mad. I needed to process what I'd done – to make some sense of it – before transmitting the news far and wide.

However, now I realise the last thing I want is to spend the night alone in a hotel room with a miniature plastic kettle and a miserable packet of biscuits.

'Kate, honey! Everything okay?' Tash picks up my call immediately. Although we message frequently we rarely phone out of the blue – especially not at night.

'Not really,' I start, my voice cracking. 'Can you talk? I know it's late . . .' As if my best friend would say, *Sorry, it's not convenient.*

''Course I can. What's wrong? Where are you?'

66

'Just down the road from Victoria coach station.'
I look around as if to reassure myself that I haven't
dreamt the whole thing. 'I've left Vince,' I add.

'My God, Kate. Really? Look, I'm at this theatre
right now but—'

'Oh, you're working. I'm sorry—'

'No, I mean I've literally just finished. I'm in this tiny
dressing room . . .' She rattles off the name of a small,
tucked-away north London theatre. 'Can you get an
Uber? Come over right now . . .'

'I will. And can I stay the night?' I'm filled with relief
now at the sound of her voice.

''Course you can, for as long as you like. You don't
even have to ask.'

*

By the time I've arrived Tash has moved from the theatre
to a late-night bar around the corner and told me to
meet her there. It's a tiny, cosy little place where, she tells
me, the cast often go, and the elderly man behind the bar
seems to know everyone. After briefly introducing me to
a group of her fellow actors, Tasha leads me over to a
corner table where we can be alone.

'Oh, Kate. My darling.' She hugs me tightly after I've
told her everything. 'I didn't realise how bad things were
and how unhappy you've been. Why didn't you say?'

'I suppose I didn't want to admit it. But I had to leave
tonight. I just couldn't be there a second longer . . .' I
pick up my large glass of white wine. Somehow, within

67

minutes, I've downed half of it already. 'I've made such a fuck-up of everything,' I continue, crying now. More tears keep coming, and no amount of deep breathing or telling myself to *stop being a big blubbing baby* is making them stop.

'Hey, it's okay,' she says gently.

'I'm sitting here crying in front of your friends—' I glance over at the group, all in deep conversation at the bar.

'No one's noticed. It doesn't matter anyway. Christ, Kate, of course you're upset. All this shit you've put up with. And I don't blame you one bit. Honestly, you did the right thing.'

'You reckon?' I wipe away my tears with my hand. 'And you don't think I'm a complete sap for moving to Shugbury in the first place?'

'Of course not,' she exclaims. 'You were willing to try it. That's pretty brave.' Now my glass is empty. She jumps up and orders two more wines. At this rate I'll be pissed, but who cares? She sits back down. 'So, Vince doesn't know you're in London?'

'No.'

I know she's thinking, *Doesn't he even care where you are?* We've been friends since we were five years old and I can virtually read her thoughts as they form. After Mum had whisked me and George to London, Tash and I had kept in touch via letters. Then at nineteen she'd arrived in London too, to study drama. (Vince says she's 'very thespy' – whatever that means.) Briefly married

68

and divorced, and long-term single, she's never wanted children but has been an adoring auntie to Edie. Until the move to Smugbury (as she and I had jokingly christened it), we'd lived just a few streets apart.

'Hey, Tash. Great to see you!' Vince would enthuse, arriving home to find us ensconced at our kitchen table. But as his gaze flicked to her wine glass it was obvious he was thinking, *Fuck, that's nearly full. She's going to be ages drinking that.* Tash would ambush him with warmth and good-natured teasing, but to me her true feelings were as clear as day.

'Stay with me as long as long you like,' she offers now. 'Move into my spare room. We can do some nice stuff together—'

'I was thinking just tonight.'

She looks at me imploringly. 'Please don't go rushing back home . . .'

'I'm meant to be working at the hotel tomorrow,' I announce, suddenly remembering. 'My shift starts at noon.'

'Just don't go in! Tell them you're sick.'

'And the bathroom door's locked!' One of Tash's friends glances around as I clasp a hand to my mouth.

'What, at the hotel?' Tash asks, looking confused.

'No, at home—'

'So?'

'So, all this time and no one's been able to use the loo,' I rant. 'At a *party*.'

'Not your problem . . .'

69

'. . . But they'll have had to, I don't know, pee in the garden, behind the shed—'

Tash splutters, and I catch a glimmer of mirth in her eyes. 'Maybe Vince has found them a bucket?'

'I'll have to message him and tell him about the knife method,' I babble.

'What?'

'It's happened before. The bathroom lock's a bit sticky. He got trapped in there just after we'd moved in . . .' I'm remembering it now, Vince hammering frantically on the door as if rats were leaping at him from the toilet.

'Don't do it,' Tash commands.

'But you can open it easily with a knife. I just need to tell him—'

'No!' She snatches my phone and places it face down between us. 'Just let go of the responsibilities,' she adds, 'and think about yourself for a change. Let Vince sort it out.'

I sip my wine, trying to calm myself and figuring that she's right. No one will die if the bathroom remains locked and there's no oat milk and Vince's book remains unfinished. While these things aren't *great* – and my entire body prickles with unease at the thought of not doing what's expected of me – I do accept that the world won't end if I don't attend to those tasks.

At least, it won't end *tonight*.

And gradually, soothed by booze and being with my best friend in the world, I sense my panic abating – although it's taking my every last shred of willpower

70

not to message Vince: *Stick the knife blade in the slot, waggle it then turn VERY SLOWLY to the right.*

We head home to Tash's Bethnal Green flat where, suddenly ravenous, I stuff my face with buttered crumpets and then tumble into the single bed in her cheery yellow spare room.

By now I'm thinking Vince must be *wild* with worry. So why hasn't he been calling me, after I hung up on him? He's lost his phone, I decide, and now he's pacing the streets, with Jarvis, calling my name and berating himself for making us move. And now, because I *really* don't want him to worry, I decide to try calling him once more.

Reaching to the bedside table, I pick up my phone and see that he's messaged me. It was sent two minutes ago, when I was in Tash's bathroom, feeling grateful that she always has the fluffiest towels, and a spare toothbrush for guests.

I stare at Vince's message, wondering if my mind's playing a trick, or if I'm dreaming.

But no, it seems I am 100 per cent awake as I read it again: *Gail's saying if it's oat milk can you get the barista kind?*

CHAPTER NINE

Vince

Vince wakes up so slick with sweat that, for an instant, he thinks something terrible has happened during the night.

He thinks he has turned into an otter.

Realising he must still be pissed, he wonders why night-time drunkenness (fun, liberating) feels so different from morning drunkenness (soiled and seedy like a pair of old underpants lying in a car park).

He rubs at his gummy eyes, remembering that Edie had been obsessed with otters for a while. He'd bought her a DVD of that movie, *Ring of Bright Water*, but of course it ended horribly with the otter being whacked with a shovel. That's not an image he wants clouding his hungover brain.

Lying very still, Vince waits for his jumbled thoughts to slide into some kind of order. Kate's the person who files things and looks after admin-type stuff around here. His book contracts, correspondence, household bills; she's good at all that. Vince wouldn't be able to tell you who supplies their gas if someone were to put a gun to his head. 'The gas board?' he'd squeak in terror. Now he needs Kate to attend to the administrative mix-up in his head: the scrappy recollections of last night, with an underlying note of paranoia.

'Kate?' he calls out. No response. Is she in a huff with him? At least he's reassured now that he's still a human and not a small, furry, water-loving mammal. So that's one good thing. However, for some reason his right shoulder and upper arm are aching horribly, and he's sweating so hard he can feel it seeping through his pores. He wants to stop it but of course he has no control over it. There's no off switch for sweat.

Is this what it's like to be menopausal, he wonders briefly? It's not normally Vince who does the perspiring around here. For the past few months Kate's been doing enough of that for both of them. She's only forty-nine. He'd assumed she was too young for all that. Wasn't the menopause something that happened to *old* ladies, like his mum and aunties, who'd chatted about seed catalogues and their varicose veins, and sat around wafting their faces once they'd hit a certain age? But apparently not. Kate had explained, rather tetchily, that she's 'in peri-peri-menopause' or something like that. All Vince could think of was Nando's. 'That's different,' she'd snapped at him. 'That's spicy chicken.' Whatever it is, she's been complaining of hot flushes lately. So what's with the corrugated vests?

'Ribbed,' she corrected him. 'It's just a nice soft layer for wearing under things.' But Kate doesn't just wear them 'under things'. She also wears them in full view – not under anything – around the house, with *leggings*, when anyone could come to the door.

If that's not bad enough, these vests were ordered from a flimsy magazine that fell out of the newspaper one weekend. His wife has started shopping from a catalogue like his nan used to! It'll be 'slacks' next. Or those felted tartan slippers with a zip up the front. To think, she once splurged £150 on a sexy slip from Agent Provocateur.

On the rare occasions when they're having sex, Vince tries to conjure up an image of *that* Kate – the 1998 version in slippy black silk as opposed to a thermal base the colour of mushroom soup. But it's like trying to progress beyond the *una taza de café por favor* level of Duolingo Spanish. His brain can't compute it. Instead – and he hates himself for this – whenever he and Kate are doing it, it's Deborah he pictures in his mind. Deborah, who he's fancied since 1982, bent over a kitchen table and clutching a spatula covered in cake mix with that long green dress hoicked up over her—

With a jolt, Vince realises he must have slipped back into a semi-conscious reverie. He rubs at his gummy eyes again and remembers now that there was a party here last night. The end of the evening is hazy, though. He vaguely recalls having a little lie-down on the bed,

74

even though some of his guests were still here. He'd only planned to rest his eyes. But he must have dozed off and, at some point, undressed fully. At some point during all that, hadn't he texted Kate about something? Something about milk, he figures, rubbing at his head. Next thing he knew, it was morning.

He checks the time – it's a quarter to ten – and frowns at the space beside him where his wife should be.

'Kate?' he calls out again, uneasiness rising in him now. Uneasiness about . . . something. He's not yet sure what it is.

What is it about hangovers and growing older? When you're young, they're almost fun, synonymous with bacon rolls and gallons of coffee and sprawling around with a bunch of mates on threadbare sofas, chuckling over the antics of the night before. Plus, hangovers make women horny; everyone knows that. The morning after was sometimes better than the night out that caused it.

It's not like that anymore. A hangover now results in complete mental collapse. 'Kate?' he shouts, sitting bolt upright now. 'Where are you?'

Silence. Perhaps she's taken the dog out? Although Jarvis belongs to Vince's daughter, it's Kate who's been doing all the walking. Feeling reassured now, he remembers that she'd taken herself off for a walk last night too. What was that all about? He opens the messages on his phone and reads the last one he sent her: *Gail's saying if it's oat milk can you get the barista kind?* Sent at 1.17 a.m. Now it's coming back to him.

Gail had wanted tea, and it had seemed easier at the time to ask Kate to fetch the milk while she was out, rather than their neighbour nipping next door for it.

Vince isn't quite sure why he thought that. But there's no reply to his request.

Frowning now, he clambers out of bed and pulls on his favourite dressing gown, grateful that the thick velour-type fabric is effectively blotting the dampness from his body. He's no sooner opened the bedroom door than Jarvis shoots in, panting with his tail wagging madly.

'Oh! What're you doing here?' So Kate hasn't taken him out after all. He's fussing around Vince now, jumping up in a manner that suggests he's desperate for breakfast.

Vince steps out into the hallway and sees that the bathroom no longer has a door on it. '*What*?' he shouts. They've been robbed! No, burglars steal jewellery, laptops, stuff like that. Not doors. So what's been going on?

Now he spots a filthy and crumpled bed sheet lying on the bathroom floor. It looks like people have been trampling on it, in dirty shoes, possibly from being out in the garden where the lawn turns to mud in the lightest of showers. More curiously still, bits of Sellotape are dangling from the top of the doorframe, as if something had been hanging there. Managing to piece these clues together, Vince remembers the jammed bathroom door and trying to smash his way in by ramming his body against it, which explains his aching shoulder and upper arm. But the door had remained shut, and Colin had insisting on rushing home for his toolkit like some screwdriver-wielding superhero. Just to rub it in that Vince hadn't known where the toolbox was kept.

Oh yeah, Colin had crowed. *Kate did mention that she assembles all your flatpack!*

Casting a cursory glance at the small pile of dog puke in the corner, Vince stomps through to the kitchen with Jarvis fussing at his heels. Here, every surface is strewn with smeared glasses, dirty plates, half-eaten sausage rolls and bowls of dismal rice and couscous. On top of the recycling bin sits a stack of frozen food boxes, and on the draining board is a smear of something white and creamy. He vaguely remembers Kate presenting some kind of dip, and his stomach shifts uneasily.

Now he's aware that the kitchen seems terribly hot, which is triggering his sweat glands again. Plus, there's a burning smell. With a jolt he realises the oven's little red light is on. It must have been left on all night. He turns it off and opens the door, reeling back as acrid smoke billows out at him.

'Jesus!' he cries out, squinting through it to identify a round, flat object sitting on a tray on the middle shelf. He grabs the oven glove, jabs both hands into it and lifts out the tray. But the glove offers virtually zero protection and he screams in pain and flings the tray and the thing on it into the sink. 'Fuck!' he yells, the smoke alarm beeping shrilly as he peers at the blackened object. Its surface is bubbled and charred, almost metallic. It looks like a component from a burnt-out car.

Vince looks around for the floor brush. He's seen Kate using it to jab at the smoke alarm on the ceiling when it's gone off before. But where is it? Why does she insist on hiding things – brush, toolbox – in weird places? 'She's gaslighting me,' he informs Jarvis, who's been observing the scene and doesn't seem to know what to make of this new information. His only concern seems to be breakfast. So Vince will have to deal with that stinky dog meat too.

He can't find the brush and the smoke alarm's relentless shrieking seems to be spearing his brain. Under Jarvis's watchful gaze he clambers unsteadily onto a kitchen chair, punches the smoke alarm with his fist and groans in relief as it falls mercifully quiet.

There, he thinks, climbing down. That's another good thing about living in a Sixties bungalow: low ceilings. He rubs at his smarting eyes and opens the kitchen window to alleviate the smell.

The day has barely begun and Vince is exhausted already. Glaring again at the incinerated object in the sink, he snatches his phone from his dressing gown pocket and calls his wife.

CHAPTER TEN

Kate

'You're . . . what?' Vince splutters.

'I'm at Euston station,' I repeat.

'What're you doing there?'

'Catching the next train home,' I say automatically, as I look around at all the people hurrying around, clutching coffees and those anaemic-looking baguettes wrapped in paper napkins.

'I . . . I don't understand,' he announces.

'Vince,' I start, 'd'you realise I've been out the whole night?'

'The whole *night*? You are kidding.'

'No, I really have.'

'You've been at Euston station all night?'

'No, I stayed at Tash's.'

'What?' A stunned pause. 'How did you get there?'

'I caught a bus.'

'A bus?' he repeats as if I'd said, 'I took a mule.' Vince

never takes buses. He claims to not understand how they work, or where they go. 'Why did you do that?' he asks.

'Because I had to get away last night.'

'Away from *what*? This is so weird, Kate. You have to explain what's going on.'

In fact, before I left this morning, Tash asked again if I'd think about staying, at least for a few days. No reason to hurry back home, she insisted. But I needed to have it all out with Vince: his attitude towards us, towards *me* – the whole mess I've found myself in.

As Tash supplied me with clean undies, a top and a jacket – and a tote bag to stash my stuff in – I felt a twinge of regret at saying goodbye. We hugged and I took the tube to Euston, having decided to head back to Shugbury by train – much faster than the bus. It felt vital to seize the moment. No more dutiful Kate, I decided. Vince would have to listen to me. I would spill out all my grievances like a dumper truck disgorging its load.

However, as I emerged from the tube into Euston station, I was already formulating a to-do list.

Explain everything to Vince in a calm way.

Call Wilma and apologise for being unable to come into work today. Say family emergency happened?

Finish Vince's book and email to Zoe, with apologies for lateness.

Clean up party mess.

Assess state of oven, deep-clean if necessary.

Walk Jarvis. Clear head. Buy carpet cleaner.

Clear up sick.

Get on with life.

It was hardly the list of a woman on fire, I realised. I couldn't imagine this being Catherine the Great's first thought, on seizing control of Russia: *That baking tray will be ruined from the burnt quiche. Better pick up some Brillo pads on my way home.* Yet this seems to be the way I'm wired now. I'm certainly not the girl who jumped aboard an Amsterdam-bound bus with Tash when we were twenty, simply because it was £12.50. I'm a robot, programmed to return to base and complete my chores.

'I'm still not getting this, Kate,' Vince announces. 'I thought you just went out wandering last night?'

'Yes, I realise that, because you somehow felt the need, at twenty past one in the morning, to text me about *barista* milk—'

'Gail's lactose intolerant!' he says defensively. 'Although I do wonder sometimes. She got stuck into that Camembert the other night. There was no stopping her then—'

'I don't mean why did Gail need oat milk. I mean, why did you feel it was okay to message me with a shopping list in the middle of the night when I could have been lying in the woods, being ripped apart by wolves—'

'There are no wolves here. And it was only one thing. Hardly a list . . .'

'Yes, I suppose you could've asked me to pick up a loaf and some eggs while I was at it—'

'Look, I'm sorry, okay?' he snaps.

'—Maybe a packet of Wotsits?'

'For God's sake. All I knew was, you'd gone out wandering—'

'Will you stop going on about me "going out wandering", like I blundered out of a care home?'

'All right,' Vince shouts. 'All *right*.'

As ill humour fizzles between us I scan the departures board, spotting a train leaving for Shugbury in twenty minutes. I spot a family hugging in a joyful reunion, and a young couple in tears, separating reluctantly.

Imagine finding it that painful to pull apart. I've been out *all night* – and my husband hadn't even noticed. Momentarily, my attention is caught by a tall older woman who brushes against me as she sweeps past. I stare after her. Notably elegant among all the people in their travelling clothes, she is wearing a camel trench and a black beret pulled down low over a sleek silvery bob. With one hand she's gripping two dachshunds' leads, and with the other she's pulling along a smart checked wheelie case.

'I'm sorry you're upset,' Vince says, adopting a martyrish tone now. 'But it wasn't exactly all fun and games here, y'know.'

'Wasn't it?' I frown. 'You seemed like you were having a *great* time.'

'It wasn't great when the bathroom door jammed shut and no one could get in there—'

'Did you have to break it?' I ask in alarm, still programmed to be the diligent wife who can't bring

82

herself not to care about damage to the home.

'Uh, I was gonna,' Vince says quickly. 'But I decided to take it off its hinges instead.'

Momentarily, I'm stunned. I'd be no more shocked if he'd said, 'And then I extracted Jarvis's problematic tooth.'

'You actually managed that?'

'Yeah. Why not? It seemed like the best option . . .'

'Wow,' I breathe.

'I am capable of operating a screwdriver,' he retorts.

'Right. Yes. 'Course you are. So you managed to find the toolbox?'

'Well, obviously, yes,' Vince says defensively. I almost feel sorry for him now, blundering about tipsily in search for the tools that I keep in his dad's old shed. (Did he *really* find them?) 'And this morning I burnt my hands,' he adds plaintively, 'when I took that scorching hot thing out of the oven—'

'The Stilton and broccoli quiche?'

'Oh, is that what was?' he asks bitterly.

'What did you think it was?'

'I dunno. A hubcap from a burnt-out car? Anyway,' he barges on, 'those oven gloves you bought are useless. Paper hankies wrapped around my hands would've provided more insulation—'

'Well, I'm sorry we don't have asbestos gloves,' I say tartly. 'You're okay, though? Not maimed or anything?'

'No, I'm not *maimed*. I'm fine. But what about you? Are *you* okay?'

'Actually, no,' I start. 'I'm not okay at all. D'you know what the most upsetting thing is, Vince?'

'No, because I haven't a clue what's going on.'

I take a deep breath, as if to fortify myself. 'The thing that's upsetting me most is that last night, even though your wife was out somewhere, you just went to bed as if everything was normal.'

My heart is banging hard.

'Well, yeah. I'd had quite a lot to drink,' he mutters.

'And then, when you woke up this morning, you weren't remotely worried that she wasn't there.'

'I just thought *my wife* must've come to bed later,' he announces, 'after I'd gone to sleep. And then, when I woke up, I assumed *my wife* had got up early and gone out—'

'To go wandering again? To buy the right kind of plant milk?' He's speaking like this – 'my wife-this, my wife-that' – because if there's one thing Vince can't bear it's people referring to themselves in the third person. It rankles him even more than the concept of brunch, with its scrambled tofu connotations, and having to get an app in order to buy a parking ticket.

'I'd just like to know why *my wife* took herself off to London,' he barks, 'when we had a party happening—'

'Vince, could you—'

'And when *my wife* might be planning to come back home—'

'Stop it,' I cut in sharply.

'Stop what?'

84

'All this "my wife" stuff—'

'You started it,' he declares.

'Well, can you just not do it? My name's Kate, Vince. KATE!' I must have shouted that bit, as several people have glanced round, including a station employee in a hi-vis jacket and the dachshund lady. Our eyes meet and I sense my cheeks burning hot.

'All right,' Vince huffs. 'Message received . . .'

'Kate?' The dachshund woman has called out my name. Now she's staring as if she knows me from somewhere, but can't place me.

I smile briskly in acknowledgement, hoping that'll be that. But instead of continuing on her way, she and the two little dogs seem to be making their way back towards me. She looks normal and perfectly nice, and not as if she'll start ranting that I'm going to hell, or try to snatch Tash's tote bag containing my work blouse and yesterday's knickers. But you never know.

I flash her another tight smile then avert my gaze, relieved when a family with a gaggle of excitable children comes to a halt between us.

'Have you had some kind of funny turn?' Vince asks.

'No, I haven't *had a turn.*'

'What is it then? Please, enlighten me!'

The man in the hi-vis jacket gives me a curious look. I realise I must look wild-eyed and verging on out of control.

'It's not just last night,' I start. 'It's the way we've been these past few months – actually *years* – with you barking orders at me as if I'm staff, which I am now. I know that—' Without warning my eyes flood with tears. But by some biological miracle, my body sucks them back in.

'Do I need to come and get you?' Vince asks. 'Do I need to get in the car and drive to London this very minute?'

'—But it's not that either,' I rant on, unable to stop now. 'It's not even the party or you laughing at my chocolate clusters. What was it you said again? That they looked like the deposits of a middle-sized dog—' I stop abruptly as the dachshund lady appears by my side. In Tash's paisley top and faded denim jacket, plus my drab work skirt and scabby old trainers, I don't *think* I look like I work here. But her apologetic smile suggests that she's waiting for me to finish my call. Does she think I can dispense travel advice?

'It was a joke,' Vince thunders. 'Fucking hell, Kate . . .'

I step away and try to merge with the crowd, and be anonymous or, preferably, invisible. *She has her talents,* said my husband who no longer finds me desirable. Now I'm picturing the two of us in our bedroom a couple of nights ago. I'd just done a full day's work on Vince's book, walked Jarvis three times and hosed him down in the garden after he'd rolled in something disgusting in the park. So I was looking forward to curling up in bed with my book.

I'd just pulled on what Vince calls my 'maiden aunt nightie' when I looked round to see him standing there, wearing just his boxers. Vince has always had a good body. It's nicely proportioned with well-shaped shoulders, toned thighs and – although it pains me to admit it – a very attractive pert bottom that a thirty-year-old would be proud of, never mind a man in his fifties. All without him putting an iota of work into it, which seems unfair. I mean, all he does is sit on it. And suddenly, the mental strain of a day's writing (contrary to what Vince thinks, it doesn't come easily) melted away. Even my annoyance at having to shampoo Jarvis – who hates being washed and snapped at me – dissipated as I looked at my husband and thought, *You are lucky, Kate Weaver. Doesn't he look good?*

Without thinking I went over and gave his butt a cheeky squeeze, just for fun. Because I'd glanced at Vince and thought, *Look at you. You're still the man I fell in love with twenty-five years ago, and I do still love you.*

'Vince,' I start, 'd'you remember when I squeezed your bottom the other night?'

'What?' I can virtually hear his brain cogs clanking, sticky with last night's alcohol.

'I squeezed your bum, remember? And you slapped me away—'

'I didn't *slap* you,' he retorts.

'You did! You shouted "OOF!" and whacked my hand away as if I were an annoying fan assaulting you in a supermarket—'

'Well, yeah. I thought you were getting a bit . . .' He clears his throat.

'A bit frisky?' I suggest.

'Yeah, and I was tired—'

'You're always tired, aren't you? You're tired of me, Vince. You might as well admit it—' With a gulp, I stop and press my hand to my eyes. I know I should finish this call and rush off to buy my ticket and catch that train. But I can't make myself do that either.

The gentle prod to my arm makes me flinch. It's that lady with the dogs, and she's looking at me with concern. 'Sorry,' she mouths apologetically, as if reluctant to interrupt my call.

I blink at her, confused.

'It *is* Kate, isn't it?' she asks.

'Er, yes.' I nod. Do I know her from somewhere?

'Sorry, but we really need to go,' she says, indicating the departures board.

'Who's that?' Vince barks.

'No one. Just a minute . . .' I turn to the woman. 'I'm not sure I know you,' I start.

She frowns. 'I'm meeting a Kate who's coming to Scotland with me as my companion?' A tinkly laugh. '*Companion*. What a silly, old-fashioned word . . .'

I smile apologetically and move away slightly as Vince rants on: 'If this is menopause stuff, maybe you should see Dr Kemp? Would that help?'

I'm about to reply, *Could Dr Kemp 'help' with the fact that I'm expected to do every blasted manual task in the house?* But instead I glance back at the woman. She has intelligent pale blue eyes and the kind of refined, mature beauty that's benefited from good genes and expensive skincare. Under the trench coat she's wearing slim black trousers, a fine pale grey polo-neck sweater and a simple gold chain. She's what you'd call *put together* – effortlessly. I believe some women are genetically programmed to be like that.

I check the departures board, realising I'll have to hurry if I'm going to catch that Shugbury train.

'What time d'you get in?' Vince prompts me. 'I'll come and fetch you from the station.'

I'm about to respond but something stops me. 'Kate?' The woman is right beside me again, looking a little stressed around the eyes now. 'I did book you through the agency, didn't I?' I blink at her, knowing I should tell her no; I'm not the Kate she's looking for. Instead, while Vince babbles on, I sense something growing in me: a sense of strength and courage that I haven't felt for a very long time. In fact, for the briefest moment I could almost be one of those heroic women from Edie's book as I say, quite calmly, 'Actually, Vince, I'm not going to catch the Shugbury train.'

'What?'

Something flickers deep down in my gut. It's a tiny spark, like when you light a rocket firework and everyone waits at a safe distance for it to go off. And now it's catching properly, flaring up as I replay Vince saying, *You're good at all that stuff that no one notices, but is actually pretty important.*

I'm handy, he meant – in the way that a small stepladder

is handy. You don't have any emotional connection with it. It's just there when you need it, although you'd rather it was kept out of sight. You certainly don't want to hang out with your stepladder or take it to bed in the afternoon and have thrilling impromptu sex with it.

The rocket goes off inside me now, shooting high above Euston station and the whole, huge London sky as I realise what I must do.

'Have you missed it?' Vince asks. 'If you run, will you catch it—'

'No, I haven't missed it. And I don't need to *run*—'

'I don't understand!' he wails.

'That's it, Vince,' I say, sensing a lightness in me as if I too have shot up into the sky where there's no book to finish or quiches to burn and I'm free to do whatever I want. 'That's all there is to understand,' I tell him. 'I'm not coming home.'

CHAPTER ELEVEN

The woman's name is Alice and the dogs are Martha (long-haired, tan/white) and Penny (russet with a velvety sheen). She tells me this in a rush as soon as I've finished my call. 'We really have to dash now,' she announces, checking her slim gold watch. 'Could you take the girls for me?'

'Erm, yes. Of course . . .' Why am I not telling Alice *right now* that I'm not who she thinks I am?

Obviously, I'm the wrong Kate!

Instead, I take the dogs' leads and hurry along at her side towards the furthest platform. 'If there's one thing I can't bear,' she adds, 'it's *falling* onto a train as it's about to depart.'

'Me too,' I say. She veers abruptly to the right and marches down the ramp towards the train, her immaculate brogues clip-clipping, trench coat flapping in her wake.

'It starts the whole journey off on the wrong note,' she says firmly.

'Yes, it does,' I agree, somewhat under her spell now, despite the horror of my own situation – the fact that I've just told Vince I'm not coming home. So where *am* I going? Toward the train, it looks like – although any minute now I'll have to hand her the dogs' leads back and say goodbye.

We've reached the barrier where Alice fishes her phone from her voluminous leather shoulder bag, and thrusts it at the young man checking tickets. He nods and lets both of us through.

'Coach G,' she announces.

'Right.' Obediently, I trot along beside her with the dogs. When we reach coach G Alice hops aboard with her suitcase, having shunned my offer to lift it on for her. Naturally, being temporarily in charge of her dogs, I have to climb aboard too.

Alice flashes a relieved smile as she finds her seat at an otherwise deserted table. 'Settle down now, girls,' she murmurs to the dachshunds who are fussing around at her feet.

'So, this train's going to Glasgow?' I venture, reading the digital display.

'Well . . . yes.' *Obviously*, her tone says as both dogs settle at her feet. Alice delves into her bag, pulls out a sort of collapsible dog bowl, and sets it on the floor. 'Perhaps, when we've set off,' she tells them, 'Kate will be so kind as to go and fetch us a bottle of water—'

'Erm, Alice,' I start, about to explain that I'm sorry but there's been a mix-up. I haven't been booked through an

92

agency as her companion on a trip to Scotland. I'm just a random woman who's run away from her husband and doesn't know what to do next.

I can't stay with my mother because she'd think I'd lost my mind, walking out on the *wonderful* Vince. And although Tash said I'm welcome to stay, her life is so full and it wouldn't feel right, landing myself on her. As I hover in the aisle, a harassed young couple tumble into the carriage, clearly having run for the train. I dip down onto the seat opposite Alice to let them pass. All around us, passengers are settling in for the journey with coffees, books and laptops.

'So, Kate,' Alice says now, leaning forward. 'We have three weeks ahead of us. Don't you have any luggage?'

I glance briefly at Tash's tote bag on my lap. 'Things were, um, a bit complicated at home,' I start.

She grimaces sympathetically. 'Poor you. I did hear a little, you know. Of your conversation, I mean. I didn't want to eavesdrop but . . .'

'No, no, it's fine,' I say quickly, wondering why I'm still parked here on this train when it's about to leave. 'But I left in a hurry . . .'

'Nothing wrong with travelling lightly,' she says with a smile. 'You know, before I booked you, it was my son who was supposed to be coming to help me. But suddenly, he couldn't do it. Too busy with work and running around after his children. Children!' she exclaims loudly, causing the woman across the aisle to shoot her a bemused look. 'You'd think they were little

93

and still needing the tops slicing off their boiled eggs. We're talking strapping teenagers. But he's always busy, busy, busy . . .'

'What was he meant to be helping you with?' I ask hesitantly.

'Everything I mentioned when I booked you,' she says briskly. 'Clearing out his grandma's house. My mother's, I mean. Only child syndrome. It all falls to you.' Alice grimaces. 'D'you have children, Kate?'

'Just a stepdaughter. Edie.' *I'm telling her this, yet I haven't admitted I'm the wrong Kate?* 'Has your mum passed away?' I ask.

She nods, apparently noting my look of surprise. I'd put Alice at somewhere in her mid seventies herself. 'I am sorry,' I add.

'Thank you, but she had a good innings, as they say. Made it to ninety-six. She was quite the character, living on her own and running her B&B . . .'

'Really? That's amazing—'

'. . . With the help of her poor, long-suffering housekeeper,' Alice adds. 'Dear Morag. An absolute stalwart. Anyway,' she adds quickly, as if catching herself, 'that's why I contacted the agency. I couldn't face tackling the house on my own. But you don't need to hear my woes, do you?'

'I really am sorry.'

'Thank you, Kate.' Alice meets my gaze, and something flickers in me. There's a *spark* between us; that thing that happens when you meet someone new, and there's a connection – like you see something of yourself in them, reflected back at you. But what is it? I can't imagine Alice being expected to cater for a party that she didn't plan, or rush to the garage for oat milk in the middle of a wet night. With her assured manner and clipped speech – there's the barest hint of a Scottish accent – I'm sure she'd tell them where to get off. Yet right now, bizarrely, I wish I *was* this Kate-from-the-agency, booked to help this proud and elegant woman to clear out her mother's house. It feels like it would make a difference – that I'd *matter* somehow. Like I used to, when Edie still lived with us and I had a job I loved.

A tannoy announcement fills the carriage: '. . . *Stopping at Preston, Lancaster, Carlisle . . .*'

'Sorry!' I say suddenly, jumping up from the seat and barging towards the end of the carriage. But even before I've reached it I'm aware of movement behind me; of this seemingly determined woman, with the dogs trotting at her ankles, not ready to let me go.

'Kate, is something wrong?' We stop in the vestibule.

I bite my lip, picturing Mum and George and me on that wet afternoon at Buchanan Street bus station all those years ago.

She didn't have a plan. She just did what felt right.

Alice is looking at me expectantly, and then she touches my arm and smiles so kindly it squeezes my heart. 'I realise you've had a stressful time today, with that call . . .'

I nod and swallow hard.

'. . . And you've come away with no suitcase or anything. You said you left in a hurry—'

'It's just all been very weird,' I blurt out.

'I'm sure it has,' she says gently, glancing down. I look down too, sensing a slight pressure bearing down on my left foot. Martha has rested her chin there.

Why not just go to Scotland? Suddenly, being Alice's companion seems a whole lot more appealing than cramming my hooves into those five-inch heels and writing Vince's book for him and wiping up his pee from around the loo area. Why does that happen anyway? Does his penis thrash uncontrollably, like an eel?

Alice touches my arm kindly. 'You *are* okay to do this trip, aren't you? Because, if you want to change your mind . . .' She tails off and looks at me.

'I, er . . . feel bad moving my foot with Martha doing that.'

Alice laughs. *She's mad,* Vince would be hissing into my ear right now. *Quick, let's get away from her.*

Yet I can't, somehow. I literally can't move my foot, which is crazy because it's not as if it's been trapped there by a paving slab. It's just a little dachshund, resting her chin on it.

The doors are about to close . . . If you're not intending to travel on this train, please return to the platform . . .

I'm pinned here by a sausage dog. *Beep-beep-beep-beep-beep!* The doors close and the train starts to move. Now my heart is racing in a way I haven't felt for a very long time. Not with frustration and anger but the thrill of doing something just for the hell of it.

Why not do this? Why not pretend to be the other Kate?

What's the worst that could happen really?

I look at Alice, and there's a beat's pause before the beaming smile floods her face. 'Let's get settled then, shall we?' she says.

'Yes, let's do that,' I say as we make our way back to our seats.

CHAPTER TWELVE

Vince

If Vince can remove a door from its hinges, he can write his own book. Well, the final bit anyway. Kate's done the rest. Okay, he didn't *actually* remove the door – Carse did that – but Vince oversaw the operation and kept everyone calm, and that's what mattered.

So, the final chapter. Hmm. How hard can it be? It's just one sentence after another, and he actually writes all the time, prepping his stand-up material. However, that's just scribbled notes; the 'broad strokes' stuff he's so good at. Details, like the correct grammar, punctuation and making actual sense, not so much.

This is Kate's area! She's the semicolon person in this marriage. (Vince has never understood what they're for.) So why isn't she here?

Frowning now, he figures that the last time he was forced to write anything 'proper' was a school essay on *Macbeth*. It still haunts him now, almost as keenly as that wooden horse in the gym hall. 'Out, out, damned spot!' Lady Macbeth had ranted. All he could think of was his mum instructing him to steam his blackheads over a bowl of hot water, which he'd tried, as he'd always done what his mum told him. He'd nearly boiled his face off. Anyway, Vince was no better at understanding the work of a playwright who'd been dead for four hundred years than at fathoming out why his wife took herself off to London last night.

She'll be home soon, he reassures himself. Gazing out of his study window, he hopes to spot Kate approaching in time to finish writing the book before Zoe, his editor, gets too cross with him. However, all he sees is Gail from next door setting off in her turquoise running gear with her blonde ponytail bouncing, the epitome of rude health. That's what you get when your fluid intake consists solely of tisanes and pea milk. Catching his gaze, she grins and waves. Vince's cheeks redden as he waves back briskly, hoping he looks like a proper writer, deep in thought – like Hemingway or Kerouac – rather than a gawping weirdo.

With stress levels rising Vince tries again to think of an opening sentence, but his mind drifts back to Kate. Or, more specifically, Kate announcing that she wasn't coming home.

Did she actually mean it? Of course she didn't. It'll be some menopause thing, he reckons. Before all this started, Vince had never known that hormones could be so problematic – causing his previously happy and generally cooperative wife to start sweating and thrashing about during the night, like she's dreaming of kicking his head in, and have her previously long hair chopped to chin length like Pam Ayres. Not that Vince has anything against Pam Ayres. But if Kate was going to turn to the literary contingency for hair inspiration, then couldn't she have picked someone like . . . he racks his brain for sexy poets. All he can think of is Sylvia Plath – and she won't do.

The menopause though, Vince reflects, gnawing on the end of a Biro. It has an awful lot to answer for. The other day he noticed a hair sprouting from Kate's chin and thought she'd be pleased when he pointed it out.

'Thanks a lot, Vince,' she said with a trace of bitterness.

'Could you get it electrified?' A reasonable question, he thought.

'What?' she exclaimed.

'You know, killed with an electrical current. Zapped at the root.'

'You seem to know an awful lot about treatments,' she declared, stomping off.

These days he can't do anything right.

Fuck it, he decides. Kate's probably sitting there, spinning out a coffee in one of those bleak cafés at Euston, making him suffer for a bit longer. For what, he can't imagine.

He stares back at the laptop, aware that time is slipping by because here comes Gail again, back from her run already! She's probably racked up 10k, and what has he achieved? Sod all. Well, of course he can't write. Not when Kate's left him in the lurch – on deadline day too. Why do books have to be so fucking long anyway? And the type so small? People don't have time for reams of text these days. Colin Carse admitted that he only ever reads when he's on the loo.

All this graft, Vince reflects bitterly, and it's going to be flipped through by a jumped-up goblin with his trousers down. Is it any wonder artists – true artists – have struggled so much with their mental health over the centuries, slicing off their ears, slugging absinthe and setting fire to their life's work? Now Vince is picturing Jack Nicholson in *The Shining*, furiously typing *red rum red rum*. It's almost appealing, the idea of going glamorously berserk in a huge, dilapidated hotel up in the Colorado mountains. It's not quite the same in a bungalow in a cul-de-sac, in what Vince grandly calls his study, which still has the peach floral wallpaper from when it was his mum's sewing room.

Apart from his desk and a crazily expensive office chair he bought when he got his book contract (because he absolutely needed to swivel on something that cost nearly a grand, right?) there is no other furniture in the room.

'Are you going to keep your stuff in boxes forever? It looks like we've just moved in,' Kate remarked a few weeks ago, referring to his vast collection of raggedy notebooks and assorted paperwork. She'd gone on and on until he'd chosen and ordered a shelving unit. But the stupid thing never turned up.

Vince sighs heavily, reflecting that Jack Nicholson's wife in *The Shining* didn't nag him about shelving units. She was too busy running around and screaming in a Seventies pinafore dress—

A sudden noise cuts through his thoughts. 'Kate?' He jumps up from his spinny chair and hurries out to the hallway. But it's not Kate. It's just Jarvis, standing motionless with something clamped in his mouth.

It takes Vince a moment to register that it's his dressing gown. Jarvis must have tugged it down from its hook on the bedroom door and is now gnawing away at it. 'Drop it! Drop it!' he yells. He's never chewed things before. Kate has been gone for less than twenty-four hours and the dog has turned against him.

He manages to tug the gown from Jarvis's jaws, ripping it in the process. Jarvis barks sharply, baring his teeth. 'Hey! Stop that!' Vince glares at him, wondering – not for the first time – what possessed his daughter to take on a dog and then hotfoot it to Maine, three thousand miles away. He'd been prepared to stand firm on the matter. But Kate had said, 'We should take him, Vince. It'll probably only be for a few months, and we know he'll be looked after properly.'

He examines his gown in dismay. It's the softest, cosiest one he's ever owned; the last Christmas present from his mum, before she died a few weeks later. Vince wonders now if this was a protest move because he hasn't let Jarvis out yet. It certainly seems personal, and tinged with malice.

With a jolt, he realises it's 12.30 p.m. Where did all the time go? He stomps through to the kitchen and, despite not having had breakfast, he grabs a beer from the fridge. Didn't all the great writers drink, to fuel their creativity? He's thinking of Hemingway again as he returns to his desk to find that Zoe has emailed him.

Hey Vince,

Just checking in. Hope all's good. We did say you'd have the book over to me by EOP? Hope you're still okay with that?

Love, Zoe x

EOP? What does that mean? Some kind of newfangled delivery method? He was just planning to email it. Or rather, Kate was. A wave of self-pity crashes over him. Couldn't she have planned her hormonal breakdown for tomorrow, when the book was done?

EOP means 'end of play', Google informs him. When *is* that? Comedians aren't generally nine-to-five kind of guys. If Vince had wanted that sort of life he'd have become an accountant.

Hey Zoe,

It's coming along great, just a few final touches, be with you really soon.

Love, V x

Vince presses send and inhales to the very top of his lungs.

He *must* finish this book, and not just to please

Zoe. He must prove to himself that he can hold things together and do it perfectly well without Kate's help. But an hour later he's no further on, and Jarvis is nudging at him with his nose, keen to go out. 'Soon, mate. Soon,' he mutters. He stares bleakly out of his study window. A heavy cloud the precise shade of a loo roll tube is hanging overheard.

Vince is overcome by an urge to call Kate. He won't, though. He's not going to keep nagging and bothering her. She's probably back at Tash's, chatting happily over endless coffees. Or maybe she's at Julian and Shawn's, their old upstairs neighbours who were always showing up with treats from the bakery for her.

She probably just needs a bit of time with her old mates, Vince decides. He knows what women are like with their besties. Vince has friends too, of course – mainly other comedians like Harry Bonomo who'd started out on the circuit at the same time as him. But they haven't really kept in contact since they left London, and at fifty-one Harry has become a father for the first time, and it's all milk teeth and the funny things his baby daughter's done, and although Vince feels guilty about it, he can't relate to him anymore.

Staring at his laptop now, he realises that the sum total of his morning's work amounts to just two words: *Chapter Thirteen.*

It's a start, he tells himself. He toys with making it bold – **Chapter Thirteen** – to add more weight to it.

It's still just two words, though. He tries upping the

type size like a child who's been asked to write a whole page describing his holiday, and thinks he can trick his teacher by doing it in *massive* writing:

Chapter Thirteen

. . . But he knows that won't fool Zoe. She's a whip-smart woman who's currently waiting in her London office a hundred miles up in the sky, and drumming her nails on her desk.

The appearance of Jarvis in the doorway gives him a start. He looks at the dog, reminding himself that *he* doesn't understand that Vince is stressed and hungover and desperately wants his wife to come home. He's only a dog, and he needs a good, proper walk, like Kate would give him—

'No!' Vince yells, jumping up from his seat. But he can't stop him now. All he can do is watch as Jarvis cocks a leg and pees, in a seemingly never-ending arc, against the study door.

CHAPTER THIRTEEN

Kate

'—*And* the peach floral wallpaper in what used to be his mother's sewing room?'

I nod. ''Fraid so. He won't let me change it.'

'So what about this water feature,' Alice continues, frowning, 'in the garden? I'm not a fan of throwing stuff into landfill, but—'

'Vince refuses,' I explain. 'I've tried everything. There's no getting through to him at all.'

Alice runs a hand over her silver bob. For most of the journey so far she's been pinging questions at me, seemingly fascinated to know more about my life. Thankfully, she hasn't grilled me about my credentials or why I signed up to an agency for this kind of work.

Of course, the real Kate – or someone from the agency – could call her at any moment and apologise for the no-show at Euston. And then I'd be rumbled and Alice would be appalled – or, understandably, furious.

Possibly even freaked out. And I don't want that to happen. Already, I've decided I like her very much.

'So it's been like living in a strange kind of limbo?' she suggests. 'As if your mother-in-law might leap out from a cupboard at any moment?'

'It sounds awful but yes.' She really seems to get it – which triggers a whoosh of guilt over deceiving her in this way. I know what Vince would say now. That I *definitely* need an urgent appointment with Dr Kemp. That what I'm doing right now is far more serious than misusing Agata's lemon balm as a salad ingredient or burning a quiche.

Yet I haven't lied directly, or tried to extort money from her. When Alice goes to the loo I quickly google agencies offering companion services on a short-term basis. From what I can gather they seem to ask for full payment upfront. Hopefully, Alice will have paid them, so there won't be an awful situation of her trying to pay *me*.

I don't want money. It's not about that. All I want is to be useful and busy and far away from Sycamore Grove, just until the dust settles.

And then I can figure out what to do next.

Alice returns from the loo and resumes her direct mode of questioning. 'So, d'you think you'll go back to Vince when our three weeks are over?'

'I'm not quite sure what my plans are,' I say quickly.

'Oh, I am sorry if I'm quizzing you.' She seems to catch herself. 'Max, my son, is always telling me off for being ridiculously nosy . . .'

'It's fine, honestly,' I reply, thinking, as long as we avoid anything relating to the *real* Kate, or the job she'd been booked to do, then I'm on reasonably safe ground. And actually, I'm flattered that someone as smart and accomplished as Alice is so interested in my life. When we moved to Shugbury, Deborah was the only one to ask what I'd done work-wise in London.

'Ugh, dusty old museums,' she'd said with a shudder. 'I was always dragged around them as a child. I dreaded it.' And that had been that. My nerves tingle a little when the same subject rears up now. However, Alice doesn't seem surprised that my career has swerved from museum curation to this seemingly unlikely new direction.

'I should have known about that,' she chastises herself, 'if I'd read your CV properly. But it was all such a rush after Max announced he wasn't coming. I couldn't be doing with Zoom interviews and there wasn't time to meet anyone face to face. And anyway, I like to trust my instinct in these situations . . .' I shift uneasily in my seat. 'I think we should have a little toast, don't you?' Alice adds with a bright smile.

'Er, yes. What would you like? I can go—' I leap up, keen for a little respite from this crazy pretence. (Am I despicable in deceiving her like this?) However, Alice is in the aisle already, holding her hand in mid-air, as if stopping traffic.

'I'll go. I need to stretch my legs. You wait here with the girls.'

While she's gone, I tell myself that, if all this becomes too much, I can confess and deal with whatever she throws at me. I'll deserve it, after all. Meanwhile, I settle her dogs who are a little agitated by her disappearance, and only relax again when she reappears.

'No champagne,' she announces, looking crestfallen. 'Only ready-mixed gin and tonics, but there *is* ice.'

'Oh, lovely. Thank you.' I pour mine over the ice cubes and take a fortifying sip. 'So, tell me about growing up in Scotland,' I prompt her, hoping to at least find out where we're going as I haven't felt able to ask. Of course, the real Kate would have known all the details.

'It's a lovely part of rural Perthshire,' she starts. 'But I was your typical only child stuck in the middle of nowhere. Lived in my own head most of the time. Loved books. They were all I cared about really. I was set on studying English literature, and when I was offered a place at St Andrews university my mother was horrified.'

'Horrified?' I exclaim. 'Why?'

'Because she had someone in mind for me to marry and expected me to produce a horde of children.' She smiles wryly.

'Wow. And you rebelled against that?'

'I did. Went through university with no help from my parents. I was pretty much cut off,' she adds. 'The only reason I've inherited the house is because there was literally no one else to leave it to. Dad had passed away a few years before.'

I nod, not sure how to respond to this.

'Did you ever go back? After you'd left for university, I mean?'

'Occasionally,' she replies, 'hoping to make amends and then to show them that I'd finally given them a grandchild, even if they'd had to wait until I was thirty-five, which was geriatric back then.' She sips her drink and smiles wryly. 'The wedding cake lasted longer than my marriage. I brought up Max on my own, which was another reason for my parents to be horrified by me . . .'

'I think it's admirable,' I say truthfully. 'So, you were working throughout all this?'

'Oh, yes. In academia. I adored the students – they were the best part. And belonging to a university, which is a bit like a family. A dysfunctional family, but a family all the same.' Is there any other type, I wonder? She laughs, but her mention of family sparks another jolt of unease in me. What am I going to tell Edie about leaving her dad?

'You know,' Alice continues, cutting through my thoughts, 'I'm so relieved I won't be clearing out the house all by myself.'

'Really?' She gives the impression that she's nothing less than immensely capable.

'Yes, absolutely. I'll tell you something, Kate.' She drains her cup. 'I didn't have the dogs until three months ago. I wasn't even a dog person really. They belonged to my best friend, Ruthie. She passed away and there was no one else to take them in—'

'Oh, I'm so sorry,' I exclaim.

'We knew it was coming,' she says, waving a hand, as if not wanting to dwell on it. 'And we had some lovely times towards the end. It happened a year ago, just after Mum passed.'

I let the information settle. 'So the house has been empty—'

'For all that time, yes.' A shrug and a resigned smile. 'I must admit, Kate, I haven't been very good at sorting things out. I've sort of been hoping it'll all magically disappear. It's *so* much to cope with by oneself . . .' Shockingly, her eyes fill with tears.

'Oh, Alice. I'm so sorry . . .' Without thinking, I reach across the table to touch her hand.

'It's fine, really,' she says. Then, in a brisker tone, she runs through what we'll be doing at the house: '. . . So it's *great* that you have all that museum experience because we'll be sorting through my parents' furniture and knick-knacks, keeping track of it all . . .'

'Yes, great!' I enthuse.

'I do remember your CV mentioned that you're an avid gardener?'

It's like a punch to my gut. Edie bought me some kind of lacy-leaved houseplant once. I'd murdered it within two weeks.

'Erm, yes,' I say, sweating now.

'And didn't it mention that you've overseen garden landscaping before?'

'I can do that, definitely.' Should I jump the train at the next station? The *only* good thing about our home

111

in Shugbury is that the garden is a plain old rectangle of grass, with a few hardy shrubs that haven't seemed to need any tending. The testicle water feature looked after itself.

'Well, there's lots to do there too.' Alice extracts a packet of dog treats from her bag and offers Penny and Martha one each.

'No problem!' I try not to appear rigid with panic.

'Oh, I don't mean tackling the whole thing yourself,' she clarifies. 'It's far too big a job. No, we'll be calling in a team, and I'd love you to manage that side of things . . .'

I gulp my G&T. 'I'm sure that won't be a problem.'

'I know it's a lot to take on,' Alice adds. 'Far more than a normal companion's role. But I went through it all with the nice girl at the agency and she was sure you'd be more than capable.' She beams now, looking delighted at the prospect of us working together. 'Oh, I'm so happy it's you, Kate. It's like fate really. You're *exactly* the person I need.'

CHAPTER FOURTEEN

In Glasgow we change trains – and stations – for which the dogs are clearly grateful. As they attend to the necessaries along the short walk, I catch myself wondering if Vince has been looking after Jarvis properly. Has he been measuring out his raw food or dolloping it haphazardly into his bowl? Has he taken him for proper walks or just released him into the garden?

Jarvis is not your responsibility! I remind myself as we find our seats for the second leg of the journey. And what a journey it is as we leave the city behind: first a patchwork of fields stitched together with spindly fences; then undulating hills swathed in dense forest, and a flat green plain sliced through with the silvery curve of a river.

Three times, Mum had brought George and me on this very journey from our Glasgow home. I picture us now, tumbling off the train as we arrived at the pretty little Perthshire town, the three of us thrilled at the prospect of a fortnight's camping – without Dad.

No shouting, and no fear. I was just a kid for most of those holidays. Then there was that last time, when we'd moved to London and George had begged and begged to go back to that Perthshire campsite one more time.

I was fifteen by then and hadn't even wanted to come. But, as it turned out, that time was the most special . . .

I've gathered that today, we are heading for that very same station. I've told Alice I've been there before; no reason not to, I reasoned. And now, as we step off the train, I'm glad I don't have to pretend – because the pastel blue clapperboard station building is still there, just as I remember. 'That used to be a bookshop,' I announce.

'The Railway Bookshop? That's right!' The smile lights up her face. 'It was the only bookshop in town and I was never out of it. It's long gone, sadly.'

'That's a shame,' I say, vividly remembering the first time we'd arrived here when I was seven years old. We lugged a borrowed tent and sleeping bags on foot, all the way to the campsite way out in the hills – with George in his buggy. This time it's a taxi, as apparently the house is a little way out of town.

'It's been a while now since Bea passed,' the driver remarks. 'Place has been all shut up for a year or so, hasn't it?' We'd no sooner climbed in than this genial middle-aged man had wanted to know why we were heading there.

'It has,' Alice says. 'We're here to clear the place out, finally.'

114

'It's so hard when your parents pass,' he observes kindly. 'You can only do these things when you're ready. So, what's going to happen to the place?'

'I'm putting it up for sale.' Alice glances down and strokes Martha's head. Each of us has a dachshund on our laps.

'Oh, right,' he says lightly. 'Not tempted to keep it?'

'I'm afraid not.' As she flashes me a knowing smile, I can't help comparing her no-nonsense approach to that of Vince, who's reacted so strongly against changing anything in his parents' house. 'We'll just rattle through it all,' she explained on the train, as she made a list in a tiny leather-bound notebook detailing where her parents' possessions will go. Auction house, various charities and – as she put it bluntly – 'the dump'. All that's fine, of course. I'm trying not to dwell on the fact that we're also bringing in a gardening team, and that it'll be my job to oversee them.

How hard can that be? I reassure myself. They'll know what they're doing, surely? A *team*, though. It seems a little excessive for a domestic garden. Must be a real mess, I reason.

More pressing still is the very real possibility of someone calling Alice tomorrow, explaining why the real Kate hadn't turned up.

'Why did you lie?' she'll ask me, aghast.

What'll I say? *I didn't lie exactly. I just wanted to help. Stuff's been happening and I needed to be very far away from home.*

Which, actually, is the truth of it. I need to be as far away as possible from Vince and that bungalow and Deborah and Agata and their sneery looks. And if I'm found out? I'll just have to throw up my hands and apologise profusely and take whatever Alice throws at me.

Anyway, I'm here now, meandering through the country lanes in a taxi as Alice and the driver chat companionably. Despite the madness of what I've done, it still feels oddly *right*. After all, the happiest times in my childhood were spent here among these hills and valleys and forests. Finally, Mum and George and I could be happy and not worry about angering Dad by doing something as innocuous as biting into an apple. 'D'you have to eat so bloody loud? You're like a fucking horse!'

It was our sanctuary, this place. We'd play hide-and-seek in the forest and cook sausages on a grill Mum made from wire she'd found in the woods, over a fire. Down a little lane, there was a table with an awning where you could buy eggs and home-made preserves. We couldn't believe that there was no one manning it – just an honesty box with a slot that you dropped your money into. And at night in our tent, George and I would be lulled to sleep by the sound of owls hooting, instead of being kept awake by Dad's roars.

Now the lane has narrowed to a bumpy single track. Dusk is falling and the lights of faraway houses speckle the hills. In the distance purplish hills are outlined against the darkening sky.

An imposing house, set a little higher than road level, has come into view. What look like formal gardens sweep gracefully towards ornate gates. Closer now I can make out turrets and spires and numerous multi-paned windows, with no sign of life behind them. Obviously once a grand residence, there's something rather forlorn about the place. 'That's some house,' I remark.

'It is,' Alice agrees with a nod.

'It looks kind of unloved, though,' I add, 'and a bit spooky. No sign of life in it at all.' There's a lull then as we slow down further, and the driver pulls up at the wrought-iron gates.

'Is this *it*?' I gasp, turning to Alice.

'Yes, this is it,' she says, as if it's a perfectly ordinary home.

'It's . . . it's not what I imagined,' I blurt out before I can stop myself, feeling bad for calling it unloved.

'What *did* you imagine?' Alice raises a brow, and my heart quickens.

'Um, I don't know. Just an ordinary house, I suppose. You know. A cottage . . .'

The driver laughs and looks round at us. 'You've never been here before?'

'No, I—'

'You had no idea what it was like? You hadn't seen any photos?'

'Er, no,' I say, wondering if *he's* realised I'm an imposter and shouldn't be here at all. I climb out quickly, still overcome by the austere yet magnificent home, set

117

on a grassy mound with forested hills behind. There's a lake in the grounds, gleaming in the moonlight, and a faded green lattice summerhouse perched at its edge.

The iron gates have been secured shut with a padlock and a thick chain. Beside them stands a rickety-looking wooden garage, and on the low stone wall a sign reads *Osprey House*.

'Guess your daughter's a bit shocked then? To finally see the old family seat . . .' The driver chuckles as he climbs out and lifts Alice's case from the boot.

'Oh, I'm not Alice's daughter,' I say quickly. 'I'm just—' I stop as she catches my eye, then pays and thanks the driver.

'Well, good luck then,' he says. Then he's gone, leaving Alice and me and the dogs at the roadside.

'This way, Kate.' She beckons me through a smaller side gate in the stone wall. Then she links my arm, pulling her case along, having set the dogs loose to scamper towards the house.

As we walk, my heart seems to lift as I replay what she said, just then, to the taxi driver: 'There's no *just* about it. Kate is my right-hand woman.' Which feels a heck of a lot better than being a back end.

CHAPTER FIFTEEN

Woken by birdsong, I take in my surroundings in the simply furnished room. It has solid country house proportions and a high ceiling with ornate cornicing picked out in off-white against pale lemon walls. There's a sturdy antique wardrobe, a scuffed dark wooden chest of drawers and a tarnished mirror hanging above the burgundy-tiled fireplace. The iron-framed bed bears a chintzy quilted bedspread that I'd pulled around myself gratefully, not even minding its mustiness, after a quick supper last night. The fridge had been stocked with essentials, apparently by Morag, Alice's mother's housekeeper. Alice explained that she's been popping in regularly, and will be on hand to help while we're here.

Despite the fact that I'd arrived under completely false pretences, I slept soundly last night, in soft flannel pyjamas kindly lent by Alice. By that point I'd gone beyond stressing about Osprey House's extensive, clearly badly neglected grounds.

Somehow, I decided, I'd figure out what to do.

Now I swivel out of bed, pad across the thin faded rug and throw open the moss green velvet curtains.

'Oh!' I exclaim out loud. Because beyond the overgrown gardens, the rolling Perthshire hills are bathed in hazy morning light. With difficulty, I manage to lift the lower half of the ancient sash window and fill my lungs with soft, cool air.

Hearing Alice pottering around downstairs, I dress in yesterday's clothes, grateful for her foisting clean underwear on me last night. I've known her for a single day and already I'm borrowing her knickers.

'Mum was still running it as a B&B well into her late eighties,' Alice explains when I find her making coffee in the kitchen. 'With Morag's help, of course. But she still presided over the place, terrorising guests.' She smirks and hands me a mug of coffee.

'It's a wonderful house,' I say truthfully.

'Come on, it *is* a bit bleak,' she insists.

'Only because it's been lying empty.'

She nods. 'It needs a lot of TLC. But that can come later when the place is cleared.'

My gaze skims the scuffed cream Aga and the enormous oak dresser stacked with crockery and glassware. Glass-fronted cabinets are filled with yet more china, and a bevy of cooking pots and utensils hang from racks on the creamy walls.

'Is this what it was like,' I ask, 'when you were growing up?'

She nods. 'Nothing's changed really. My parents

didn't believe in upgrading anything until it literally fell apart. So, d'you fancy eggs before I give you a tour? I think Morag's left us some. She has a smallholding—'

Before I can answer she's produced a basket from somewhere, filled with eggs, and now she's cracking and scrambling and brushing off my protests that I could do it – because aren't I here to help?

'Not to cook for me, Kate,' she admonishes, good-naturedly. 'You'll have your work cut out, believe me.'

I smile, relieved that she's apparently keen to get on, rather than asking me anything difficult – like why did I sign up with an agency? What kind of people have I 'companioned' for? If I let myself, I'd be a fizzling ball of anxiety. So again I push those fears away, wondering instead why Vince hasn't been in touch since our conversation at Euston yesterday. He hasn't even messaged me. I *did* tell him I wasn't coming home – but he must have thought I meant, 'I'm not coming home just yet.'

Unless he really doesn't care?

Maybe he's sitting it out, waiting for me to crawl home, humiliated and full of regret. I'm trying not to think about his book that I was supposed to finish yesterday, or our garden table that's no doubt still cluttered with bottles and cans. (What will the neighbours think!) None of that would have happened if I'd just said, 'No, Vince, I'm not making a buffet' and tipped a load of Wotsits into a big receptacle – like the washing-up bowl! That would've done! – and banged it on the kitchen table and been done with it.

'Let's go, Kate.' My thoughts dissipate into the dusty air as, with breakfast over, Alice whisks me on a tour of the house, with the dogs trotting along at our sides. In the drawing room, the powder blue walls are hung with muted oil paintings of stags and eagles and sheep being herded across hillsides. The tiny study leading off it is entirely filled with books, most of which seem to be gardening manuals of some kind.

Perhaps I can *cram* my brain with plant knowledge?

A utility room leads onto an overgrown kitchen garden. Amidst the tangled weeds a carved stone bird of prey – presumably an osprey – regards us coldly from its plinth. 'Let me show you the rest of upstairs,' Alice says. The elegant curved stone staircase leads to the L-shaped landing and a succession of bedrooms, all eerily still and clearly uninhabited for a long time.

'This is my little den,' she explains as we step into a box room. Extremely basic, and a little claustrophobic compared to the other bedrooms, it's furnished with a single bed, a waist-high cupboard and what looks like a child's desk at the window.

'Wouldn't you rather sleep in one of the other rooms?' I ask.

'I'm fine in here,' she says quickly. 'So, shall we head into town? I'm guessing there's a few things you'll need to stock up on . . .'

'Oh, yes please.' I glance down. 'I *hate* this skirt,' I add without thinking.

'Did you have to wear it for work?' She looks bemused.

'Er, yes,' I say quickly, relieved when the subject is dropped, and we head outside.

Wilma from the hotel messaged yesterday. *Where are you? Are you coming in today or not?*

I was poised to call and explain, gushing apologies, that I wouldn't be in for my shift – or indeed ever again. Then I pictured those heel-lacerating shoes and the guests who'd made such a fuss about a winged insect floating in the swimming pool. ('We didn't pay to swim with bugs!') Fuck it, I decided, and replied simply: *I'm not coming back*. Wilma's lengthy and furious response wasn't pleasant, and I barely skimmed it before deleting it from my phone.

At the main gates now, Alice wrangles the padlock and untangles the hefty chain. Beside it, in the dilapidated garage, sits her mother's car.

'Held together with sticking plasters and hope.' She chuckles. 'But Morag's made sure I'm insured to drive it, and you can be too if you're brave enough.'

'Yes, I can do that.'

'It'll be handy,' she says as we lift the dogs onto the flaking tan leather back seat, and climb into the front of the grey saloon. 'Like a driving a bus,' she announces as we set off.

An easy silence settles as I take in the smudgy greens and hazy purples of the landscape. In the distance a loch shimmers, narrowing to a river spanned by a pedestrian suspension bridge. Then suddenly Alice takes a sharp turn – her driving is a little erratic, even gear-crunchy, but perhaps that's the car? – and we're parking up in town.

Immediately, I'm thrown back to those camping holidays with Mum and George. The compact arrangement of independent shops and quaint cafés, set around a single high street, is vividly familiar. I clearly remember the ornate town clock and drinking fountain. Local businesses are heavily weighted towards tea rooms and outdoor shops, as if eating cake and walking it off is what really matters around here.

'There's a little boutique at the top of the town,' Alice offers, 'and a charity shop. That's your choice for clothes, I'm afraid. It's not exactly a fashion mecca.'

I smile at that – 'Honestly, I'd expected better!' I joke – and Alice laughs, because the town is delightful.

'I'll walk the dogs by the river,' she adds. 'Shall we meet at noon by the clock?'

'Great,' I say, and watch her striding away determinedly in flat boots, her camel trench and a woollen beanie pulled low over her silvery bob, with those ridiculously pretty dogs. I've learnt now that her home is a flat in West Hampstead. ('A shoebox but I like it!') It's not exactly surprising. I can easily picture her in the chichi neighbourhood, marching across Hampstead Heath and having coffee or a G&T with friends. It's trickier to imagine her growing up here, where the community noticeboard is all bowls tournaments, a meeting about 'the conservation of trout and salmon in transitional waters' and a raffle to raise funds for the community centre's roof.

On the train Alice mentioned that she's seventy-six. ('All this fuss about ageing,' she scoffed, 'like it's a battle. I lost Ruthie. That's the alternative, isn't it?') Although she might fit the demographic, I can't imagine her attending 'soup-and-roll for seniors' events hosted by the Baptist church. Clearly, she's something of a powerhouse, keen to have Osprey House ready for sale as soon as possible. That's why she needs help, and as long as I can get away with this, I'm determined to give as much of myself as I can. Because I'm grateful, I decide. Grateful that she was there at Euston at that precise moment and it all just happened. It hardly seems believable.

I start to explore the town, perusing gift shops filled with local crafts and cuddly Highland cattle toys. There's a cosy-looking Italian restaurant and a tiny cinema. The old-fashioned newsagent has a postcard carousel in the doorway and a poster in the window advertising birdwatching and salmon-fishing trips. Yet it's a proper working town too, with a butcher's – the queue snakes along the pavement – plus a fishmonger, a hardware store, and more cafés and bakeries than I can count.

I spot the village hall, and my heart does a little flip. That last time we came here, when I was fifteen, there was a ceilidh in that hall – a night of traditional Scottish music and dancing. And other things happened that night too. Mum had danced with local men, and I'd had a little adventure of my own.

125

Smiling at the memory, I check out the town's sole boutique. As it turns out to be pretty much cashmere and tweed, I switch my focus to the charity shop.

'That's you all stocked up,' announces the cheerful, pink-cheeked woman at the counter as she bags up my selection of jeans, T-shirts, sweaters and a sturdy outdoor jacket. Toiletries are amassed at a supermarket, along with multipacks of knickers and socks, and I buy a leather purse and canvas shoulder bag in a gift shop.

Still with time to spare, I venture down a side street where the sweet aroma of hot chocolate and toasted teacakes drifts out from a café. I pass a fishing tackle shop with an array of fishing flies in the window, mounted and framed like rare butterflies, and an inviting-looking pub festooned with hanging baskets. There's a short row of single-storey cottages, all with brightly painted front doors and tiny, immaculate front gardens. Then, just as I'm about to turn back, I spot another shop at the end of the street.

It's a second-hand bookshop, no bigger than one of the cottages, with a bow window and a hand-painted sign above. Clearly, it was a home at some point. *Off the Rails Books*, the sign reads, gold lettering gleaming against blue.

When Mum whisked George and me to London, I'd only been allowed to bring three of my books. Now here I am in Scotland without any at all. Tiny brass bells tinkle above the door as, with my heart quickening in anticipation, I step into the shop.

CHAPTER SIXTEEN

Neatly filled bookshelves stretch up to the ceiling. Old-fashioned table lamps glow invitingly in the alcoves. I start to browse, expecting someone to appear from the back. But no one comes. There's no sign – or sounds – of life at all.

After buying up an entire wardrobe for my stay here, a sense of calm settles over me as I set down my bulging carrier bags. Soon I discover a second room behind the first, and yet another leading on behind that. The place is a treasure trove of unexpected nooks and book-lined corridors linking the rooms.

Objects have been placed on the shelves, in gaps between books, to reflect the different sections. Leather-cased binoculars and a sketchbook of bird drawings, its pages yellowed with age, nestle on the natural history shelf. Victorian ink bottles and antique spectacles are arranged in the fiction section.

'You museum types,' Vince often teased me. 'You say "It's so beautifully curated" when you mean it's been set out quite nicely.' *Curated* was definitely on his list of mockable words. Shocked at how quickly I've begun to think of him – of us – in the past tense, I carry on browsing. His interest would dwindle rapidly in a shop like this. 'I'll wait outside,' he'd say. 'Will you be long?'

'Just go off and do something else, Dad,' Edie would retort, if she was with us. And she'd catch my gaze, and deliver an eye-roll and we'd laugh. Trying not to think about Edie either – because I'll have to tell her what I've done very soon – I head back through to the shop's front room, just as the brass bells tinkle again, more brashly this time, and a young woman barges in.

Immediately, the cosy home library vibe evaporates. She shuts the door with unnecessary force, stomps to the counter and plonks herself down behind it with a heavy sigh. She doesn't acknowledge me. She just pulls out her phone from a pocket and frowns at it.

'Hi,' I start. In a little shop like this it's too awkward not to say anything.

'Hi.' It's brief, reluctant. No eye contact.

'I love your shop,' I add. 'It's so beautifully, um . . .' *Don't say 'curated', you'll sound like a prat*, '. . . set out.'

'It's not mine,' she remarks.

'Oh, right.' Still no eye contact, and no further information supplied. Her face is chalk pale and murky shadows lurk beneath tired-looking eyes. I'd put her at late teens, early twenties at the most. Her dark brown hair is piled up on her head and secured haphazardly with a plastic comb. She's wearing a faded black top

128

with a splodge of something on the left shoulder, and the kind of tight expression that suggests she'd rather be anywhere but here.

Should I point out the stuff on her shoulder? It could be bird poo, and if I was carrying that around with me I'd be grateful if someone let me know. But it's hard to tell, and her hostile vibes, which have killed off any remaining desire to browse, are propelling me towards the door.

A flurry of sudden activity catches my attention. She's disappeared from view and, judging by the sounds, is rummaging for something under the counter. I pause to study local guidebooks by the door. The girl reappears with a clingfilm-wrapped sandwich. She tugs off its wrapper and devours it in enormous bites. She's acting like it's the first thing she's eaten all day, and I'm wondering now if perhaps she's not supposed to eat at the counter, and wants to guzzle her lunch before her boss appears.

The sandwich is finished, and now a Twix appears, plus a sugary doughnut from a brown paper bag. There's more eating happening in here than in the tearoom a few doors down. As she chomps into the doughnut a jet of red jam spurts out, hitting both her top and the counter. 'Ugh!' With a groan she uses the paper bag to dab at both the counter and herself, seemingly ineffectually.

'Don't you hate it when that happens?' I remark, trying to convey sympathy.

'Uh. Yeah.' She looks at me briefly as if I have no

business being here, browsing books, in a *bookshop*. How weird that this delightful shop is being staffed by a powerful customer deterrent. A little disappointed now, I'm about to leave when the door is opened again, this time by a tall man with wavy mid-brown hair, smattered with a little grey. Carrying a huge box that covers the lower half of his face, he props the door open with a broad shoulder. Then, before I can offer to help, he swivels and sets it down on the shop floor as the door closes behind him.

'Hi,' I say.

He straightens up and smiles. 'Hi,' he says. 'D'you need help with anything at all?'

'No thanks,' I reply, aware of the dramatic change in atmosphere from the moment he walked in. 'Just been having a browse,' I add. 'It's a lovely shop. I could get lost in here for hours.'

'That's the idea.' He's handsome in a rugged, unaffected way; tall and slim, in faded jeans and a sweatshirt, with soft grey-blue eyes. 'Take your time,' he adds. 'And if there's anything you're looking for . . .' He turns to the girl. 'Everything okay, Liv?'

'Yeah.' Apart from the jammy blob on her chest, all evidence of the counter picnic has gone.

'Any sales while I was out?'

'Nope.'

'Any customers? Phone calls?'

A terse shake of the head.

'Right. So, if we could price up these, that'd be great,'

he says, breezing over her minimal communication. 'They're mostly history. A couple of nice editions of classics too. And some poetry. Lovely family, they were. Sorry to see their books go but they're downsizing and won't have the space. So, I've another pick-up to do later,' he adds.

'Okay,' she murmurs vaguely, as if it's of no concern to her what he does.

Now I detect a glimmer of exasperation, but he seems to gather himself quickly. 'Did you offer our customer some coffee, Liv?'

'Uh, no, Dad.' Ah, his daughter's been manning the fort.

'Would you like some?' he offers. 'There's a pot made . . .'

'Better not,' I say reluctantly. 'I'm meeting a friend soon.'

'Well, next time then, if you're in town for a while?'

'Yes, definitely,' I say as something occurs to me. 'Your shop's name. Off the Rails. Did it used to be on the station platform?'

'It was, yeah. Not in my time, but the guy who set up the shop started off there. Then the building needed refurbishing and he wasn't sure if they'd let him move back in once it had been done. So he found this place. And when he retired I took it over from him . . .'

'Well, I love it.' I smile, glad now that I hadn't left a moment earlier. 'I remember it,' I add. 'The Railway Bookshop, I mean. I came on holiday here as a child.'

'It was a real gem, wasn't it?' He grins too. 'I was obsessed with the place. My parents rationed my visits to one a month. I had to make do with the library in between times.'

I chuckle. 'That sounds familiar . . .'

'So are you on holiday here?'

'No, I'm actually, um . . .' How to put it? *No, I'm assuming someone else's identity and actually conning an older lady who's shown me nothing but kindness?* But then, he's not here to interrogate me. He's just a bookshop man being friendly to a customer. 'I'm kind of working,' I reply.

'Oh, really? Whereabouts?'

'It's . . . well, um, it's a bit out of town. I'm helping to clear out a house to get it ready for sale.'

'Right. Well, if there are books I'm always happy to have a look. Here's our card. The number's on there if you need us . . .' He fishes one from a box on the counter and hands it to me. 'I'm Fergus,' he adds.

'I'm Kate. And thanks,' I say, slipping it into my pocket.

He reaches below the counter for a coffee pot and fills two chunky pottery mugs. 'Here you go,' he says, handing one to his daughter. 'That'll perk you up a bit.' Then to me: 'Sure you wouldn't like one?'

I hesitate, checking the time on the wall clock behind the counter. There's just enough time, I decide, reluctant to leave just yet. 'Oh, why not? Just a quick one—' But the words have barely left my mouth when my phone trills in my skirt pocket. Without checking the caller's name I answer it, expecting Alice to say she's waiting for me.

Except it's not Alice. It's Vince, who seems to be shouting – but I don't know what about.

CHAPTER SEVENTEEN

'I can't hear you,' I say. 'You keep cutting out . . .'

'I said *viss-ate-my*—'

'Vince, you're all muffled. I don't think there's a very good signal—'

'. . . I said JARVIS ATE MY DRESSING GOWN!'

'Okay! No need to shout!' I look around at the man and his daughter, give them an apologetic grimace and quickly leave the shop.

'I'm just saying,' Vince says hotly.

I've travelled four hundred miles from home and this is the most pressing matter. Although, of course, he doesn't know where I am. For all he knows I could still be at Euston station. I stride away from the bookshop, along the narrow side street and back towards the main hub of the town. 'That's unlike him, isn't it? To eat a non-food thing? I hope he's all right—'

'Yes, *he's* fine,' Vince exclaims. '*He's* absolutely tickety-boo, thanks for asking . . .'

'Vince—'

'*I'm* not, though—'

'Is it mendable?'

'Mendable? You tell me! Only thing I know is, we were having a perfectly nice time at our party, and then you'd stormed out—'

'I don't mean our *marriage*. I mean your dressing gown. Is it a big rip or just a tiny hole—'

'I haven't examined it forensically,' he announces. 'I mean, yes. It's pretty sizeable . . .' He exhales. 'Look, I wasn't going to call you. I figured you needed some time to cool off or simmer down or whatever the hell's going on. I didn't want to bother you,' he adds with a martyrish edge. 'I just wanted to tell you—'

'About your dressing gown?' I cut in.

'No! Well, not just that. We need to talk, don't we?'

Something seems to clench inside my chest. I've reached the town clock now, where there are benches and ornamental flower beds. I place my shopping bags at my feet. 'I know we do,' I say tightly.

'Sorry,' Vince mutters. 'I've just been having a pretty stressful time with work and everything, and Jarvis peed in my study yesterday as well . . .'

'Did he?' I exclaim, shocked at these sudden changes in his behaviour. I've never known him to have an accident indoors.

'. . . So there was that to mop up,' Vince goes on. 'Why couldn't Edie have a goldfish instead of this *mammal* with all its assorted emissions?'

He's trying for a joke, but it hangs limply. The town

is growing busier now. People are in and out of shops and cafés, carrying paper bags of baked goods and in one case a giant bunch of sunflowers. 'Did you clear up the sick?' I ask.

'What?'

'Jarvis's sick on the hall carpet.'

''Course I did,' he mutters.

'And did you manage to finish the book and send it off?' Ridiculously, it still feels like *my* job, *my* responsibility. It's like being trapped in a too-tight garment in a changing room that you can't pull off.

'Um, not quite, but I'm almost there . . .' He sounds calmer now, and more amenable. Perhaps he's coping without me after all.

'So, Zoe was okay about you missing the deadline?' I start, but Vince leaps in.

'Kate, I'm not worried about deadlines right now. I mean, it's not my priority, okay? 'Cause I have other things on my mind, like you telling me yesterday that you weren't coming home.' He takes in an audible breath. 'Did you mean it?'

My heart thuds hard. 'I . . . I don't know, Vince. I just haven't been very happy lately. Well, for a long time. I've been miserable actually, for ages now. I've tried to talk to you but we never seem to get anywhere and I just can't carry on—'

'Can't carry on with what? With me?'

'Don't keep shouting over me like this,' I say firmly. 'I'm trying to explain things. This is the problem, you

136

see? I don't feel listened to, or even seen. I'm like this floating ghostly thing, and I can't—'

'Just come home, Kate. Get the first train you can. Or I can come and get you—'

'Vince, I'm not in—' I start.

'We'll make things better,' he announces. 'I promise. Look, I'm sorry if you've felt taken for granted or whatever, or if I upset you by laughing about those chocolate things, the crispy dollops for the festival. They weren't that bad. *I'd* have eaten them—'

'Vince, you wouldn't!'

'I would! Honestly. Well, if I was *starving* I would . . .' He snorts. 'Who cares about baking anyway? It's become like this competitive sport. You're not very good at it, but you're good at lots of other things, aren't you? Like, um, er . . .'

'Vince, this isn't about my chocolate clusters,' I say firmly, but he leaps back in.

'Tell you what. How about I book you a half-day at a spa with a fluffy robe—'

'*What*?'

'A nice spa thing. Wouldn't you like that? I could ring a few places, sort something for later this week, once the book's finished. I can call right now. Shugbury Spa's meant to be nice. Deborah said it was. She had a hot stone thing or something like that. Scorching rocks put on her naked bum—'

'Vince, I don't need hot rocks on my—'

'I thought it'd be relaxing for you?' he says, in a

women-there's-no-pleasing-'em way.

'And I don't need to be told what Shugbury Spa's like,' I remind him sharply. 'I work there, remember? At least I did . . .'

'You mean you've quit?'

'Yes!'

'Oh. Right.' A beat's pause. 'But this would be for *leisure* . . .'

'Oh, would it? So I wouldn't have guests complaining about finding a pubic hair in the shower?' A man unloading a tray of loaves from a van spins round and smirks.

'Go somewhere else then, if it'd be awkward,' Vince huffs. 'Just give me some ideas.'

I want to explain that women don't want to have to 'give ideas' about gifts. They don't want a bottle of handwash either, which is what he gave me at Christmas as if I was his Auntie Joan. But suddenly the signal's gone, and when he calls back I ignore it. Now Alice is approaching with the dogs, her face breaking into a wide smile.

'Gosh, you've been busy.' She glances down at the bags. 'Did you find everything you need?'

'Yes, everything,' I reply.

'Great! You *are* efficient, just like they said. Let's head back then, and get started. Ready?'

'Yep, I'm ready.' *I can do this*, I tell myself. I can be the Kate that Alice needs me to be. And as for Vince? He didn't even get around to asking where I am.

138

CHAPTER EIGHTEEN

Vince

Vince wakes on a grey Wednesday morning and glances at the space in the bed where Kate should be. It used to be a regular king-sized bed. Now it feels huge, as if the mattress has been extended by at least three metres on her side.

Kate's always here beside him. That's the thing. Since they've been together she's never been one for nipping off on girls' holidays, the way some of his friends' partners still do. She seemed to flush all of that out of her system in her early twenties, on all those jaunts she went on with Tash. He's heard about them getting drunk and stoned and dancing all night, tottering back to crummy hotels in the breaking dawn. Kate was actually wilder than he was. But that's all way in the past, and he honestly thought she was perfectly happy with the way things have turned out.

Clearly, though, she's not. He replays her reaction

yesterday to his offer of a half-day spa visit – with a hot stone treatment! – and wonders what he said wrong. Aren't women supposed to adore being slathered in oils and mud? Vince feels like he doesn't know anything anymore.

Aware of a hollowness in his belly, he lurches out of bed with uncharacteristic decisiveness. Naked, he snatches his dressing gown from the hook and pulls it on, registering the ragged hole at the front.

Jarvis greets him in the hallway in a blur of panting and tail wagging. This display of unbridled joy feels inappropriate, considering that Kate's had some kind of hormonal meltdown. But then, a spaniel can't be expected to understand marital difficulties. He can't even be relied upon to distinguish a pane of glass from an open space, the silly mutt. On more than one occasion he's made a dash for the garden and thwacked his head against the patio door.

In the kitchen now, Vince looks around in dismay at the party debris that's still littering the table and worktops. A seed of irritation fizzles inside him, as if a horde of gatecrashers had broken in and caroused in his home while he was sleeping like a pure, sweet baby. They didn't even bother to clear up! Of course, Vince has to accept that there were no gatecrashers apart from Sue Stone of the unfeasibly large radishes, whom he didn't remember inviting. More shamefully still, the mess has sat here for three days.

Well, of course it has, he thinks irritably. Kate's not

140

here and Vince has had his book to finish and the dog to look after and God knows what else. Meanwhile, thinking positively, End of Play came and went yesterday and no lightning bolt struck the house. Zoe hasn't even emailed again. Maybe she's off sick? It seems wrong, hoping that she's come down with something. But he's thinking a heavy cold or food poisoning. 'Not bacterial pneumonia or anything like that,' he tells Jarvis, who gazes quizzically at him.

Thus reassured that he hasn't wished death upon his editor, Vince scoffs a withered sausage roll that's been sitting out on the worktop since Sunday and lets Jarvis out into the garden. Grass is grass, right? Garden or park; it's all the same to a dog. As Jarvis tinkles against the double-orb water feature, Vince checks his emails on his phone. *Still* nothing from Zoe. Yeah, she's definitely sick, he decides. He calls Jarvis back in and heads through to the kitchen, where he peers into the fridge for a tray of that incredibly expensive Rover's Kitchen dog food that the Shugbury vet insisted he has.

There isn't any. The food actually comes frozen, and defrosting it is – or *was* – Kate's job. Of course Vince hasn't done this with everything that's been going on. But it's fine, he reassures himself. He boils the kettle and dumps the tray of rock-solid meat in the sink on top of a pile of dirty dishes. 'Well, my wife *did* leave me,' he announces out loud, as if a council inspector has burst in to grill him about why he hasn't washed up.

He sloshes the entire kettle of boiling water over the

141

meaty slab. This seems to have zero effect. He considers hacking it to bits, using a hammer or an ice pick or whatever the heck's in the toolbox. He tries to picture what Kate used, when she built that *Pinntorp* table and *Malm* chest of drawers, then remembers that he doesn't know where the toolbox is hidden. First thing he must do, when she comes home, is ask where things are!

Briefly, Vince considers serving Jarvis the meat in its frozen state. It'd be like a savoury ice lolly, right? It seems like a brilliant idea, actually – and if Kate were here he'd ask her to look into marketing it as a concept. A meaty brick that your dog can lick indefinitely! Genius, Vince reckons. But then he worries that ingesting frozen meat might damage Jarvis's insides, and he couldn't live with himself if anything bad happened. So he knocks that idea on the head.

'Microwave!' Vince shouts, as if he's just discovered penicillin. He can defrost it that way. 'Who needs Kate?' he asks Jarvis, aware that he's already started to act in a way that he wouldn't want others to witness. Even the dog seems wary around him, as if he's not entirely happy about being here without Kate.

He's not the only one, Vince thinks darkly. He thrusts the tray of meat into the microwave, sets the timer and launches into the task of clearing up the party mess. Bottles and cans and food debris – including the couscous garnished with perfumed leaves – are lobbed into a bin liner. Should that have been a warning sign? Kate's sudden urge to sprinkle potpourri over food?

142

After pausing for breath Vince deliberately loads the dishwasher in a way that Kate would hate, with everything shoved in any old how.

Next, having built himself up to the final task, Vince scrapes the dog sick off the hall carpet with Jarvis watching keenly like some mean-eyed supervisor on a factory floor. *That's better*, he decides. He is getting on with stuff now, seizing the day. 'Carpe diem!' he shouts, startling the dog. 'Or is it *carpet* diem, the deodorising shampoo for all your rug-cleaning needs?' He didn't really use carpet shampoo because he couldn't find any. He just squirted it with the hideously expensive lavender handwash he bought Kate for Christmas, which she seemed somewhat underwhelmed by. What *do* women want these days? Not handwash or even a half-day spa package, it seems.

Ping! goes the microwave. That's Jarvis's breakfast defrosted. However, something has gone badly wrong because the thin plastic tray has melted and warped. 'Fuck,' Vince mutters. Rather than risk his safety with the frankly substandard oven glove, he manages to lift it from the microwave by means of two spatulas, and transports it gingerly to the table.

It hasn't merely defrosted. It's cooked like a fat rectangular burger from a fast food joint in hell. Jarvis ate a dressing gown so surely he won't turn up his nose at this. But what if chemicals from the melted plastic have leached into the meat? The last thing Vince wants is to poison his daughter's dog. 'The middle bit's probably

143

okay,' he tells himself. Thus reassured, he finds a small casserole dish and forks the 'safe' parts – i.e. the interior parts – into it, and bins the melted tray. It's a tactic he used to employ with mouldy cheese back in the day. With scant regard for health and safety, he'd slice off the fuzzy bits and happily scoff the rest, confident that it wouldn't kill him and might even do his immune system some good.

Of course that stopped when Edie moved in. Kate, who took to her stepmother role with enthusiasm and ease, announced, 'We're *not* pretending that mouldy food is okay to eat.'

Already, with the kitchen reasonably tidy now, Vince feels a lot better. He forks half of the casserole dish's contents into Jarvis's bowl and watches as the dog sniffs it before consuming it in small, sporadic bites.

He seems to know it's not right. That's ridiculous, Vince decides. He's a dog, not a Michelin restaurant inspector. Back in his study, he tries to settle into writing. Another hour spins by, with Vince doing little more than rubbing at his face, until a sharp rap on the front door – and then the sound of it opening – ejects him from his swivel chair and he scrambles towards it.

Kate has come home! And now *everything* is going to be all right—

'Hi, Vince.'

'Oh! Deborah. Hi.'

Already in his hallway, she steps back and gives him a curious look. 'Hope I'm not interrupting anything?'

'Er, no. No, not at all,' he blusters, raking at his hair. 'It's fine. I was just, um . . . working.'

'Oh, right.' She's wearing a Breton top and jeans, and her russet hair is coiled neatly on top of her head, with tendrils flowing down at her cheeks. It's the first time in his life that Vince has been disappointed to see her. 'It's just, I have a day off and I'm in organising mode,' she clarifies as he makes them coffee in the kitchen.

Thank Christ he cleared up. The sound of the dishwasher, rumbling away on its cycle, seems to say, 'Nothing untoward has happened here. Everything is normal.' Apart from the casserole dish of dog meat, and a jam jar of cutlery that Kate had set out for the party, everything else has been put away.

'Is Kate working today?' Deborah asks.

'Yeah, yeah, she has a shift, yeah.' He can't face going into what's really happened, and Deborah being all concerned and *involved*, in the way he knows she would be. Much as Vince likes her, he's aware that she loves a gossip, and that the news would whip around The Glade like a freak hurricane: *Have you heard, Kate walked out on Vince? Well, she was acting weird at their party . . .*

Deborah's nostrils quiver. 'Mmm, something smells good in here!'

'Just been doing a bit of cooking,' he says quickly, wondering how many fibs he'll manage to cram into their conversation.

'You are good, cooking from scratch when you're so busy. Did you manage to finish your book?'

145

'Almost.' He senses his cheeks flushing.

'This is your second one, isn't it? You're *amazing*, being able to write them, on top of your gigs and everything . . .'

He shrugs, feigning bashfulness. He hasn't actually had too many gigs lately. 'It's just stream-of-consciousness stuff really,' he says.

'Well, it seems to be working brilliantly. But here I am, babbling on, taking up your time! What I wanted to say is, d'you fancy coming over for dinner next Saturday night? Both of you, I mean . . .'

'Next Saturday? Not this one?' he barks in panic.

She looks at him strangely. 'Yes, a week on Saturday. Just a casual supper. Not busy, are you?'

Vince makes a quick calculation: that's ten days away. Surely Kate will be back by then, and they'll have smoothed everything over and life will be normal again.

'No, I'm pretty sure we don't have anything on . . .'

'Well, check with Kate, would you? Just so I know the numbers.'

'I will,' he says stiffly. 'Erm, is it for anything special?'

'Book festival planning committee,' she explains. 'I know you're not on it but you're an integral part of it now. I thought you'd have loads to offer, and we could get the ball rolling nice and early for next year . . .'

'Sounds great,' he enthuses, aware of the three-day-old sausage roll's greasy residue still clagging the interior of his mouth. His phone trills from his study. That'll be Kate saying she's okay now – she's over her 'little wobble' as he's started to term it privately – and is on her way home. 'Sorry, better get that,' he says, dashing through and snatching his phone from his desk.

Not quick enough to take the call, though. And it's an unknown number. It's probably Tash or one of Kate's other friends. Maybe Kate's phone has run out of charge and she's using theirs. He calls the number, and the recorded voice tells him it's an energy supplier babbling on about something. Is it their one? Vince has no idea. Their gas could be piped in from Pluto for all he knows. Bills are Kate's job. *We're busy helping other customers,* the voice says, *but please don't hang up. Your call is very important—*

Vince hangs up.

'Well, I'll leave you to crack on,' Deborah says brightly, back in the kitchen.

'Great! Well, good to see you,' Vince says with a note of relief. He doesn't want Deborah or anyone else hanging around right now, picking up on the fact that things aren't quite right.

She stands up and jabs a finger towards the casserole dish on the workshop. 'That's delicious, by the way.'

'What?' He swivels and sees the fork lying beside it.

'Hope you don't mind but I had little try of your tagine. It's so good, Vince. Did you make it, or Kate?'

'Erm, I did,' he squeaks, sweating now.

'Well, it's *really* flavoursome.' She beams at him. 'Hmm, yummy. You've given me inspiration for next Saturday night.'

CHAPTER NINETEEN

Kate

I'm good at the stuff no one notices but is actually pretty important. That's what Vince always said. It never felt like much of a compliment. But Alice notices how well we fall into working together, and says we're 'a real team' as we pack up her mother's clothes.

There are sturdy waxed jackets, thick Aran sweaters and exquisitely beaded gowns. Bea was obviously a practical and hard-working woman who also loved a dash of glamour. Photos of her are dotted around the house; a beautiful but austere-looking woman, with flinty eyes and a mouth always set in a firm line. Alice's father looked like more of a genial sort, and I'm struck by Alice's timid expression – a fair-haired wisp of a girl – in the childhood photos arranged on the living room mantelpiece.

However, I'm still keenly aware that I'm an imposter who shouldn't be here at all. As if to compensate, I fling myself into the sorting and packing, stopping only for brief cups of tea and a sandwich when Alice demands it. 'You need a break, Kate,' she insists. 'You've been at it for hours!'

'I'm fine, honestly,' I say, showing her the colour-coded system I've devised, marking items with Post-it notes according to where they'll go. Bric-a-brac – of which there is an enormous amount – will be packed up for charity, and collectables sent to auction in Perth, along with prized pieces of furniture.

'So impressive,' Alice observes. 'I do remember the agency saying you were a bit of a miracle worker.'

'Really?' My smile sets, and I'm almost tempted to blurt out, *I'm so sorry. I'm not Kate from the agency. I've told you a whole bunch of lies and I'd better pack up and leave right now.* But then Alice touches my arm, saying, 'It's such a relief, having you here. I'd be so miserable and depressed, doing all of this on my own.'

So maybe it doesn't matter that I'm the wrong Kate?

'I'm glad it's not too painful for you,' I say truthfully.

'Not at all. So, what next? The books, maybe?'

'Yes,' I say eagerly. 'I'll call him now.' I've already told her about meeting Fergus, and that our beloved Railway Bookshop lives on in the form of Off the Rails Books.

As my mobile signal's iffy inside the house I call him from the landline. It's a pleasant surprise when he answers immediately. 'I can come out tomorrow,' he says, 'when I've closed the shop.'

'Great. Thank you,' I say, already looking forward to

his visit. I can't help being intrigued by the man who's kept a second-hand bookshop going in a little country town.

'Oh yes, it's a real gem,' agrees Morag, Bea's housekeeper, when she pops in with gifts of more eggs, plus a seeded loaf from the bakery that Alice had mentioned she loves. She's a sparky woman with ruddy cheeks and grey hair cropped no-nonsense short, and my heart lurches when I hear Alice tell her, 'Kate's going to take charge of the gardens. You won't recognise the place when she's finished!'

In a panic, I step outside, leaving the women chatting, while I call every gardening company I can find. But no one can take on the job at such short notice; not even Morag's recommended guys who, seemingly, 'everyone' uses. 'Sorry, love. We need more time to plan for a big job like that.' I wonder how the real Kate would have handled it. Surely, being an avid gardener wouldn't have made it any easier for her to magic up a team out of thin air?

I sip my mug of tea, scanning the weed-choked borders and overgrown lawns and almost wish I could call her. After all, even though Alice booked her in a hurry, she recognised an impressive CV. How would mine compare?

Kate Weaver
Phoney. Lunatic.
Career history:
Museum ass-cure.

Part-time hotel spa receptionist and small-town cul-de-sac misfit.

On a happier note, there's been no call from the agency, so perhaps I'm on safe ground now? And Vince hasn't called again either, which is a relief. I just want to get on with the job in hand.

It's so good to feel properly useful and the hours fly by. Before I know it, we've done two full days of sorting, and a couple of bedrooms are empty already, and any minute Fergus is due to arrive.

I'm not sure why I'm poised for his arrival. He's just the bookshop man, coming to take a look at Bea's home library. And he'll probably be in and out in five minutes flat.

*

Only, it doesn't happen like that.

I'm bubble-wrapping paintings upstairs as Alice welcomes him in. '. . . So nice to meet you, Fergus. I was delighted to hear there's still a bookshop in town . . .' Her animated voice drifts upstairs, mingling with his warm and friendly tones. Then their voices fade as she takes him through to her mother's library. A bizarre realisation hits me: I want to be there too. But I can't go muscling in. Alice is taking care of things and I'll just get on with stuff up here.

Even so, I'm aware of working quietly, ears pricked, as I move on to wrapping Bea's butter-soft leather gloves in tissue paper.

It's not just Alice and Fergus's voices that are drifting upstairs. There's also an aroma of roast chicken and my stomach growls hollowly. Having made so much headway already, Alice decided we'd celebrate with a proper roast dinner tonight.

'Kate?' she calls out. 'Are you up there?'

'Yes?' I stride out onto the landing to see her and Fergus looking up at me.

'Hi,' I start, as if I hadn't realised he was here. 'Are the books any good to you?'

'Yeah.' He nods. 'I'm taking them all. Thanks for calling me—'

'Rather than the dozens of other bookshops in town?' I say, and he laughs.

'Well, yeah. There is a benefit to being the only one. But I think my customers will love them anyway. There's a lot of keen gardeners around here . . .'

'And he's given me a very fair price,' Alice adds with a smile. 'So I thought it was only right to ask him to join us for dinner. I know it's a bit impromptu but is that okay with you, Kate?'

'Of course it is,' I say, wondering why I'm actually delighted, and wishing now that I wasn't quite so grubby and dishevelled as I head downstairs.

'So kind of you,' Fergus says, as Alice brings dishes to the table and I lay an extra place.

'It all looks delicious,' I enthuse, at which she flaps a hand dismissively.

'It's nothing, really.' Yet her 'nothing' is a perfect roast

152

chicken scented with rosemary, which she'd managed to pluck from the undergrowth in the neglected kitchen garden, plus roasted new potatoes and a delicious salad. So simple and seemingly effortless – like her fashion sense.

'I remember this place being a B&B,' Fergus offers as we tuck in.

'Yes, that's right,' Alice says, pouring water for him – as he's driving – and wine for us. 'It was hardly the Ritz but my parents had their regulars,' she adds. 'As you know, there weren't too many options around here if you couldn't splash out on the big grand hotels.'

'Yeah, definitely,' he says. I find myself wanting to know more about his life, growing up around here. I know about his daughter, Liv, but there's been no mention of a wife or a partner. If he's single I'm sure, as a handsome bookseller, he has a host of admirers.

'But then TripAdvisor happened,' Alice adds with a grimace, 'and there were plenty of guests who weren't too impressed by the standards. Or by my mother, actually.'

'What did she do?' I asked, intrigued. 'I mean, what did they object to?'

Alice smiles and sips her wine. Already I've gathered that she regards a decent Sauvignon, plus candles at the table, as essential to any evening meal. 'She was hardly the genial host, shall we say . . .'

I catch Fergus trying to keep down a grin and wonder what's amusing him. His blue-grey eyes sparkle now in

153

the candlelight. Clad in a burgundy T-shirt and jeans, his build is lean for a man of his age – I'd put him at about fifty – although his shoulders are broad and his upper arms nicely muscular. He seems to notice Alice's expectant look, and chuckles. 'You did hear the odd thing,' he starts.

'What kind of thing?' I ask.

'I shouldn't say really,' Fergus says quickly.

'Oh no, do,' Alice insists. 'Please.'

'Well,' he offers, catching my eye briefly across the table, 'there was the time when Bea ordered a couple to go straight up to their room after breakfast, and pack up and leave immediately because they'd complained about the toast . . .'

'The toast?' I exclaim.

'Don't tell me,' Alice says, laughing. 'It was stone cold, like my mother.'

'Well . . .' Fergus laughs. 'Allegedly. But you know how gossipy it is around here . . .' He turns to me. 'So, whereabouts are you from, Kate?'

'Glasgow originally,' I reply, 'then London. This past year I've been in a little Buckinghamshire town.' I spring up and clear the table, keen to avoid further questions about my life. It's bad enough, keeping up the pretence with Alice. I'm not sure how I'd deal with direct quizzing from Fergus across the table.

'And how are you finding it up here?' he asks, getting up to help too.

'I love it,' I say truthfully.

'You know it, though, don't you? You mentioned in the shop that you'd had holidays here?'

'Yes, that's right.' I nod, flattered that he remembered. 'They were some of the happiest times of my life. And you obviously love it here too?'

'Well, I'm still here,' he offers with a smile and shrug. As the talk turns to books, it strikes me how much all of our tastes coincide, and also how easy Fergus is to be around. The chatter is constant and I find myself forgetting that I'm not really Alice's 'companion' (at least, not the one she booked). Then the chat moves on to our grown-up children, and Alice points out how funny it is that we have just the one each (because of course Edie feels like my child in every way that matters). Alice tops up my glass and says, 'Next time you come, Fergus, it's a taxi home for you.'

'Yep,' he says and laughs.

Of course, running a bookshop, he's bound be easy around people, I remind myself. But there's something terribly attractive about a man who's relaxed and comfortable in his own skin.

'You said you'd come back to the shop for a proper browse,' he reminds me, as I start to make coffee.

'Oh, I will. Definitely.' Then, as I set out the cups, my phone vibrates on the worktop. There are several messages from Vince. I've been so engrossed in the work here, it's the first time I've checked it all day.

Hey just wondering how it's going.
Hope you're having a good day.

All okay down there?

He must assume I'm back at Tash's, or at another friend's place after my little jaunt to Euston. And he's resisting barraging me with calls and demands to come home. Instead, he's playing the long game, giving me 'space'.

And now another message appears.

I was thinking if you'd like a full day at a spa I could organise that?

I blink at it, then glance back quickly at Fergus, catching myself feeling . . . not guilty exactly. But as if Vince might be watching me somehow, from four hundred miles away in Shugbury, while I'm having an extremely enjoyable evening with another man.

But not *just* with another man! Alice is here too – she invited him – and why shouldn't I make new friends? Proper ones, that is, who make me feel happy and relaxed and more like my old self. The best of myself, even, rather than somehow lacking as a woman. There have been no subtle put-downs tonight.

As I pour our coffees I remember Deborah popping round sometime in November last year. The talk had turned to Christmas plans. 'D'you make your own Christmas pudding, Kate?' she asked.

'No, I just buy ours,' I replied.

'Oh, I do admire the way you cut corners,' she trilled. 'And I know not everyone's into Christmas, the way I am.'

Excuse me! Had I said I wasn't 'into' Christmas? I

love it actually. I especially loved it when Edie was little. We'd strewn our flat with fake snow and put out mince pies for Santa, all that. It was so much fun. However, I've never believed it must involve buying a zillion ingredients – including suet, as if it's wartime – weeks before the big event, and then mixing or grinding them or whatever the fuck you do.

And then of course Deborah made one for us. Or for Vince really, because he'd mentioned how much he'd loved his mum's. 'It really isn't difficult, Kate. There are plenty of recipes online!'

That 'recipes online' thing again – as if, when faced with a computer, I'd mistakenly think it was a peculiar-looking TV!

What a relief it is to be far, far away from all that, I decide, 'relaxed' from two glasses of wine now and wishing I'd politely suggested where Deborah could stick her pudding. But never mind that because I've left that place – and my marriage, I decide rashly as Fergus finishes his coffee quickly and gets up from the table.

'I'm on baby duty tonight,' he explains. 'So I'd better get back.'

Ah, so he's not single. Of course he's not. He's a complete catch.

'You have a baby?' Alice asks brightly.

Fergus chuckles. 'Finn's not mine. Well, he *is*. He's my family, absolutely. But he's my daughter Liv's little boy and they live with me and I suggested she went round to her friend's later tonight, to get a bit of time off . . .' *With*

157

me, he said. Not *with us.* I don't know why I homed in on that detail.

'I do hope we haven't ruined your plans!' Alice looks genuinely perturbed, as if she'd bound him to a kitchen chair and forced her delicious roast dinner on him.

'No. Not at all,' he says firmly. 'This has been lovely. I did message Liv to say I'd be a bit later. She said I need a social life too—'

'Well, I'm glad,' I say quickly, before I can stop myself.

Fergus smiles warmly, protesting that he doesn't need help with the boxes of books, and insisting on carrying them all out to his van himself. As we see him out I catch Alice looking at me in a bemused way. Or perhaps I'm imagining it?

'Lovely man,' she muses, as we watch him climb into his battered blue van. 'Isn't he, Kate?'

I look at her and can't keep down the smile as Fergus waves, before pulling away. 'Yes,' I reply. 'He really is.'

CHAPTER TWENTY

Vince

Kate wasn't bowled over by Vince's offer of a *full* day at a spa. At least, he assumes she wasn't. By the next morning she hasn't even deigned to reply, or to the other messages, which he only meant as friendly and caring and not pressurising at all.

Why won't she message him? Is he being punished for something? If so, what?

He's also baffled as to why the working week has spun by and there's been no further email – and no calls – from his editor, despite Monday's EOP deadline.

Has the whole world forgotten he even exists? Is he just a dog-feeding serf now?

Several possibilities have been swirling around Vince's mind:

- Zoe is seriously unwell. If this is the case, he can't help feeling that it's actually his fault. He's

159

wished it on her for his own deadline-dodging convenience.

– Or she's left the company and no one has bothered to tell him.

– Or Zoe has died.

None of these options are making it any easier to finish writing his book. Vince wishes now that he wrote children's books. Like those board books Edie loved as a baby, each page as thick as a biscuit with about three words on. Or cloth books – the kind that are washable – with no writing in them at all! *That's* the kind of author he should be, he thinks manically. The sort that doesn't have to do any writing at all!

His phone pings with a text.

Could you send me that tagine recipe sometime? Thanks, D xxx

Back in normal times Vince would have been delighted to receive a message from Deborah. The inclusion of the familiar 'D', plus three kisses, would have ignited a little flame of delight in him, and caused him to drift around like a big happy hot air balloon for the rest of the day.

Shame he's too agitated to enjoy it. Of course he's relieved that Deborah appears to be very much alive and unharmed (unlike poor Zoe, who he now imagines to have an exploded gall bladder or something, and hooked up on life support) after ingesting dog food two days ago. Yet he definitely hasn't felt like himself since Kate took herself off. She didn't even seem to care that

Jarvis had savaged his dressing gown. Does this mean she doesn't love him anymore? Meanwhile, he's been trying his hardest to go about his business all week, making pleasantries with neighbours, and texting his daughter as he normally does. Just chatty stuff. Edie's news, mainly. He can't bear to tell her that Kate walked out, because she'll be all worried about him and start going on about getting some 'talking therapy' that all her friends seem to have these days. Feelings, feelings, feelings – according to his daughter they should be unleashed in front of strangers for a colossal fee. There's no need to worry Edie anyway. Because Kate will be home at the weekend, he tells himself.

It's probably her menopause. Vince reckons she just needs to 'get through' it – as if it's as simple as shaking off a heavy cold – and then everything will be normal again. But when he googles it on this wet, grim Friday afternoon, he learns that the whole hormonal rumpus can go on for *years*. A decade even! With Deborah's Planning Committee Dinner looming like a terrible court appearance next weekend!

He needs to calm down, Vince decides. He can't just sit around waiting for his wife to come home. A knock at the door sends his blood pressure skyrocketing – but it's only the guy to read the meter. He laughs when Vince babbles that he doesn't know where it is, and strolls calmly to the little cupboard by the front door and flips it open.

'Wife away?' the man asks with an infuriating grin.

After seeing him out, Vince realises he's starving and there's sod all fresh food in the fridge. He will *not* plummet into a tinned-soup lifestyle like some hapless kid, newly arrived at student halls. He decides to do an online shop, but he doesn't know the password Kate uses to log in. Then he decides to order more dog food as they're almost out of that too, but he can't find it online and he doesn't know where Kate gets it from. Defeated, he hoofs it off to town (he's had a couple of beers already), deciding to take Jarvis with him so he has a proper walk for once.

On the way a brilliant idea comes to him. He stops and does a quick bit of googling, his heart lifting as skims the various options. He pictures Kate's face when he tells her: full of joy and gratitude at how inventive he's been. Already, he's giving himself a virtual pat on the back.

Of course she'll bloody love this!

For extra reassurance, he calls his old mate Harry Bonomo, who sounds amazed to hear from him. 'Vince! Mate! It's been such a long time . . . How *are* you?'

'Yeah, y'know. Busy, busy. How's Michele and, uh—' From his scrambled brain he can't access the baby's name. The pause dangles ominously.

'Yeah, great. We're all good. Just bashing on, y'know . . .' Back in the day, Vince and Harry had been virtually inseparable, boosting each other through those soul-sapping early years of trying to get gigs. They'd even shared a flat for a time, living on beer, Cheerios and cigarettes. Vince has a sudden sharp craving for those days, when he didn't have to worry about deadlines or the fact that he might have unwittingly killed off his editor. 'How's Kate?' Harry asks.

Vince inhales, about to say, 'Great!' But he knows there's no point in lying if he's about to ask his friend's advice. Kind, sorted Harry, who fell in love with Michele, fifteen years his junior and – judging by his social media – seems to be living a charmed life. So he tells him about Kate leaving, and how he proposes to put things right.

'Aw, Christ. Sorry to hear that,' Harry says.

'It's just a blip,' Vince says quickly.

'Yeah. She probably needs a little break. Let her have a bit of headspace and everything'll be fine.'

'That's what I was thinking,' Vince murmurs as Jarvis cocks his leg against a bench.

'And who wouldn't need a break from you, mate?' He's trying to lighten things, as he always does.

Vince forces a laugh. 'Yeah. Ha-ha. Who could blame her, eh?' He senses Harry's attention wandering, and now he's aware of a female voice in the background, and a baby crying. Clearly, Harry wants to finish the call. Michele probably needs him to do something. Unwilling to let him go, Vince barrages him with questions about work and tours, surprised to hear how well he's doing, and accidentally lets slip that he's having trouble finishing his book.

'Small piece of the elephant,' Harry says.

'Huh?'

'You know. Just take it piece by piece, chipping away at it. You'll soon have it done.'

'Yeah.' Vince feels a little better now. He misses all of his old mates, the gang all crammed around scruffy pub tables and laughing and shouting over each other, whole Sunday afternoons and evenings spinning by like that. Who does he have around here, bloke-wise? An insufferable sports coach and Lenny, the well-meaning but patio-obsessed GP, always offering to lend him his jet-washer machine to blast off stubborn lichen.

Still, Harry's still there for him, even with the baby shrieking now like a terrible car alarm in the background. Did Edie used to scream like that? Vince can't remember. He's probably blotted it out.

Over the din, he explains his brilliant idea for coaxing Kate back home. Although he can hardly hear Harry at all now, Vince is pretty sure his old best mate said, 'Yeah, she'll love that, mate.'

'You really think so?'

'Yeah, yeah. Definitely.'

Vince is about to thank him and pass on his love to Michele and, uh – the baby. But Harry seems to have disappeared into a vortex of bawling, so Vince lowers himself onto a roadside bench and calls his wife.

CHAPTER TWENTY-ONE

Kate

I stop outside Off the Rails bookshop and stare at my phone. Vince's name is displayed. Answer or ignore? What if it's something urgent? He can message me, I decide, jamming it back into my jeans pocket.

I hadn't planned to come back so soon. But Fergus did remind me last night that I'd promised to return for a more leisurely browse. Plus, I was in town anyway, dropping off some of Bea's bric-a-brac at the charity shop. I'd also planned to scour every noticeboard in town for gardening firm flyers as Alice is 'keen to get things started', as she put it. 'But I'm sure you'll find someone. I have every faith in you, Kate.' The pressure is mounting and, short of getting out there and tugging up weeds by myself, I really don't know what to do.

Fergus is chatting to an elderly customer as I step inside. It strikes me how glad I am that he's here today as he greets me enthusiastically. 'Kate, meet Joe,' he says.

'One of my best customers. Kate's helping to clear out Osprey House,' he adds.

'Brave woman.' Joe chuckles.

'Oh, not at all,' I say truthfully. 'I'm enjoying it actually.'

'So, are you a friend of the family?' he asks.

'Erm, not quite,' I say, trying to avoid fibbing that I'm hired help. Because I absolutely *don't* want to lie outright. 'I just got to know Alice recently,' I add.

'Y'know, I didn't ask how you two met,' Fergus remarks.

'Oh, we just kind of fell into each other,' I babble, aware of my cheeks burning.

'Really?' He looks surprised. 'That was lucky.'

'Yes. Yeah, it really was.'

Those blue-grey eyes are fixed on mine. 'Did you meet in London?'

'We did, yes,' I say hurriedly. My heart is racing, and I'm aware of both Fergus and Joe giving me curious looks. But I *can't* lie. I just can't. Then, thankfully, Joe remarks, 'You had to do the same thing with your folks' place, didn't you, Ferg? The clearing out?'

'Yeah, a few years ago now,' he replies.

'It's hard to let go of stuff,' Joe adds, and Fergus agrees.

'I kept the important things.' He catches my look with a smile. 'My excuse was, their old bits and pieces would add a bit of personality to the shop . . .'

'You mean the binoculars and things on your shelves?' I ask, relaxing a little now.

'Yep, exactly. I was going for a sort of museum feel. They were Mum's. She was a real nature person—'

'Aye, she was that,' Joe says fondly.

'. . . and the ink bottles and nib pens were Dad's,' Fergus adds.

'He wrote the parish newsletters,' Joe explains. 'Anyway, this is the best bookshop for miles around.'

'I'm sure it is,' I say, smiling now. 'It's really special.'

'Although I thought he'd lost his marbles when he took it on,' Joe adds with a smirk.

'Everyone did,' Fergus concedes. 'Liv still thinks that now.'

'And no wonder. Her mad dad, driving all over Perthshire buying up books . . .' Joe laughs.

I'm itching to ask, *Why does Liv work here?* She didn't seem to be relishing her job. But then, as if sensing my curiosity, Fergus explains, 'Liv's just giving me a hand temporarily. I needed the help and, well . . . she'd been going through a tricky time.'

'Oh, has she?' I ask.

He nods, reaching for the coffee pot, and looks round at both of us. 'Like one?'

'Yes please,' I say, although Joe declines.

He pours our coffees and continues, 'I thought it'd be good for her to have a job, earn money, and get a break from the baby for a few hours here and there.'

'And Helen had upped and left you,' Joe teases.

'Well, yeah.' Fergus nods. 'There was that. Deserted me for glittering London . . .'

'Can't keep your staff, Ferg.' Joe grins.

'Hey, she'd done eleven years!' he says in mock-protest.

'Murderers get less,' Joe chuckles, and I learn that Helen had been something of a stalwart in the shop.

'Super-organised in a way that I'm not,' Fergus explains. 'Kept us on the straight and narrow. Banned me from buying book collections that we'd have no hope of selling.'

'How's it working out with Liv in the shop?' Joe asks.

Fergus pauses as I picture the girl's bleak demeanour, and the jam spurting at the counter. 'It's . . . well, it's *working*, I s'pose,' he concedes with a wry smile.

'It's hard working with family sometimes,' I suggest, thinking of Vince and me. *You'll be working with me, not for me. Big difference,* he said. And later, when Joe has gone and we're having a second coffee, Fergus tells me more about how his family situation came about.

'So, Liv's mum died when Liv was sixteen,' he explains. 'It was very sudden so, as you can imagine, everything was thrown up in the air.'

'I'm so sorry,' I exclaim.

'Thank you. It's okay. She had an aneurysm – it literally happened out of nowhere. I mean, we weren't prepared. Not a bit.'

'I can imagine,' I murmur, sipping my coffee and feeling a little shellshocked, yet also honoured that he's sharing this with me. After all, we barely know each other. 'How was it for Liv?' I ask. 'I mean, I know that would be terrible at any time. But at sixteen . . . it's such a tricky stage.'

'Yes, it really is. And what happened was, our previously studious girl decided to leave school at the first opportunity and not go to uni or college or any of that. I mean, that had been the plan, to apply for Edinburgh if she got the grades. But all that went out of the window,' he continues, pushing back his wavy hair. 'She found herself a boyfriend and next thing I know I'm a granddad—' He breaks off and smiles. It's not a stoical, making-the-best-of-things smile at all. He looks genuinely happy.

'And . . . how's that turned out?' I wrap my hands around the mug, glad there are no more customers in here, that it's the two of us. I get the impression he doesn't talk about this often, especially to someone he barely knows. And I can't remember the last time I met a stranger and felt, almost instantly, that there's a connection; that we could be genuine friends. In Shugbury, with Deborah and Agata and the rest, it felt like the harder I tried to fit into their world, the more they pushed me away. Yet here in this cosy shop, crammed from floor to ceiling with second-hand books, I feel entirely different.

I feel, I realise, with a tingle of surprise, as if I've come home.

'She's actually a fantastic mum,' Fergus explains. 'And of course I'm completely besotted with Finn to a ridiculous degree.'

My heart lifts at that. His daughter's lucky, I decide,

169

despite the tragedy of losing her mum. 'I'm sure you are,' I say.

'But she's struggled,' he goes on. 'She's only nineteen – Finn's just had his first birthday – and her relationship broke up. So on the days Finn's with his dad, or his other grandparents, she does a few hours in the shop. I think it is helping her a bit. Anyway, enough about me,' he says quickly with a smile. 'So . . . what about your situation?'

I know what he means. Whether I'm single, which would be a reasonable assumption, given that I'm working up here and Vince's name hasn't come up. So I find myself telling him – skating over the details – that I kind of left home, and hadn't planned it and somehow, here I am, helping Alice to move on with her life. The part that I'm avoiding – that I'm here under false pretences – fizzles and burns in my gut.

'Wow.' He pauses. 'Sounds like you've been through a lot too.'

'Not really. Not compared to you.'

'Oh, we all have our stuff, don't we?' He grins and adds, 'You probably came in for a browse and here I am, distracting you—'

'Hardly,' I say with a smile. But I look around anyway, selecting a handful of novels, wishing I could tell him what really happened on Monday at Euston.

'Let me know if I can help with anything while you're here,' he says as I pay.

I hesitate as he hands me the brown paper bag of

170

books. 'Actually, there might be something. I don't suppose you know any gardeners around here?'

'To tackle Osprey House's gardens, you mean?'

'Yes. At least, as much as can be done in a short time . . .'

'Like one of those revamp-your-home-in-a-day type shows? But for the outside?'

'Exactly,' I say, laughing. 'A spruce-up, I suppose. First impressions and all that.'

'Let me have a think and I'll call you. You have my number, right? Could you send me yours?'

'I will,' I say, 'and thank you.' As I leave the shop, setting the bells above the door tinkling, I realise I'm feeling a little more like my old self. I'll fix the gardening problem somehow. Everything will be okay, I can feel it.

And much later, as sleep folds over me in the pale lemon room, I remind myself that I arrived here less than a week ago. Right now, that hardly seems possible. But already, I'm beginning to remember who I am.

CHAPTER TWENTY-TWO

Vince

Deborah's dinner party is galloping towards Vince like a racehorse at the Grand National. One of the loose ones without a jockey that seem completely out of control and look like they might run amok and trample everyone.

Vince fears horses. He always has. From the wooden kind in the school gym to the flesh-and-blood type with wild eyes and flaring nostrils, they're all terrifying to him. Right now, Vince wishes he could find a small cupboard to climb into, where he'd hide until the book festival planning committee dinner was over.

Yet he can't do that. For one thing, he has a gig this week, in a decent London venue, which he's actually grateful for as things have quietened down a little of late. It'll be weird, being so close to Kate, yet being unable to see her. But he's determined that he won't pester her or beg to meet up. Normally he'd stay the night with Harry in Clapham. But now there's the baby and Vince isn't sure he can handle seeing Harry and his wife being besotted with each other and cooing over their daughter and everything being perfect.

Instead, he books a chain hotel in Holborn and heads straight to it after the gig. At one a.m. he's still lying on top of the bedcovers with the lights on, gazing around at the cheap desk and bland art and thinking, *This wouldn't be depressing if Kate was here. It'd be fun.* At least it would have, when she seemed happy with him. They'd have had a few drinks and come back and had a lovely session on crisp hotel sheets and laughed at the purpleness of the lighting and the industrialness of the shower gel. 'In a wall-mounted pump dispenser so we can't nick it,' she'd have said.

Vince checks the time again. An air-con unit, or some kind of machinery, is growling ominously and there's no way he'll be able to sleep tonight. Another worry is Jarvis, who's staying with Gail and Mehmet next door. They hadn't seemed keen but it's only one night and aren't neighbours supposed to be, well . . . *neighbourly?* Wasn't that one of the reasons he'd been so keen to move out to his parents' house, where people were kind and considerate instead of flinging their filthy mattresses onto the road?

'As long he settles at night,' Gail said, pulling a face when she finally agreed to the arrangement. 'I need my full eight hours' sleep, Vince. Otherwise I can't function.'

'Of course he does,' Vince reassured her. He's a good dog, when he's not savaging dressing gowns and peeing in his study. (Of course he didn't mention that.) Why are some people so preoccupied with sleep and plant milk and why is everything so fucking difficult now?

'Oh, Kate,' Vince groans out loud. Hours and hours spin by in the bleak hotel room. Finally he crumbles and decides to send Kate just one carefully composed message.

It takes him forty-five minutes to get it right.

Hey honey. Hope you're having a nice fun time wherever you are. At Tash's presumably? Well that's good because I had an idea and you can mention it to her. That spa thing. Thinking maybe you don't want to go on your own? Not much fun that. I should've realised, sorry. I know I'm a fuckwit sometimes. So I looked into some places and how about you and Tash go together? For a whole weekend as a treat? There's a place where you can get covered in paraffin—

His phone pings with an incoming message and in shock he sends the text. Shit, that didn't sound right. It sounds like he wants to douse her in fuel and that's not what he meant.

He checks the new message. *Could you send me that tagine recipe? Want to order quality lamb at Lawson's.*

What's Deborah doing, bothering him about recipes at this hour? Lawson's is the best butcher's in Shugbury. Vince's mum would never go anywhere else. But it's Wednesday night – actually Thursday morning; he can hear what sounds like bin lorries out – and he's lying alone on a hotel bed that feels approximately the size of Belgium and he's not exactly in the mood for sharing recipes.

The planning committee meeting isn't until Saturday night. A 'casual supper', Deborah said it would be. How much preparation is needed? He thinks of Kate, flinging together an immense pile of food for their party guests with no warning whatsoever.

There was no phoning in an order to Lawson's then. No wittering about 'quality lamb'. She tore into the task, albeit with a whiff of resentment – and, okay, she'd left him immediately afterwards. *And* the food was weird. (Were the two connected, he's wondered? Should her 'couscous surprise' have warned him of impending marital collapse?)

All the same, Kate had always just got on with it. She gets on with everything that's thrown at her, he reflects now: being a stepmum to Edie, and rising up the ranks at the museum and moving out to Buckinghamshire and being his back end and working at the spa hotel, with those idiots who can't be bothered to take a pumice to their own stupid pampered feet.

His heart seems to twang as he tries to brush off the awful suspicion that whatever he's done – and he still can't fathom it out – might have screwed things up forever.

So no, tagine recipes aren't top of Vince's concerns right now. Exhaling forcefully, he files Deborah's request under the 'irksome things I'd rather not deal with' part of his brain, where an awful lot of stuff seems to go these

175

days. Like rehanging the bathroom door. He'd rather not deal with that either, even though he's growing tired of having Jarvis sitting there, staring at him, whenever he's on the loo.

Their relationship seems to have intensified. Well, of course it has. Vince is now the dog's primary carer: a role he never signed up for, no matter how much he loves his daughter and wants to make her happy. Now, whenever Jarvis's unwavering gaze is fixed upon him, Vince imagines a message being transmitted:

So you think it's okay to switch from my special raw meat to cheap kibble, hmm?

Feeling hollow now, Vince dozes fitfully then gathers himself up and checks out and catches the first train back to Shugbury. Back in Sycamore Grove, he tells Gail that the gig was brilliant, thanks, and takes Jarvis home. At least someone seems happy to see him. And then, despite being dizzy with exhaustion, he decides to take Jarvis for a huge walk all the way into town to pick up a fresh loaf, milk and some expensive cheese in order to prove that he's functioning properly while Kate's away.

Can't have her coming home to find nothing but a spongey courgette and a bit of grizzly old cheddar in the fridge!

He'll also clean out the fridge, he decides. *And* scrub the bathroom until it's gleaming. The whole house, in fact. He'll clean it to within an inch of its life. Is that why she's so angry with him? Because he doesn't clean the toilet? Feeling determined now, he buys his groceries in town then marches homewards. He has nearly reached the bungalow sprawl when he spots Colin Carse jogging towards him. *Keep going,* he wills his neighbour, returning the waved greeting. *Don't let me break your stride!*

Colin stops, panting lightly. 'Hey, Vince. You look a bit tired. How's it going?'

'Great,' he enthuses. 'Really great.'

Colin seems to give him a look of concern. 'Haven't seen Kate around for a while. Doesn't she normally do the dog walk?'

There's a lot that Vince enjoys about The Glade: the peace and quiet, the attractive gardens. What he's not so keen on is the fact that people notice everything that goes on.

'She's, um, not been feeling too good,' Vince blusters.

'Oh, really?' Colin frowns. 'Nothing serious, I hope?'

'Just a bit under the weather. A virus, probably.'

'Well, I hope she's better soon—'

'I'm sure she will be. She was a lot perkier this morning.'

'Ah, good. Well, give her my best,' Colin says, resuming his jog – Vince's cue to speed-walk home before anyone else can grill him about Kate's whereabouts. Letting himself into the house, he sighs in relief, wondering if Jarvis was fed this morning. He didn't think to check. That's another thing Kate's good at, he realises now: keeping track of the details, project managing their life. Without her, everything feels like a big, blurry mess. He's had his neighbour eat dog food and barely managed to achieve a stroke of work. Even his meals have ceased to happen at proper mealtimes. He's been existing on Wotsits and beer and is already developing a bit of a paunch.

Yawning now, Vince scoops the cheap food into Jarvis's bowl, reflecting that at least his meaty farting has ceased. Kate will thank him for it when she comes home.

He's just flumped onto a kitchen chair with a coffee when Deborah messages him again. *Sorry to hassle. Could really do with that recipe. You're both coming on Saturday, yes?*

'You're both'. The most couply phrase from coupledom. *I'm not sure if we're both coming,* he wants to reply, with a sudden urge to come clean instead of all this dodging and fibbing, *because Kate doesn't seem to want to communicate with me at all. So who knows what her Saturday night plans might be?* But he can't do that, as he needs to pretend to Deborah and, more importantly, to himself that everything is normal. And so, quickly googling recipes, and not even registering the lack of kisses on Deborah's message, he sends her the link, with a curt message:

Here you go. Pretty simple if even I can make it.

Thanks, she replies. *Hope it's as delicious as yours!*

And that, he hopes, will be that.

CHAPTER TWENTY-THREE

Kate

The former guest rooms have been emptied and thoroughly scrubbed, leaving just the bare wooden floors and pale-hued walls. Now, on the upper floor only Alice's box room, my lemon room (already it feels like mine) and a bathroom have been left intact for the duration of our stay. We've had the boiler man here, and a joiner fixing several windows and a woman from the auction house, valuing the mahogany pieces in the drawing room, which have now been taken away. People come and go. There's all this activity and then it dies down again, the house feeling emptier still. Yet the whole process is making the place seem less austere. Without the heavy sideboards and bookshelves – so much looming dark wood – it seems to be opening up, allowing the light to flood in.

'It feels,' Alice tells me, 'as if *life* is being breathed into this house.' She's so happy, and obviously relieved, as if a weight has been lifted from her shoulders, that I don't feel quite as guilty about the deceit. There's been no word from the agency, or the woman who was booked to do the job. In fact, I hardly think of myself as an imposter now. I'm almost allowing myself to believe that *I'm* the real Kate.

As for the garden, Fergus called me on Saturday, saying, 'Are you coming into town anytime soon? There's someone I'd like you to meet.'

Rory isn't a gardener as such. He's a kind of everything-guy: nineteen years old, apparently hard-working and up for earning some cash, and the father of Liv's baby. He was already at the shop, with baby Finn cocooned in a sling on his chest, when I arrived.

'Oh, he's a beauty,' I exclaimed.

'Thanks.' Rory smiled. Tall and wiry with shaggy dark hair, he unclipped the sling and handed the baby to Fergus.

'Best baby in the whole of Scotland,' Fergus said, while Rory delved into his rucksack for the baby's bottle. As Finn was passed back to him it struck me how relaxed the two men seemed together; one not much more than a boy in a striped T-shirt and paint-speckled jeans, perching on a chair to feed Finn.

'So, Fergus said you might be looking for work?' I ventured.

Rory nodded. 'I don't have a lot on just now.'

I glanced down at the baby and caught his eye, and we laughed. 'I wouldn't say that.'

'Yeah, well, I can help you out if you need me to. And I can get some mates together as well. Fergus said the grounds of that big old house need a bit of tidying?'

I hesitated. Was he really up to the job? Last thing I needed was a pile of teenagers turning up and being incapable and Alice wondering why I'd hired them. But somehow, I trusted Fergus's judgement.

*

True to their word, on the dot of nine on Monday morning, four young men tumbled from Rory's dad's truck with an assortment of tools and two lawnmowers and a great deal of banter.

'So, what first?' Rory asked.

I looked around the garden in panic. Where to start? 'What d'you think would be best for you guys?' I asked.

'We could divide up and give all the borders a really good weed?'

'Yes! Great. Perfect.'

Then, later: 'Kate, what about the roses?' Rory indicated the border adjoining the house. *Please don't ask me about rose care!*

'Can I get back to you?' I asked. 'There's something I need to take care of . . .' I scuttled inside, because the thing I needed to 'take care of' was finding out what the heck you do with a badly overgrown rose garden. I could have called my mum, who has a tiny but much-loved garden. But she doesn't know I've left Vince. I haven't told her yet – simply because I can't face her wrath.

'You're so lucky, Kate!' she often tells me. 'What I'd have given to have what you have. And Vince worships you!' Does she really think so? Because if he does he has a weird way of showing it with his snippy comments about my 'maiden aunt nighties' and 'old lady knickers'. Mum doesn't know, of course, that he'd decided it'd be more convenient all round for me to pick up some oat milk on a wet, cold night rather than Gail strolling the arduous twenty metres or so to her own fridge. Or that he'd taken to flinching whenever I had the audacity to touch him in bed, as if I've poked him with a stick daubed with poo—

I shoved all that stuff from my brain as I read about dormant buds and pruning hard with extremely sharp secateurs. Back outside, I gathered that Rory's gang didn't have any secateurs, let alone sharp ones. So that necessitated a quick drive to a garden centre, and by the time I came back, Alice was chatting amiably with the lads.

'The box hedges? Oh, that's well beyond my knowledge,' she announced. 'You'll have to ask Kate about that.'

Now four days have flashed by, the borders weeded, edges trimmed, lawns mown. The grounds have started to take shape, no longer fuzzed over by weeds, and my 'managing' of the project has so far amounted to keeping the team fuelled with mugs of tea and bacon rolls and bluffing my way through their questions. At least the boys are hard-working and cheerful, and by the end of the week Alice is delighted. Next they'll tackle the kitchen garden, and trim all the hedges and re-lay the paths. 'What d'you think we should do about the pond?' Rory asks me, within earshot of Alice.

I have absolutely no idea what they should do about the pond! Then I remember taking Edie to the city farm, where we'd learnt that ponds are a vital habitat for an enormous variety of species.

'I think the best thing is to make it look a bit tidier,' I say, quickly. 'All kinds of creatures will be living in there and we don't want to disturb them . . .'

'My thoughts exactly,' Alice agrees.

'Great.' Rory nods. 'Easier for us!'

My thoughts turn to Edie. We've been messaging as we always do, as if nothing untoward has happened. Her young life is focused on the here and now, on whale conservation and the new friends she's made out in Maine. I haven't told her I've left and, presumably, Vince hasn't got around to it either.

Is it up to me to take responsibility for letting Edie know, in the way that I took on all of the homework supervision and making packed lunches and ensuring that school trips were paid for on time – not that I ever minded any of that – on top of our household admin and maintenance to the point of building every item of flatpack that ever came into our home? Maybe, if there's a difficult conversation to be had, Vince could take responsibility. He's Edie's father after all. And I'm all done with responsibilities for now.

That's why I ignore a bizarre message he pings me, just as the guys are packing up their gardening tools at the end of a blustery Friday afternoon.

Hey sorry to bother you. Do we have any ras-el-hanout?

Is this code for something? Or a joke? If it is, then I'm not getting it. I hadn't even realised he'd know what it was. Perhaps he's expecting me to focus my laser vision across four hundred miles and see right into the kitchen cupboard where our spices are kept?

I shoot back: *What's this about Vince?* I'm wondering now about his state of mind. There was that other weird message – the one about covering me in paraffin. Charming!

Nothing important, he replies. *Deborah's having a festival planning committee dinner tonight. What shall I say about you not being there?*

I start to type *I'm sure you'll think of something.* But before I send it my attention is caught by Fergus's van as he turns into the driveway.

'Just thought I'd see how the boys have been doing,' he says as he climbs out. Just like when he came to buy Bea's book collection, I'm surprised by how happy I am to see him here.

'They've done an amazing job,' I tell him. 'I can't thank you enough.'

'Oh, it was nothing. I'm glad it's working out.' His grey-blue eyes catch the late afternoon sunlight as he pauses. Then Alice appears in the garden and Fergus says, 'I wondered if you two fancy coming into town tomorrow? Just for a bit, for a break? I was thinking we could have a quick lunch at mine, then there's a bit of a mini-festival happening by the river. A few bands and stuff . . .'

'That sound great,' I enthuse, all thoughts of the spice cupboard forgotten.

'It's usually a fun day as long as it doesn't bucket down,' he adds, 'and all the boys'll be there.' Rory and his mates, he means. But later, when we're alone in the kitchen, Alice insists: 'I'm going to give the festival a miss. You don't want me hanging around like a spare school dinner.'

I laugh at that. 'You're not a spare school dinner! How can you say that?'

'Well, I plan to enjoy the garden tomorrow and maybe do a little bit of pruning myself,' she says firmly, 'now we can see where the actual plants are.'

I look at her, trying to figure things out. 'What about lunch? Fergus invited both of us . . .'

She shakes her head. Then she adds, with what's definitely a mischievous twinkle: 'No, *you* go. I think a bit of time out, having fun, might be exactly what you need.'

CHAPTER TWENTY-FOUR

Saturday turns out to be perfect for the festival. The sky is unblemished blue and the Perthshire landscape is a paint chart of glorious greens. After a week of bluffing my way through Rory's gardening queries, it's a relief to step away from all that.

I'm filled with a sense of delicious anticipation as Alice drives me into town. Insisting that it's no trouble, she drops me at Fergus's end-of-terrace cottage. There's a tiny, neatly kept front garden, and a yellow climbing rose adorns the whitewashed stone wall. After she's driven away, I pause before knocking on the glossy red front door.

I'm going to Fergus's for lunch. I'm a little nervous now, in case it feels awkward without Alice being there – although I did text to let him know. It's no big deal, I tell myself. He's just being friendly as people are around here. Every time I'm in town now someone smiles and waves in recognition, or stops for a chat. People are curious about what's happening with Osprey House –

but not prying or judgemental. It's a far cry from the disapproving vibes of Sycamore Grove.

'Sorry about the mess,' Fergus apologies as he welcomes me in. 'It's always a bit chaotic around here . . .'

I follow him through a cosy living room walled with bookshelves to a cheerfully cluttered sunflower-yellow kitchen. 'It's not a mess,' I insist. 'It's homely and lived in.'

'Ha. That's a good way of putting it. Shabby chic, maybe? Does anyone say that anymore?' He grins and turns to the stove.

'I'm sure they do. Anyway, after two weeks in Osprey House it's lovely to be in a normal-sized house . . .'

'Oh, that's good. Please, have a seat. This won't be too long.' He reaches for a wooden spoon from an earthenware pot.

'Something smells good,' I say, installed now at the kitchen table.

'Just a pasta. My go-to,' he explains.

'Lovely.' My gaze skims the room, which he clearly tries to keep orderly. Numerous jars and bottles are neatly lined up on shelves, and logs are stacked in a wicker basket by the wood-burning stove. There's a vase of garden flowers on the table, and I wonder if Fergus put them there because he was expecting visitors. Or maybe they were Liv's touch?

There's also no doubting that a baby lives here. The wood burner is cordoned off by a sturdy fireguard, and

187

a wooden box in the corner overflows with a menagerie of soft toys.

'How is it, the three of you living together?' I ask.

'Busy,' Fergus says with a smile. 'We're a little gang really. We make it work. But for such a small person Finn has a heck of a lot of stuff . . .' He clears a scattering of books from the table – I spot *The Very Hungry Caterpillar*, a favourite of Edie's – before swinging back to the counter to throw a salad together, while insisting that he doesn't need any help.

'I remember it vividly,' I say.

'How old was Edie when she moved in with you?'

'Just turned two,' I reply, impressed that he remembered her name, and conscious that we haven't talked any more about me leaving Vince. Perhaps he doesn't want to pry. Or maybe it hasn't occurred to him to ask anything else. Edie has always teased me about my burning need to know all about other people's lives.

'The thing is, I remember it vividly too. With Liv, I mean . . .' Fergus starts to dish up our lunch: tagliatelle with olives and parsley and freshly grated Parmesan. Then comes a big bowl of salad, a carafe of water and a sourdough loaf. It's simple but delicious and I can't help being impressed.

I also register that Fergus has had a haircut, more close-cut now. It makes his face look leaner, his eyes and cheekbones emphasised. 'So, it feels like it's all come round again pretty quickly?' I suggest. 'The baby stage, I mean?'

'You could say that.' His smile reaches his eyes as we start to eat. 'Sorry – I haven't offered you wine. Would you like some?'

'Later, maybe,' I say, then catch myself. Am I now suggesting I'm hanging around until evening?

'There'll be a bar at the festival,' he explains. 'It gets pretty lively later on.'

'Sounds fun!' I smile.

An easy pause settles, then he says, 'So, just another week to go? With Alice I mean?'

'Yes, that's right.'

'D'you have another job lined up? She mentioned she booked you through an agency. D'you always do this kind of work?'

'Erm, I'm not sure what I'm doing next,' I say quickly. 'I mean, I don't have any plans . . .'

He looks at me curiously across the table. I *so* want to tell him, just to be honest and not squirming inwardly, as I am now. It doesn't seem right or fair when he's being so hospitable.

Why did I even start this? Why didn't I admit to Alice, right at the start, that I wasn't who she thought I was? Perhaps she'd have said, 'Well, never mind. The other Kate hasn't turned up so why not just come anyway?' Then there'd be no deceit. As it is, I can feel something happening between Fergus and me – the beginnings of a friendship, of course that's all it is. *Get a grip on yourself, Kate!* And I can't confess now. He's so open and straightforward. And he'd think

189

I'm despicable or mad and I like him too much to risk that.

The realisation hits me. This is crazy. I can't have feelings for someone, not so soon after leaving home. I'm forty-nine years old and I left Vince two weeks ago. Fergus is just being friendly and hospitable, I tell myself firmly. But then I catch his glance, and there's a weight to the silence between us. I can tell he's curious about me.

'It all happened pretty quickly,' I start. As you know, 'I'd just left my husband, and then this job came up at just the right time . . .'

His expression settles into one of concern. 'That can't have been easy.'

'No. No, it wasn't. I hadn't planned it at all . . .' Now I wish I'd said yes to wine. But as I start to explain how things were with Vince and me, it feels okay to share it with this kind, attentive man, in his kitchen with sunshine streaming in, and a single knitted bootee lying on the floor by the fridge. I tell him about the move from London to Shugbury, and how I'd had to leave my museum job. I tell him about Vince being a comedian, and how I'd been working for him, and even about Vince's book-in-progress that I still wonder, occasionally, if he's managed to finish.

'I've heard of him. Haven't seen him though,' Fergus adds, almost apologetically. 'I'm a bit out of the loop. I mean, even before Finn, the shop's been an all-consuming monster. There's literally been no time for anything else in my life.' Does he mean girlfriends? I get the distinct impression that there's been no one since his wife died.

He forks in some tagliatelle and I sense my shoulders relaxing.

'You love it, though?' I suggest. 'The shop, I mean?'

'Oh yes, of course. I couldn't do it otherwise. It's hardly a route to riches and things have a been a bit perilous sometimes. But whenever I've thought of selling up, things have picked up – and I've thought, okay. Just one more year. So we keep going . . .'

'I'm so glad you have,' I say.

He smiles, and it's so warm and genuine it seems to squeeze my heart. 'Oh, me too. So, was it a case of wanting to be somewhere far from home? Is that why you took the job at Osprey House?'

'Kind of,' I say. Isn't that true really? That's precisely why I hadn't jumped off that train at Euston.

'I think it's very brave of you,' he adds.

I rest my fork in my now-empty bowl. 'That's what Alice said too. I'm not sure if it is.'

Fergus gets up and clears our plates. 'I'm sorry. It's probably the last thing you want to talk about. I didn't mean to pry.'

'You weren't at all,' I say quickly. '*I* started it . . .'

'No, I think *I* did . . .'

We catch each other's eyes and laugh at the absurdity of our conversation. What would it be like, I find myself wondering, to just be my honest, open self with him?

Instead of nurturing a secret that I wish I could share? 'It's just been a bit . . . complicated,' I add.

'I can imagine.' Fergus starts to wash up, brushing off my offer to do it: 'Hey, you're my guest!' Then he makes a quick call, checking in with his daughter – 'Be along in a minute. Everything okay?' – and we set off.

CHAPTER TWENTY-FIVE

The festival is in full swing already. A band is playing on stage, and people of all ages are milling around the riverside area, from the elderly to excitable children, in the golden afternoon sun. There's face-painting, a bouncy castle *and* a home-baking stall, although no towering red velvet sponge as far as I can see. We head for the bar, where I insist on buying our beers after Fergus cooked me lunch, and then find ourselves a spot to watch the folk band on stage.

Judging by the crowd's enthusiasm, they are local favourites. Aromas from a pizza stall waft over us, and soon we're joined by Bea's former housekeeper, Morag, and Rory and the gardening team and clusters of others who I'm introduced to. I try to remember names but there are so many, it's impossible. Instead, I relax and let myself be pulled into the music and lively but laid-back atmosphere.

It seems as if Fergus knows *everyone* here. As he introduces me to yet more friends and neighbours, it reminds me of the museum crowd and how we'd go out to celebrate on the flimsiest excuse. I've missed *people* so much. Real, warm people, who don't make assumptions about the kind of person I am. And today I don't have to worry about dodging around why I ended up here. I'm just Kate who's come up from the south to help clear out Osprey House.

'Shame you're not here for longer,' Morag remarks, clutching a slice of pizza and a beer. 'Alice too. It's so nice to see a bit of life back in that old house.'

'It *is* a shame,' Fergus says, as we find ourselves alone again. 'You've fitted right in here, haven't you?'

'I hope so,' I say with a rush of happiness. I only wish I didn't have to hide my lie from Fergus – but what alternative is there? Even if he understood my reasons, there'd be the risk of something slipping out, and Alice finding out – and I can't bear for that to happen now. Occasionally, though, I wonder: what happened to the real Kate?

Then my attention is caught by Liv, who's arrived with Finn and passes him over to Rory. 'Good luck!' Fergus gives her a quick hug.

'Thanks, Dad.' She grimaces.

'Liv's up next,' he explains, turning to me.

'You mean on stage?'

'That's right. She's a singer,' he starts, but she laughs awkwardly, brushing him away.

'Kind of. Not really.' Her mouth twists and she flushes.

'She's a brilliant singer,' Fergus offers, 'but I'm not allowed to say that, am I? Not allowed to have an opinion—'

'*Daaaad*.' For a moment that could have been Edie there, joshing with her father. Then she's hurrying away and we watch, transfixed, as she sings a handful of songs without embellishment or vocal tricks. She seems utterly at ease up there, in a simple black dress and Birkenstocks, her long glossy dark hair loose. A teenage girl alone with just a microphone and an acoustic guitar. I glimpse Fergus watching her, and the pride that emanates from him fills my heart. Of course, Vince has always been proud of Evie too. But I wonder how he'd have coped if there'd been an unplanned teenage pregnancy, and if mother and baby had lived with us.

He'd made a big enough fuss when Edie had announced that she'd be moving to the States. 'We *can't* have Jarvis. I don't want a dog, Kate. This is so unfair!' We'd argued then – out of earshot of Edie. Okay, it might not have been what we'd imagined. But what other choice was here?

Fergus just gets on with stuff, I reflect. But then, he's had to. His wife died, and he had his daughter to look after – and a bookshop to run – on top of his grief.

Liv finishes her set to enthusiastic applause and comes to find us again. There's no surliness today; no acting as if she'd rather be anywhere else but here.

'You were brilliant,' I tell her.

'Really? Are you sure?'

'Really,' her father says firmly.

'Thanks!' She beams at us, then scampers off again, disappearing into the high-spirited crowd. Then, gradually, it all starts to thin out. Fergus and I fetch another beer from the bar and find ourselves sitting on the grass, alone together at the river's edge.

It's seven-thirty already. The afternoon has spun by and now, I realise, I don't want the day to end. Fergus has already mentioned that Peter, the taxi driver, will be on hand later if I need a ride home. We sit in easy silence, watching golden light dance on the river.

With the festival over, a beautiful stillness settles over the Perthshire hills. I'm aware of the closeness of Fergus. His strong profile, his long legs stretched out in front of him.

And I can sense the steady thud of my heart. Then he turns to me and says, 'So, did you enjoy the day?'

I nod and smile. 'It's been wonderful. Thank you.'

'Hey, nothing to thank me for.' His smile crinkles his eyes, and his gaze catches mine for a moment. It strikes me suddenly that, back in Shugbury, Deborah's planning committee dinner will be starting around now. And Vince will have to explain why I'm not there. Will he tell the truth, I wonder? Or perhaps everyone already knows? I quickly push the thought away and sip my cool beer with Fergus beside me as the sky turns honey-gold.

Never mind home, I tell myself. I'm all filled up with music and people and happiness, and I feel so lucky to be here. Almost like that teenage girl again, hauled up to Scotland by Mum – because George had demanded it: 'Just one more holiday at that campsite. Please!'

I'd thought it would be boring. At fifteen I was far more interested in my friends, and boys, than being in a tent with Mum and my brother and cooking sausages over a fire. But up we'd travelled, and it had turned out to be the best trip of all.

I'd been so happy then. Everything had felt so thrilling and new – as if a whole new world was opening up to me. And now, as I glance at Fergus, I realise that feeling is still in me. 'Fancy a stroll, and maybe a stop-off at the Boat Inn?' he suggests now.

'I'd love that,' I say, as we get up and start to stroll along the riverbank.

Maybe that feeling has been there, buried deep inside me, all along.

CHAPTER TWENTY-SIX

Vince

Vince is so *not* in the frame of mind for Deborah's planning committee dinner. He's considering feigning illness – or faking his own death like that guy with the canoe.

But what if he's spotted moving around in his own house? Will he be driven to lying on the floor with all the lights off? Living here, he's come to realise, there is no bloody escape.

Why hadn't they just stayed in Bethnal Green? No one cared what you did there! You could drop dead in the street and people would just step over you! There was no Colin Carse, telling you the right way to unhang a door, or constant flyers being posted through the door asking you to sweep up your hedge clippings and not put bird food on the ground and whatever-the-fuck else – Vince loses track of it all. Suddenly he has an overwhelming urge to rewind the clock so they'd be back in their old flat, with Shawn and Jules from upstairs forever popping in and guzzling their wine and making Kate howl with laughter.

It doesn't help that, earlier today, Deborah was plaguing Vince with messages: *Could I pop round for some ras-el-hanout?*

What the fuck? Was that code for some kind of exotic sex? In normal times he'd have been in a stew of excitement. But with all that's happened lately, Vince wasn't sure he could cope with any startling developments. His response was a curt '?'

A spice mix, she replied. *Forgot to get some and am cooking now. Assumed you'd have some from making yours?*

From making his what? Oh, of course. The mythical tagine that's going to taunt him until the end of time. *Sorry used ours up,* he fibbed in reply.

Damn. Anything I can use instead?

What was this? Some kind of terrible test?

A blend of the major spices should do it, he replied. Then he tucked his phone away in his desk drawer where it could no longer harass him, and pictured his lies, stacked up like Jenga bricks: a great wobbling tower that the slightest wrong move could send toppling down.

Still, it's no big deal, he reminds himself now, as he buttons up his smartest shirt and checks that nothing untoward is sprouting out of his nostrils or ears. (He's let personal grooming slip of late.) It's only a casual supper to chat about book festival stuff.

In fact, he decides, as he gives Jarvis a friendly head ruffle as he sets out, he doesn't even have to stay for the duration. He can show his face briefly, explain that Kate's been under the weather with a virus, and that he thinks he's getting it too. Or – another idea hits him – she had to rush off to London to tend to her mother who'd fallen off a stepladder while trying to change a lightbulb. *We've told her to ask a neighbour to help instead of insisting on doing it herself!*

Does that sound feasible? As Vince heads down the street, clutching his bottle of red wine on this warm and somewhat humid Saturday evening, he decides instead to say that Kate's away on a retreat. An open-ended retreat – meaning he doesn't know when she'll be home.

She's taking a bit of time out to find herself. Never mind that he normally pours scorn on people who talk like that, about 'finding' anything that's not a tangible object like, say, their car keys. Yep, that'll do, he decides.

He's the last one to arrive at Deborah's. Everyone is already quaffing Prosecco and picking at 'nibbles' – tiny bread discs adorned with various daubings, as if squeezed from paint tubes. Obviously, Kate's absence is commented upon immediately. Lacking confidence in his fibbing abilities, Vince mutters vaguely that something came up, and she's sorry she couldn't make it. Hopefully that'll be that, he decides.

However, once dinner is served, and everyone is

tucking into Deborah's tagine, Vince senses gusts of suspicion wafting from her every time she glances at him.

She knows, he realises. Any minute now—

'So,' she booms – her voice is the kind that 'carries' – 'where *is* Kate tonight, Vince? Is everything all right at home?'

His heart clangs like a can kicked into the road. He opens his mouth, about to spout hogwash about a retreat or a virus or elderly ladies teetering ill-advisedly on stepladders. *And then she fell and dislocated her shoulder!* But he can't do it. It's all tangled up in his brain (retreat? Virus? Stepladder?) and as his cheeks burn, it all tumbles out of his mouth. Not the tagine, which is probably delicious, even without the crucial spice mix. No, the truth is what splurges out, in front of his neighbours and platters of flatbreads and salads and glasses of red wine.

'So, I might as well tell you. Kate's actually gone.'

They're all staring at him. Sporty Colin, Deborah, Gail and Mehmet, Radish Sue, and Agata and Lenny Kemp. All those eyes boring into his skull. Vince feels utterly exposed, as if he's blundered into Deborah's immaculate dining room having forgotten to put on his trousers.

'Gone?' Gail repeats. 'You don't mean . . .'

'Oh, no. Not *gone*-gone,' Vince blusters.

'Oh my God, Vince.' Deborah clasps a hand to her chest. 'I thought . . . you know. Something *awful* had happened . . .'

201

Well, it has, of course. 'No, she's just left me. So maybe it's not *that* awful, when you think of alternative scenarios . . .' His attempt at lightening the mood seems to miss its mark.

'When did this happen?' Colin asks, frowning.

'Um, a couple of weeks ago . . .'

'Vince, mate.' He slaps an unwelcome hand on Vince's shoulder. 'Really sorry to hear that.'

'You should've said something,' adds Agata. 'It's far too much to carry around all by yourself. We're all here for you any time. Honestly, Vince. You don't have be alone with this.' Her eyes widen with concern.

And now everyone's commiserating, with Gail asking how he is *really*, and if there's anything he needs . . . 'I mean, anything,' she gushes.

'I did wonder,' Deborah offers, with a pained expression, 'if Kate was all right at that party of yours.'

'Didn't seem like herself,' Colin offers sagely, and Vince prickles with annoyance. He barely knows Kate. How dare he have an opinion on her!

'Was there some kind of trigger?' Gail asks, seemingly oblivious to kind, sensitive Dr Kemp shooting her a look. 'I mean, were there any signs that she was *deeply* unhappy?'

'Erm, I'm not sure,' Vince starts.

'Was she depressed?' barks Radish Sue.

'I, er, don't know—'

'Maybe Vince doesn't want to delve into the details right now?' Lenny Kemp says quickly.

'No, of course,' Gail says, fork poised with a fat chunk of lamb on it. 'So, d'you think you'll be able to work it out? I mean, is it just a break, or a permanent separation—'

'Shall we talk about committee business now?' Lenny asks in his reassuring yet authoritative doctor's voice. *Take these twice a day and come back in a week if there's no improvement.*

'After dinner, Lenny.' Deborah smiles tightly and turns back to Vince. 'So where *is* Kate?'

'Erm, she's staying with a friend in London,' he mumbles. 'At least, I think she is. I guess so.' He shrugs.

'Well, this is really good tagine!' Lenny announces, and Mehmet murmurs in agreement.

'Vince's recipe,' Deborah announces brightly. And finally, everyone resumes eating, making a great show of how flavoursome it is, and how clever Vince is to know the recipe.

'Well done, Vince,' Agata offers, patting his hand. He didn't even make it!

'It really is very good,' adds Radish Sue. 'And I don't normally do spicy food . . .'

Spicy food? Vince thinks derisively. There's probably one particle of cumin in it. And suddenly he's overcome with an overwhelming desire to jump up from his chair in this savagely coordinated dining room, which looks like a John Lewis room set, the kind his parents would admire at the Milton Keynes branch when he was a child and he'd stand there, desperate to leave as it felt like they'd been admiring that coffee table for eight hundred years and they'd promised him that they'd pop into Thorntons before going home.

And now here he is, literally a three-minute walk from the house he grew up in, with people who think a lamb stew that, frankly, tastes only of gravy, is 'spicy'. People whose apparent concern over his collapsed marriage is actually barely disguised glee.

Because finally something has happened around here! It's more exciting, even, than the Walkers' new conservatory or a new bin collection system being implemented by the council!

'Always thought you two were rock solid,' announces Gail, even though she's barely known them for two minutes.

'Me too,' Colin agrees. 'D'you think it's her age or something?'

'What d'you mean?' Vince stares at him. Deborah is up out of her seat now, clearing away serving dishes and the remains of the salads, with sidekick Agata gathering up the bowls. But all the movement and clattering seems to fade away as Colin goes on.

'Well, it is quite a tricky life stage for women with their oestrogen going off.'

'Really?' Vince blinks at him. 'Does it go off, then? Like milk?'

'Hope you all have room for brownies,' Deborah trills, sweeping off to the kitchen with the diminutive Agata at her heels.

'Well, yes,' he blusters. 'You do hear of it happening.'

Vince blinks slowly. 'You hear of *what* happening, Colin?' *There's a doctor in the room*, he wants to shout. If anyone's equipped to talk about menopausal symptoms, shouldn't it be him?

'*You* know. The emotional side of all the changes-type stuff . . .'

'Erm, d'you think we should move on now?' Lenny suggests, twiddling the stem of his wine glass. 'This is all very personal stuff and I really think it's between Vince and Kate—'

Why am I here? For the second time tonight Vince has an overwhelming craving for their old Bethnal Green life. *Why did I drag Kate away from the job she loved and all her friends? Where we brought up Edie and it was all so diverse and accepting and you could go about your daily business without the laser beam of the whole sodding neighbourhood on you, whereas here you only have to wear a fucking hat and it's on the front of the* Shugbury Gazette—

'So, how about we discuss what went well with the festival this year?' Lenny suggests in a louder voice. 'And then the aspects that maybe didn't work so well?' He turns, beaming, to Deborah and Agata as they reappear in the dining room. 'Deborah, you were saying we could probably charge more for teas and coffees next year?'

She doesn't seem to care about hot beverage pricing. No one is even registering that he spoke. Because the entire focus of the planning committee is on Vince, who has turned to Colin and said, in an eerily mild tone, 'D'you mean it might be Kate's menopause? Is that why she's left me?'

His neighbour reddens and looks down. 'I'm just thinking, you know. With the right hormonal treatment—'

'D'you think that's what happened to *your* wife?' It comes out more fiercely than Vince intended.

'Sorry?' Colin blinks at him.

'I mean, is that what caused your wife to leave you, Colin? Did her oestrogen "go off" too?'

'Hey!' he barks, aghast.

'Because, y'know, we're in a public forum here and if you'd like to talk about it, if you'd like the whole committee's take on it—'

'Vince!' Deborah exclaims. 'Please!'

Colin looks stunned and Radish Sue is glaring at him. 'I don't really,' he mutters. 'It wasn't the easiest time of my life, you know. Most of my friends realise that.'

For a moment, the room falls silent. Then someone clears their throat, and Mehmet mutters something conciliatory to Colin, and Vince looks down at his hands and the checked shirt that Kate bought him recently and it wasn't even his birthday.

A chair scrapes. Vince is overwhelmed with a sudden urge to cry. Instead he gets up from his seat, muttering that he needs the loo. And as he leaves the room he hears Lenny announcing, 'Well, I thought the marquee people were great this year. Who says we book them again?'

206

CHAPTER TWENTY-SEVEN

Kate

We find an outside table at the Boat Inn and spot Liv with friends across the pub's garden. 'It's a night off for her,' Fergus explains. 'Finn's with Rory overnight.'

'She's lucky,' I venture, 'having you to support her. I can see how close you are.'

'We've grown that way,' he says, 'although, believe me, we had our moments when she was younger . . .'

'Was she a handful?'

'And the rest . . .' He grins and breaks off as she makes her way to our table, clutching an almost empty glass.

'Hey, Dad,' she says. 'All right?'

As she glances from him to me, a flicker of panic ignites in me as I wonder if she's okay with this. With her dad having a drink with a woman, that is. Perhaps it's a little weird for her. 'Another beer?' he asks me.

'Erm, yes please. If you are . . .'

'Coke for you, Livs?'

She laughs and her cheeks flush. 'I'd better. I've had a few . . .'

'Never have guessed,' he teases, then he's gone.

Immediately, she plonks herself onto the seat beside me. 'Thanks for being so nice about my singing.'

'Honestly, I loved it,' I tell her. 'Have you always been into music?'

'Mum was a singer,' she says, which takes me aback a little.

'Oh, really?'

'I don't mean professionally. But she sang in pubs and stuff around here. I wanted to go to music college,' she adds. 'But my plans kinda changed . . .' A wry smile crosses her face.

'Right,' I say. 'Finn's a beautiful little boy. But I know it's not easy . . .'

She pulls her chair a little closer. 'D'you have children?'

'I have a stepdaughter, Edie. None of my own. But Edie's mum was young when she had her too. Just twenty, and she was working as a model—'

'A model? Wow!' Liv exclaims. She has a finely boned face with defined high cheekbones and full, pink lips. Her eyes are the same soft bluey-grey as her dad's.

'Yeah. She was doing really well too, but that all stopped,' I tell her. 'She was happy, though, I think. But she was the only one in her group to have a baby so that was hard.'

'Yeah, it is.' Liv nods and presses her lips together.

Without warning her eyes fill with tears.

'Liv, are you okay?' All of sudden I want to pull this girl in for a hug. I don't, of course. She might not be the huggy type and, besides, I barely know her.

'I'm fine, honestly.' She blinks them away quickly. 'Just a bit drunk.'

'Well, it's been a big important night . . .'

'It's just, I wasn't prepared for it, y'know? What it'd really be like. How hard it is . . .'

'I can imagine,' I murmur. A small pause settles. Fergus has been a while, I realise. The pub's probably packed – or maybe he's got chatting in there. 'And you're working in the shop too,' I add.

'Uh-huh. That was Dad's idea to give me a break from the baby. Rory's pretty good. A good dad, I mean. He does his share. But Dad thought it'd be a good idea for me to do something else too. 'Cause it was all getting a bit much for me—' Her eyes fill up again and she blinks the wetness away. 'Sorry! I'm really going on, aren't I?'

'You're fine,' I assure her, suspecting she misses having her mum around, now more than ever.

She smiles, pushing back the long dark hair that's brushing her cheek. 'I feel bad,' she adds. 'About Dad, I mean.'

'Why?' I ask in surprise.

'He's so kind,' she announces, meeting my gaze directly. 'He's, like, the kindest man I know . . .' As if to reassure herself that he's not within earshot, she glances towards the pub's doorway. 'And he's paying me to work

209

for him, of course. So I should be grateful . . .'

'Sounds like there's a "but",' I suggest, and she nods.

'Yeah.' Her mouth twists. 'I hate it.'

'Really? Working in the shop, you mean?' I picture her sullen face that first day I ventured in, and the doughnut jam spurting.

'I don't mean I hate the shop,' she says quickly. 'It's a lovely shop. Dad's worked so hard to build it up . . .'

'But . . . you don't want to be there?'

'Yeah. No. No, I don't. Finn's only just turned one. He's my baby and I want to be with him. It was hard at first, and I had postnatal depression and I couldn't handle the crying and how you never get a break. So working with Dad seemed like a great idea. An escape, you know? Just for a few hours.' She pauses. 'But I'm much better now. I'm *fine*. And I don't want to be in the shop—' She breaks off again, pulling a mock-fearful face. 'Don't tell him I said that, will you?'

'Of course not. But why don't *you* tell him?' I ask, genuinely confused. From what I've seen of Fergus he seems like an understanding, supportive dad.

'Because he's always saying what a difference I've made, and how much it helps him, with me being there,' Liv continues. 'After Helen left he'd have to shut the shop every time he needed to drive somewhere to pick up books from a house clearance or whatever. Or he'd have to do all that in the evenings or on Sundays when the shop's shut. He was always either working or driving or lugging boxes about. He was running things all by himself . . .'

'You mean he *needs* you?' I offer.

'Well . . . yeah.' Liv nods, and I wonder how to phrase what I want to say.

'I'm sure he values you,' I start, 'and you're *great* in the shop. But why not just explain all of this to your dad?'

She looks tentative. 'You think so?'

An image forms in my mind then, of me, climbing out of the bathroom window in Sycamore Grove on a wet Sunday night, and walking to town and boarding that bus – because somehow I knew it was what I needed to do. 'I do, honestly. Really, Liv. Life's too short to not be doing what you want to be doing—'

Fergus appears then, and places our drinks on the table. 'Sorry I've been so long.'

'You were talking to everyone,' Liv chastises him. 'You left Kate all alone!'

He laughs and hands her her Coke, and I hope he hasn't noticed my face flushing. 'See you later, then.' Liv jumps up, and turns to me. 'And thanks.'

'See you, Liv,' I call after her as she hurries off.

Sitting next to me now, Fergus gives me a quizzical look. 'What was she thanking you for?'

'We just had a bit of a chat,' I say lightly.

A bemused smile flickers. 'That's nice. It's quite unusual. She can be a bit of a closed book, can Liv . . .' And then – it's barely detectable but I catch it – he looks at me in a way that says, *And so can you.* But the

211

moment passes, and we settle into chatting about what's left to do at Osprey House.

'And you don't know where you'll be working next?' Fergus asks.

'No,' I reply. 'I do know that I'm not going back, though. Back to Vince, I mean.'

Until I said it, I wasn't 100 per cent sure. But I know now. I *can't* go back to all that. 'Right,' Fergus says carefully. 'Does he know you're in Scotland?'

'No, he doesn't.'

'So . . .' He frowns, looking thoughtful. 'You don't *want* him to know where you are? I mean, did you have to escape—'

'Oh no, it wasn't like that,' I say quickly. 'I wasn't in danger. It wasn't a scary, got-to-leave-this-house-type situation.' I catch his steady look. It's as if he knows that I was part of that kind of situation once, and know the difference.

'Vince hasn't actually asked where I am,' I explain. 'He's just assumed I'm at Tash's – that's my oldest friend – because in his eyes, that's where I'd go.' As I tell him this, I wonder if Vince ever really knew me at all.

We finish our drinks and find Liv to say goodbye. Then slowly we stroll into town. 'I'd better let Peter know I'm ready to go home,' I say, even though I'm not really. I could talk to Fergus all night.

'You're calling it home already,' Fergus observes with a smile.

'I am, yes. It sort of feels that way.' I catch his eye

and have to look away because I'm not sure what's happening here. Two weeks ago, I left Vince. I can't have these kinds of feelings for someone else.

Quickly, I text Peter, as arranged, and a few minutes later we see his taxi approaching along the main street. 'Thanks for a lovely day,' Fergus says, touching my arm.

'Thank *you*,' I say, realising that, now I know about Liv's true feelings, I'm keeping *two* secrets from him. But none of that matters as his arms wrap around me, and he envelops me in a hug.

As we pull apart my heart seems to soar high into the inky night sky. 'Night, Fergus,' I say, still tingling with the feeling of him so close to me.

'Night, Kate,' he says. I climb into the taxi and wave as we pull away.

'Have a good day?' Peter asks, catching my eye in a rear-view mirror.

'The best,' I say truthfully. 'It's been the *best* day.'

CHAPTER TWENTY-EIGHT

Vince

At just gone midnight Vince lets himself into his house, clips on Jarvis's lead and slopes out into the night. He might as well take him to the park and back, he decides. Filled with self-loathing, and that hefty tagine he can barely remember eating, he hopes it'll make him feel better.

As Jarvis insists on stopping for what seems like around sixty tiny pees, instead of emptying his bladder in one time-effective motion, progress is extremely slow. And weirdly, Vince is shimmeringly sober, despite having knocked back a vat of wine at Deborah's.

Finishing his book. Getting drunk. These are just two of the things he seems incapable of, as he adjusts to life without Kate. He doesn't seem to be able to behave properly in company either. What made him tell everyone about her leaving him? It's out there now, no doubt being transmitted throughout The Glade and beyond, to Shugbury Old Town and probably all the way to Milton Keynes at this very minute.

As Jarvis sniffs around the park in the cold light of the sole streetlamp, Vince replays the terrible evening before making his way back to his empty house. That stuff he said to Colin – about his wife leaving him. How mean of him. It was bullying, really. And after all that humping-the-horse stuff he endured at school, Vince has always despised bullies.

Next day, scared of seeing any of the neighbours, he skulks around his house feeling like someone in solitary confinement. Really, he wants to call or text Kate, but he no longer knows what to say to her. He's getting desperate now. He needs to know what her plans are, and if he's somehow blown things forever. He can't even call Harry because his old friend will be busy on a Sunday doing fun family things. And Vince can't be that suddenly needy friend, who's started calling his old mate just because his life's turned to shit. He will *not* be that person.

Vince is aware of an ache inside him and wonders if his heart is actually breaking. And then first thing on Monday morning his phone rings, and he levitates out of bed, as if stabbed with a cattle prod, in his hurry to answer it.

'Hey, Vince. How's things?' It's Zoe, his editor at the publishing house. Zoe to whom he was meant to submit his finished book two weeks ago.

'Great!' It comes out all ragged and hoarse, the result

of not having spoken to another human since Saturday night. 'How're you?' he manages.

'Really good,' she enthuses. 'Amazing weather this weekend. Hope you've been enjoying it?'

Was it amazing? Vince has no recollection whatsoever. 'Yeah, it's been lovely. So, um . . .'

'Great,' Zoe cuts in. 'So, I just wanted to say . . .'

'Erm, look, I know I'm a bit late with the book, Zo.' Is it okay to call her Zo? He's never done that before.

'Well, actually, Vince, the reason I'm calling is to tell you—'

'The thing is, it's nearly finished. I just need a bit more time—'

'Please don't worry about it,' she says firmly.

Vince blinks, momentarily stunned. 'Oh, really?'

'Yes. Not at all. Just take your time with it and see how you go . . .'

'*Really?*' Vince croaks.

'Honestly, yes. Don't stress. We're not in a hurry for it at the moment. Or actually at all. I mean, there's no rush. So just finish it in your own time, okay?'

Anxiety prickles at him now. He can do it *in his own time*? Has his hilarious take on the absurdities of modern life plummeted to the realms of some vague homework assignment? 'I'm sure it's going to be great,' she adds. 'I'm so excited to read it!'

He doesn't know Zoe that well. Through their handful of face-to-face meetings, and a few chats on the phone, he's gathered that she's just moved out from North London to Hertfordshire and is married to her university boyfriend and ran this year's London Marathon in under five hours. Beyond that, it's a void.

But Vince has been around the block, and he knows when his act is going well, and when he's tanking, and he knows when people are sucking up to him just because he's a little bit famous now, or they want to be genuine friends.

He's developed this radar over the past few years. He's pretty certain that Kate has been having a whale of a time in London with her old mates, and that she and Tash are sitting around in pyjamas in Tash's kitchen right now, chatting and laughing just like old times.

And he knows, as much as he can ever know anything, that Zoe is lying to him.

Much later, at around two a.m., Vince wakes with a start, sensing that something is different. For two whole, empty weeks he's been horribly conscious of the empty side of the bed. He's tried to fill it, splaying out his arms and legs in order to inhabit maximum space. But it's felt odd and awkward – like trying to mimic someone else's walk.

However, at this moment it feels less empty than it has in recent times. In fact it feels almost normal, like it used to, with his warm, softly breathing wife in it.

He must be imagining it because Kate has left him, just like Colin Carse's wife left him, the only upside being that Kate isn't shagging a driving instructor.

She might be, he reflects, for all he knows. She might be going through all the manoeuvres at this very moment. Yet the thought soon dissipates, and he is soothed once again by the closeness of another living being.

Vince can hardly bear to look.

'Kate?' he says softly.

He can hear breathing: a gentle in and out. In and out. The tension of that terrible Saturday night, of upsetting Colin and having nothing to contribute to the planning of next year's book festival – as well as today's bizarre conversation with Zoe – seems to leave his chest. Now he's thinking, what kind of man is he to have commented on the hair he'd noticed poking out of Kate's chin? Or expected her to throw a buffet together the minute she'd come home from work? He'll be kinder – far kinder – from now on. He'll never make disparaging remarks about her corrugated vest or massive pants. He won't even say she looks good for her age, as he did recently – which had her looking as if she'd happily take a bread knife to him. And now, having vowed to turn over a new leaf, he flops an arm over the soft warm furry—

Furry? Vince jolts fully awake, realising a line has been crossed. At some point during the night, he has been taken advantage of. For a moment he's poised to shoo the interloper from his bed and shut the bedroom door firmly. But then, it feels so good to have the warmth of his body close by, demanding nothing; not recipes or ras-el-hanout or that he shares the details of his marriage break-up with the neighbourhood. Even the faint whiff of not especially fragrant breath is weirdly pleasant. So instead he murmurs, 'Make yourself comfortable, why don't you?' Then, edging a little closer to the slumbering hound, Vince falls soundly asleep.

CHAPTER TWENTY-NINE

Kate

Stunning 6 Bedroom House For Sale

Osprey House is a magnificent baronial home set in a rural Perthshire location within beautifully landscaped gardens. Having previously operated as a B&B, the house could equally be an idyllic family home.

'So our work here is done,' Alice announces.

'It is. And doesn't it look amazing?' I say.

'Not too shabby, I suppose.' We laugh at her understatement. After days of dark, brooding skies, the sun had burst through obligingly when the estate agent's photographer arrived. The house looked spectacular against the sweeping hills, all traces of gloominess gone.

Installed at Alice's laptop at the kitchen table, we're checking the estate agent's advertising before it goes live, and the glossy brochure is printed. The slick young woman in a pinstriped trouser suit had assured us that 'a premium property like this deserves top-level marketing material to attract the right buyer'. She was confident that it would be snapped up.

'So much of this is thanks so you,' Alice says.

'Oh, not really,' I protest.

'No, it's true,' she insists. 'You've worked so hard and used your initiative . . .'

'Have I?' I'm unused to so much praise.

'Yes! Just look at the garden, Kate . . .' She points towards the kitchen window. 'You knew, instinctively, that there wasn't time for Rory's team to relandscape the whole grounds. So you had them focus on what would make the biggest impact, and leave the rest wild. The contrast is lovely. So natural,' she enthuses. 'I've never been a fan of formal gardens anyway.' Then the dogs start nudging at us to go out, and we step outside.

'I've loved it here,' I say truthfully. 'Honestly, Alice, it's been wonderful. The three weeks have flown by.'

And now it's almost over. The thought squeezes my heart. We've been so frantically busy this past week that I haven't had a chance to pop into town – or, more specifically, into the bookshop. Fergus has texted occasionally, asking how we were doing in putting the final touches to the house. It was thoughtful but each message made me realise, with a sharp pang, how much I'll miss being here.

Then, just as Alice steps aside to admire the climbing roses, another message comes: *Liv's just told me she doesn't want to work in the shop anymore.*

Oh no, why? I reply, feigning surprise.

Something about life being too short not to be doing what you really want to do . . . very wise. Not like her at all! As I blink at his smiley emoji, thoughts start to turn over in my mind.

Alice rejoins me on the newly laid gravel path. 'So I'll tell the agency how delighted I am,' she says.

'Great. I'm just glad you're happy . . .' I inhale the fresh, sharp air. I could tell her now – come clean about everything. It would be a relief, frankly. And isn't she due a refund anyway, as the real Kate hadn't shown up?

We fall into an easy silence as we walk, with the dogs scampering ahead. There's the distant baa of a sheep, and a crow calling out, sharp and urgent, perched on the fence. I glance at Alice – this kind, smart and accomplished woman – and am aware of the thud of my heart. Then I start, 'Alice, I wanted to say something, about working for you. You see, I—'

'Oh, hasn't it been fun, Kate?' she cuts in, blue eyes glinting. 'I didn't expect that at all. I thought it'd be hell, actually. Clearing out my dead mother's things! God . . .' She shudders, then brightens again. 'You know, Ruthie had always planned to come up with me and we'd tackle it all together. We'd make a holiday of it, we said. Maybe travel further north when it was all done, as a reward to ourselves. Ruthie had always wanted to go to Orkney. It's where her paternal grandparents were from – a little fishing town there with cobbled streets.

You know how you talk about doing something and then you realise you've run out of time?'

She tails off and I link my arm in hers, surprised by how much she's shared. Until now she's barely mentioned her friend, whose dogs are currently investigating the lavender beds.

'I'm so sorry you lost her,' I say.

She presses her lips together and nods. 'Then Max was meant to come up,' she reminds me. 'I mean, I haven't asked much from my son over the years!' She laughs dryly. 'But things got in the way – work, family, whatever. I was furious with him at the time, you know? But he has his own life. Why should this old place be his priority?' She shakes her head, as if exasperated with herself for being annoyed with him. 'And then there was you!' She beams at me, her face lighting up now. 'How lucky am I? And after all you'd been through, leaving Vince, you were still prepared to do this job with me. *You* didn't let me down . . .'

'I'm glad I could help you,' I say. My insides twist with guilt. But it's true, isn't it? I was right there when Alice needed someone. Perhaps I should feel proud – not ashamed – of what I've done. If the agency people don't even know, and just assume the real Kate did the job . . . then maybe Alice will never find out that I've deceived her?

'I thought you were an angel,' she continues, 'standing there at Euston station with that little leopard-print tote bag, in quite an *unusual* outfit . . .' Despite everything, I

223

can't help smiling at that.

As we head back towards the house, my gaze sweeps the grounds. Somehow – miraculously, it seems to me – Osprey House shines out now, like a painting, newly framed to be shown off to its best advantage. Next week the place will be on the market. Alice has yet to book our return train tickets for our journey back down south. I've explained that I'm in no immediate rush, and she feels the same. 'We deserve a few days' rest,' she added. Yet even so, I'm aware that the end of my time here is surging towards me, faster than the scudding clouds above.

'We can treat this place like our holiday home,' she says with a smile, as we step back into the hallway.

I stop and look at her. 'Alice, I know you weren't terribly happy here when you were younger. But still, this must be a huge thing to you. To put it on the market, I mean.'

'Well, I suppose so,' she says, with a trace of reluctance. 'And these past three weeks, with you here, I have felt a little differently about the place . . .'

'Really?' I ask in surprise.

She nods. 'We've breathed new life into it, haven't we, Kate?' The waver in her voice suggests that perhaps she does care about this house after all.

'Yes, I think we have. But . . . are you absolutely sure about—'

'About going home? Yes, Kate. Of course I am.' She sounds determined now.

'I mean . . . about selling the house. D'you feel it's the right thing to do?'

Her mouth twists, and pink patches appear on her cheeks as she touches my arm. 'Kate, darling. It's the *only* thing to do. So, what d'you fancy doing this afternoon?'

Somehow, after all the activity this week, I sense that she'd enjoy some alone time here with her dogs in the house. So, having checked that it's fine with her, I borrow her mother's ancient car, and rattle along the country lanes, stopping whenever the mood takes me.

I drive without even thinking about where I'm going, passing dense, dark woodland and rivers shimmering like ribbons of silk. I drive Bea's shabby saloon along single-track roads into the hills, getting lost on several occasions when there's no phone signal, so no Google Maps – just the sharp cry of a hawk above.

Stopping in a lay-by, I open the car door and gaze out over the valley below, filling my lungs with crisp, cool air. Somewhere down there was a campsite. Seeing that I have a phone signal now – rare around here – I check Google Maps. But nothing shows up. I drive on, hoping to spot the lane that led towards it, thinking my brother would love to see a photo of it, if I can find the place. But of course, I was fifteen the last time we came here and it's probably not there anymore. It was little more than a clearing in the forest anyway. So, instead of continuing my search, I pull over again and make a call.

'Hi, Fergus,' I start. 'Just wondering if you're at the shop today?'

'Hey, Kate. Yes, I am. I'll be here all day. Everything okay?'

'Yes, I'm good,' I say. 'I was just thinking of coming into town. There's, um . . . something I'd like to talk to you about, if you're free. Is it okay if I drop in?'

CHAPTER THIRTY

Alice didn't head back down south the week after Osprey House had been put on the market. 'I'm kind of enjoying it here,' she explained, 'without all the looming furniture and clutter. It's like a totally different house. I'll just make myself scarce when the estate agent's doing viewings.'

I haven't gone either. I'm still living in Osprey House, as Alice has insisted I stay there – until it's sold, if that's what I want. 'I'll be out of your hair soon, I promise,' she's joked.

Now, finally, there's no deceit surrounding the work I'm doing – because I have a new job. That day I'd looked for the campsite, Fergus and I discussed how I could step into Liv's shoes and help out in the shop.

I know it's working out because Fergus is appreciative and tells me all the time. And as July tips into August, and then gradually the trees turn copper and golden, I'm still here. Alice is too. We cohabit happily, sharing our news when I return home after work.

One evening, out of the blue, Vince messages me.

The bed feels huge without you. Just that, a simple statement of fact.

I'm sorry, I reply. It's all I can think of to say.

Or maybe it's me that's shrinking?

He means it as a joke, I know him well enough to understand that. But it seems so sad. The only response that feels right is a short row of kisses: *xxx.*

And it strikes me that he still hasn't asked where or how I am.

Meanwhile, my life has taken on a new shape. If Fergus is out and about, I man the shop. Or I'll drive all over Perthshire and beyond to check out collections of books that are no longer wanted. I can usually tell pretty quickly whether they'll be of interest for us. For instance, *Your 2007 Libra Year*, or a raggedy edition of *Naming Your Baby* – not so much. Ditto out of date DIY and car manuals: those hefty tomes that would clog up our shelves. Instead, we look for quality fiction and anything about nature, the outdoors or with a Scottish slant.

As we work together I try to push all those thoughts of how attractive Fergus is, and how perhaps there's some kind of frisson between us, out of my mind. Because I'm probably imagining it – and isn't he friendly to everyone? Besides, although he never acts this way, he *is* my boss.

On a bright and crisp September afternoon my heart actually flutters when I'm presented with a vast

228

collection of natural history books in a remote cottage way out in the hills. 'Of course we'll take them,' I tell the elderly man.

'That's great,' he says. 'I'm downsizing, you see. Won't have room for them anymore.' He pauses and laughs. 'And I suppose my poaching days are over.' I pay him in cash, as he requested, already looking forward to sharing this new consignment with Fergus.

'*A Salmon Glossary . . . The Secret Life of Foxes . . .*' Fergus reads titles out loud later, clearly delighted. Tonight, I offer to stay on after closing to sort and price up our newly acquired books. There's a record player by the counter – old jazz records Fergus picked up along with a book collection. Now and again one of us gets up to change the record, and then we fall back into a comfortable silence.

Sorting and cataloguing. It's not so very different from museum work. We check for damaged or missing pages, and pencil a price on the inside cover. As we work on, way past closing time, I become aware of something else happening.

I'm conscious of the closeness of this man whose shop is his passion. The two of us are sitting cross-legged on the floor, with mugs of tea and crackly music playing, surrounded by piles and piles of books.

'We don't need to sort this whole lot tonight,' Fergus says apologetically. 'I mean, please don't feel you need to stay. It's almost eight . . .'

'I'm actually enjoying it,' I say truthfully. 'And it's a

big job, isn't it? It's a lot easier with the two of us.'

'Well, I guess it is really,' he admits. 'And anyway,' he adds quickly, not meeting my gaze as he flicks through a book, 'it's much nicer, you being here.'

Trying to keep down a smile, I realise something has tilted a little tonight. I can sense a charge, like electricity between us, as the hours go by. 'I love being here,' I say. 'You know that.' And he looks up and our eyes meet, and we hold each other's gaze, just for a moment.

'I'm glad,' he says, getting up to make more tea.

Now Fergus looks thoughtful. 'So, what about you? Where will you live now that Osprey House is on the market?'

'I can stay on there for the time being,' I say. 'Although Alice is making noises now about heading back south . . .'

'You don't have to stay in that big house on your own,' he adds.

'I'm not sure where else I'll go,' I tell him, checking the time. It's half past ten on this cold, wet night. In the warmth of the shop I hadn't even noticed time spinning by.

'Even in the short term it's a drive for you, isn't it?' he adds. 'Coming into town, I mean . . .'

'It is.' I smile. 'Alice says I can keep on using Bea's old car, but I'm not sure it's going to hold out much longer. And I must admit, the house might be a bit . . .' I try to find the right word.

'Spooky?'

'Yes, sort of. It'll definitely feel very big and empty without Alice.'

'And those ferocious guard dogs.' He chuckles, and something turns inside me. It feels so comfortable and right, hanging out together like this.

'Well, there's a flat upstairs,' he explains. 'It's pretty basic and it hasn't been used for years. After Jane died, I thought about letting it out. Then I had in my mind that Liv and Rory might need it after Finn was born. But . . .' He shrugs. 'That didn't work out.' He talks about Jane in passing now and again, quite easily. I've gathered that they were teenage sweethearts, together since school. 'It seems crazy having it lying empty,' he adds. 'We could clear it up, give it a lick of paint. Rory would help. You'd be welcome to move in there, if you'd like to . . .'

My heart seems to lift. 'Are you sure about that?'

'Absolutely, yes. You might want to see the place first, though. I mean, it's not quite the grandeur you've become accustomed to,' he teases.

'It's a really kind offer,' I start. 'I mean it. Thank you.'

He shrugs as if it's nothing. 'It just seems to make sense. We could make a start on the place next week, if you like? No pressure, though. Maybe you'd like to think about it . . . but shall I show you now?'

'Why not?' I say. So we head up the narrow staircase in the alleyway next to the shop. The flat isn't nearly as bleak as Fergus made out. It's tiny, yes – just a minuscule kitchen, living room, shower room and bedroom. But all the basics are here – bed, chest of drawers, tiny sofa, table and two chairs – and I can't think that I'd need anything more.

'It's perfect,' I say, wanting to hug him, overcome by his thoughtfulness. Instead, I try to push away my racing thoughts and say, 'You know, Fergus, I think I'd be really happy here.'

232

CHAPTER THIRTY-ONE

Vince

As is his custom these days, Vince lies very still on waking. He is conscious of the warmth and steady breathing of Jarvis lying on the bed where Kate used to be.

Before all this – before he lost his mind – he'd no more have licked a spilled takeaway off the pavement than allowed a dog on the bed. But he's different now. He hardly recognises himself.

'I know Jarvis is completely happy with you and Kate,' Edie said last time they spoke. He still hasn't told his daughter that he's here alone now. Announcing it, Vince feels, would be like admitting that Kate isn't coming back. And he's not ready to accept that yet.

And *is* Jarvis happy? He seems to be, spread out like a lord, snoring softly with his head on Kate's pillow. Obviously, if Kate doesn't come back, then Jarvis can't stay here because Vince will be touring, when his agent gets his arse into gear and actually secures him some work. Things are awfully quiet at the moment. Thank God Vince had some savings to live off. But it's fine for now, the dog being here. Better than being alone anyhow. And now Vince has made the switch to kibble instead of that rank, stinking meat, he's no problem really.

With no pressing need to get up, Vince drifts back into sleep, snuggling closer to Jarvis until a sharp noise jolts him from his reverie. Triggered by the sound, Jarvis leaps from the bed and charges to the closed bedroom door where he stands, barking urgently.

'Hey, fella,' Vince says, rubbing at his eyes. 'Just someone outside.' He's no longer scared that Zoe's going to turn up, force her way into the house and stand over him until he types 'The End' in his book. Clearly now, she doesn't give a stuff when he finishes it. But who *is* that outside, rapping loudly on his front door? Because that's what the noise is, he realises. *Rap-rap-rap*! For a moment Vince's entire body is flooded with relief. Kate's back! Scrambling naked out of bed, Vince knocks over a full glass of water from his bedside table and curses loudly as he grabs his ripped dressing gown from the hook on the door and pulls it on. Thus attired, he hurtles out of the bedroom and through to the hall with Jarvis barking excitedly, thrilled by the sudden activity.

Shit, where are his keys? 'Hang on!' Vince shouts to the human-sized shape on the other side of the frosted glass door. *Is* it Kate? The kitchen clock tells him that it's ten-thirty and he cringes at the thought of her seeing that he's not even dressed.

'Just getting my keys!' he announces, darting to the kitchen, and then the living room, cursing himself for not having proper places for things and always putting them there. He can't even blame Kate for hiding them, like she did with the toolbox.

'Keys, keys, keys,' he rants, sparking another barking frenzy.

Spotting a telltale glint between the sofa cushions, he grabs the metallic bunch and swoops back to the front door. Kate's back! He'll never again expect her to cook for him. He'll festoon her with lavish feasts!

Vince stabs his key into the lock and jiggles it, pulling open the door in a dramatic motion that seems to startle the short gaunt man standing there.

'All right, mate?' he says, stepping back. It's a delivery guy with a plaster across the bridge of his nose, thrusting an electronic device at him.

'Uh, yeah,' Vince says distractedly.

'Sign here?'

'Ah. Thanks.' Vince coughs to clear his throat and waggles a finger across the screen. The man doesn't even thank him. He just rubs at his blond stubble and saunters back to a scuffed white van, leaving Vince to frown at the enormous flat box that's been left propped up against the house.

'What's this?' he asks Jarvis. But of course the dog doesn't know. Baffled, and feeling oddly cheated, Vince manhandles the thing inside. He leans it against the wall in the hallway, next to the bathroom door that's still propped up there, after the party that he can hardly bear to think about these days. He must rehang it sometime, and have a proper functioning bathroom door once again, so he can do his business without Jarvis sitting there staring at him. But how? Vince has no idea how to hang a door, any more than he knew how to *un*hang it.

Frowning, he studies the parcel's label, which offers no clue as to its contents. He rips off copious brown tape and pulls the box apart messily. Looks like furniture of some kind. Huge slabs of something that mean nothing to him. There's a document inside, sheathed in clear plastic, and he pulls it open. Now he realises it's the shelving unit that Kate went on at him to order many months ago, when life was normal. 'You could make your study more of a functioning place,' she suggested. 'If we're going to be here forever—' he caught the pain in her voice there '—we'd better make it our home, Vince. I mean, somewhere that feels more like *ours*. So how about we choose some things to put in it?'

It's like a stab in his heart to think of that now. Vince has always been immensely fond of 37 Sycamore Grove, filled as it is with memories of birthday teas and a glittering silver Christmas tree that his father had hauled down from the attic every year, and the aroma of Sundays roasts, his mother's baking and her powdery perfume. He's tried to pretend he's okay these past few months, and that the place still feels like home. But it can never be home without Kate.

He's picturing her now at the scratched old kitchen

table in their Bethnal Green flat, with an open bottle of wine and a candle flickering and Tash, Shawn and Julian all gathered around, laughing, sharing stories and jokes.

Julian always said the same thing whenever Vince walked in to find such a gathering happening: 'Pull up a chair, Vincey. Come and join us. Good to see you, man!' Vincey. A word to set his teeth on edge. He'd meant well, though, Vince reflects. He was only being friendly and trying to bring him into the fray. Why was Vince so prickly about Kate's friends? He can't understand it now.

He turns to glare at the shelving unit, partly pulled out of its box. He can't just leave it sitting there, can he? It might even bring order to his fractured life. As Vince pictures it all built and neatly storing his work papers, his spirits start to rise. *That's* what he'll do on this bleak wet Monday morning. He'll build the fucker and Kate will come back and be amazed, and realise how deranged she was to run away.

CHAPTER THIRTY-TWO

Kate

We work away – Fergus, Rory and me – scrubbing and rollering fresh white paint over grubby magnolia walls. The radio's on, the kettle on a rolling boil. Alice has dropped by to man the shop, which she seems delighted to do. It feels like a real team effort.

By late afternoon the first coat is finished and we stop to admire our handiwork. 'It's looking good,' Rory offers.

'It really is,' I say with a surge of pleasure.

'Think you'll be comfortable here?' Fergus asks. 'I'll bring bedding over, and towels, crockery, all the things you'll need . . .'

'That'd be great.' I beam at him, suddenly transported back to when Tash and I moved into our first shared flat. It was bare and basic – actually this is much nicer – but that sense of newness is the same. Then I'm remembering Ingrid, my friend and manager at the museum. *There'll always be a job for you here. Nothing has to be forever if you don't want it to be.* I'd hugged her and taken one last look around our displays. I knew every exhibit intimately: every china doll and matted bear and wooden rocking horse. It was impossible not to cry as my work friends all gathered after we'd closed, and threw a party for me in the museum.

It had felt like an ending then. However hard I convinced myself that I was doing it for my marriage, and that life didn't have to be perfect – didn't being a grown-up mean compromising sometimes? – I couldn't push away the hollow feeling in my gut.

But this feels different. It feels like the start of something – a new chapter beginning in this tiny but bright and welcoming flat overlooking the pastel-painted cottages across the street.

'Let's finish up,' Fergus says. 'We can let this coat dry, and maybe do the next one tomorrow—'

'I'm up for that,' Rory says amiably.

'Me too,' I start. 'Maybe we could—' I break off as my phone rings and I grab it from the windowsill.

Vince. I stare at his name in panic. Weeks have flown by without us speaking. Has something happened? Something serious that he really needs me for? Clutching my trilling phone, I hurry downstairs and out into the street. 'Vince?' I say.

'Kate. Hi. How are you?' As if we are colleagues who haven't spoken in a while.

'I'm . . . I'm okay, Vince. I'm fine . . .'

'Great. Look, I don't know if it's all right to ring you. I've tried not to hassle you, I really have—'

'You're not hassling me,' I say firmly, striding away from the shop now. Alice is still there but it's nearly closing time. An awkward silence hovers. 'So, um . . . is there something—'

'Erm, yes. There is. Look, I'm sorry to call you. I'm sure you're having a great time with Tash. I just wanted to ask—'

'Vince, I'm not at Tash's,' I cut in.

'Oh, aren't you?'

'No. I'm actually not in London . . .'

I sense him frowning, his forehead crinkled, a look of bewilderment in his eyes. 'Where are you, then?'

'I'm in Scotland,' I say.

It seems to take a moment for him to digest this. 'Scotland?' he repeats.

'Yes.'

'But . . . why?' Like buses and brunch, 'The North' is another thing that Vince doesn't understand, and has no desire to interact with, especially after his torturous Highland hike for the TV show.

'I took a train here,' I reply, 'from Euston. The day after I left . . .'

'You're kidding me!' he splutters.

'No, I'm not kidding.'

'God, Kate. You could've told me,' Vince announces. 'I assumed you were with Tash!'

'That's it,' I exclaim. 'You just assume, Vince. You

haven't actually asked since I left.'

'Well, that seemed like the most logical thing,' he says hotly. 'So, what is this then? Some kind of pilgrimage to your childhood home?'

Anger rears up in me. 'Of course it's not! D'you seriously think I'd want to visit that house?' Where Dad terrorised us all, is what I mean. Where Mum stopped buying apples because the sound of crunching enraged him.

'Well, *I* don't know. Anyway, I didn't think there was anyone left up there,' he adds, in a calmer tone.

'What, people? In Scotland? There are a few, yes—'

'I meant your family,' he says.

'No, there isn't,' I say flatly. 'Everyone's gone.'

'So . . . who are you with?' A pause. 'Kate . . . you haven't *met* someone, have you? Is that what this is all about?'

'Of course not,' I retort. But then, I have, haven't I? I've met a lot of people up here. So, just to stop him from making assumptions, I share the bare bones of my encounter with Alice at Euston station. I tell him that I've been working for her – no, not for her. *With* her. We were a team. And, even though I miss out the bit about stepping into the 'real' Kate's shoes, Vince still thinks this utterly mad. But perhaps it makes him feel a little bit better, too: the implication that this is about me losing my mind, rather than anything being wrong with our marriage.

A silence hangs heavily. 'I'm sorry,' I start, 'if this

is hard for you. I know I haven't handled things brilliantly . . .'

'As long as you're okay,' he says quietly.

I bite my lip as a group of four women make their way down the side street, chatting and laughing. A bunch of friends on a girls' getaway, by the look of it. 'There's a lovely bookshop down here,' one of them announces. 'Let's see if it's still open . . .'

'I'm okay, Vince,' I say, stopping now at the corner of the street.

'Well, that's good to hear.' *Because I'm not*, is the subtext.

'I'm assuming you haven't said anything to Edie yet,' I add.

'No. No, I haven't. Have you?'

'No, Vince. I think it should come from you.' I pause. 'Is that all right?' Guilt twangs in me, deep in my gut.

'Yeah, I s'pose so,' he says gruffly.

'Okay.' I pause. 'So, I have a few things to do now—'

'Can I just ask you something?' he blurts out.

My heart quickens. 'Er . . . yes?'

'This, uhh . . . this thing's arrived.'

'What kind of thing?'

'A flatpack thing,' he mutters.

It takes a moment for me to register this properly. A flatpack thing. Was this the reason for his call? 'What flatpack thing?' I ask.

'Remember that shelving unit you nagged me to order?'

'I didn't *nag* you, Vince. I just suggested that you might consider having a piece of actual furniture in your study instead of a row of dented cardboard boxes—'

'Yeah. Yes, you did. Well, the thing you *encouraged* me to buy to turn my working environment into a sleek and highly efficient nerve centre of creativity—'

'It's finally arrived?' I start to walk back to the shop. It's still open, a little past our normal closing time. Alice must have let the women in for a browse.

'It has. Yeah.'

My gaze alights upon the bookshop's window display. We've just redone it, Fergus and I. The selection of natural history books is set off with an autumnal arrangements of twigs, fir cones and coppery leaves. Beyond it, I glimpse Alice and Fergus and the women all chatting animatedly.

'Have you built it?' I ask.

'Erm, not quite yet. I, um . . . just wondered . . .' Vince clears his throat. 'D'you know where the tools are?'

'The toolbox, you mean?'

'Yeah.' He sounds sheepish.

'It's in the shed, under that old chest of drawers of your dad's. But you probably won't need it, if it's just basic flatpack. There are screwdrivers in the kitchen drawer – Phillips and flathead – and there should be an Allen key in the packet—'

'What packet?' he asks.

'The *packet*, Vince. There's always a packet of little bolts and things along with the instructions—'

243

'No,' he says forcefully. 'There aren't any instructions. I've pulled everything out and checked a hundred times—'

'Are they hiding under the label on the front of the box?'

'No! I've checked that too.' *I'm not an idiot,* his tone says.

'Well, I don't know what you expect me to do from up here.'

'I thought you might know,' he says in a quieter tone. 'I thought . . . y'know. You might have some tips.'

I exhale slowly, picturing Vince surrounded by panels of MDF. 'Just approach it methodically,' I start. 'And don't rush. Think about it carefully instead of barging at it like a maniac. You know you can do it if you take it step by step.'

'Right,' Vince says cautiously, as if I am issuing instructions on how to deliver a baby.

'And don't panic or get angry or try to ram things together that won't go.'

'Okay. Fine. I won't.'

In the pause that follows I sense him rousing himself for the task ahead. 'And that's it, Vince,' I conclude, pushing open the bookshop door. 'They're all the tips I have.'

CHAPTER THIRTY-THREE

Vince

Vince has always enjoyed raging against IKEA. The terrible one-way system, guiding customers through the store like scented-candle-seeking zombies, stumbling for Daim Bars and hot dogs in that weird, pillow-stuffing bread that he'd still be picking from his teeth next time they went. Around twice a year, Kate would badger him to go. He might have huffed and moaned, dragging his feet through the marketplace like a teenager forced to look at Renaissance paintings in a gallery. But at least he'd gone. So he can't have been *that* bad a husband, can he?

If only this unit had come from IKEA, then at least he'd have the satisfaction of being able to complain bitterly about the company (albeit with only a spaniel as his audience). But it didn't. Rebelliously, ignoring Kate's suggestions and the helpful links she'd sent him, he'd gone for an unknown cheaper brand.

Hence the lack of instructions for the piece of crap. Muttering about the injustice of it all, Vince lugs the various components through to his study and stares at them. He's found the famous 'packet', although there's nothing in it that could possibly be an Allen key. It's just metal nuts and bolts and whatnots. They might as well be mammoths' teeth for all the use they're going to be.

Vince feels foolish now for calling Kate. Ridiculously, he'd expected her to come up with some miracle solution: a spell he could chant, to make the unit self-construct. Now it's apparent that that isn't going to happen.

And she's been in Scotland all this time, cleaning out some dead woman's house! Why hadn't she told him? Vince fetches a beer from the fridge to try and settle himself, and turns to Jarvis, who's been watching him intently. 'It's not rocket science,' he announces.

You know you can do it if you take it step by step. With Kate's advice still ringing in his head, he starts to try and fit things together. However, the pieces are huge and surprisingly heavy, and at one point the biggest section topples over and slams into his legs. Maybe this is how it'll end for him. He won't collapse dramatically on stage, to a collective gasp in the packed venue, as he has fantasised occasionally. He'll merely be found flattened on the dingy blue carpet in his mother's former sewing room, beneath a pile of MDF.

'Fuck it,' he says out loud, gulping his beer and raking at his hair. With ceilings a mere foot above his head – at least it seems that way, especially today – the bungalow can feel claustrophobic. Back in London, their flat had high ceilings and big, spacious, light-filled rooms.

Another beer down, Vince adjourns for a lie down on the sofa. He dozes fitfully, feeling even more irritable as he wakes. He checks the time, baulking at how late it is. Ten past six already and he's achieved precisely nothing!

Craving air, Vince gets up and grabs a third beer from the fridge. Then he strides to the front door, flings it open and stands there, sipping from the bottle and surveying the street. Weak sunshine has broken through the greyness, and the evening is unseasonably warm. At the sight of Agata Kemp, pedalling towards him on her bicycle, he stands up straighter and tries to rearrange his expression from one of quiet desperation to something more neutral. As if he's just enjoying a beer on his doorstep – and why not? – rather than trying to anaesthetise himself.

'Hello, Vince!' Agata comes to a halt in front of his house.

'Hi, Agata. You're putting me to shame, cycling about on your bicycle,' he says inanely.

A quick, bright smile. 'I'm trying to cycle to work most days,' she says.

'Good for you!' He knows she works with Deborah in an office in the old town, doing something with the council. Town planning or roads or something like that. Designing car parks maybe? He should know more about it, but feels that too much time has elapsed now to ask either of them what they actually do.

'I really must dust my bike down,' he adds.

'Oh, what d'you have?'

'Um, a foldable one,' he says, flushing slightly as, in truth, he'd splurged an enormous amount on it, lured by the idea of being an urban warrior cyclist in London. He'd lost his nerve after an elderly lady with a wheeled shopping trolley had yelled 'Wanker!' at him when he'd jumped a red light.

It's a jungle out there, he'd realised. Not so much here, but since the move to Shugbury the bike hasn't emerged from the shed.

'We could go for a cycle sometime,' Agata says. 'There are some lovely routes around here.'

'Yeah, definitely,' he says, trying to sound as if this is something he'd love to do.

Agata steps off her bike and smiles at him. She has a slight, boyish build, wears her fair hair in a crop and has an air of lightness and efficiency about her. He remembers now that Kate had gone on about her perfect macarons at the baking stall, and he can picture it now; that she'd approach such a task with thought and care. Not like Kate with her boxed cake mixes.

'So . . . how have things been?' she asks.

Beyond passing pleasantries, they haven't spoken since Vince humiliated himself over Deborah's tagine. 'Oh, not too bad,' he says, 'considering . . .'

'That's good.' He wills her not to quiz him any further. 'What've you been up to today, then?' she asks.

'Building some shelving thing,' he fibs, not that he

248

wants to impress her especially. But it sounds better than, 'Nothing.'

'Oh, right.' She smiles, showing perfect little teeth. 'How have you got on?'

'Erm, not too well,' he admits, before he can stop himself. Then, thinking to hell with it, he adds, 'It's actually more Kate's department than mine. The building-things thing, I mean.' He shrugs and senses himself reddening.

'Oh, is it?' Her smile edges towards sympathy now. 'I can't imagine it's been easy lately, Vince.'

'No, you could say that.' He shrugs and sips his beer.

She stands there for a moment, clutching the handlebars of her bike in the weak early evening sunshine. She's not one of those zippy, coiled-over-the-handlebars cyclists. More the sitting-bolt-upright type, wearing a spotty dress and cardigan and those old-fashioned flat shoes with a strap across the front, which fasten with a kind of button. (Baby Janes? Is that what they're called?) Of course Agata's bicycle has a wicker basket at the front, containing a small bunch of pink tulips – and it's definitely a *bicycle*, not a bike.

'To be honest with you,' Vince adds, 'I haven't even got started. With the shelving, I mean. It doesn't seem to make any sense . . .'

'D'you want some help?' she asks.

'Oh no, I wouldn't want to bother Lenny with that . . .' Catching her bemused look, he realises his horribly sexist mistake.

'I didn't mean Lenny,' she says with a tinkly laugh. 'He's a clever guy but building stuff isn't his forte. No, I meant I'll give you a hand if you like. I actually enjoy it.'

'Oh!' Embarrassment floods his veins. But why not accept her offer? He hasn't made any headway all afternoon. In fact he's been dangerously close to fetching the meat tenderiser and battering the thing to pieces. 'Well, yeah,' he adds. 'That'd be great, if you have the time.'

'I'm a free agent this evening,' Agata says, already climbing back onto her bike. 'Give me half an hour to grab some dinner and I'll come back with my tools—'

'Hang on,' he calls after her. 'D'you *need* tools?'

'I have my methods,' she announces gaily, and pedals off.

CHAPTER THIRTY-FOUR

Kate

It wasn't supposed to be just Fergus and me having dinner in the pub. We'd asked Alice too, and Rory, planning to treat them after helping out with the flat and the shop. However, Alice zoomed off, and Rory wanted to give Liv a break by helping with the baby, so it ended up just being the two of us, tucking into the pub's famous steak pies. 'Well, why not?' I remarked. 'We've earned it.'

'And no point in sitting around watching paint dry,' Fergus remarked with a smile. We had a second beer, and although I'd have been fine normally I felt a little giddy as we left the pub.

Now the air is fresh and sharp after a sudden shower. 'Fancy a walk?' I suggest. 'It's a lovely evening.'

'I'm up for that,' Fergus says. So we stroll along the riverside, watching ducks on the river and swallows soaring above. Instead of looping back, the way Alice would have with the dogs, we carry on walking until we are out of town.

Fergus tells me about the day his wife passed away; how she'd felt a little poorly but they hadn't really thought anything of it. 'Next thing, Jane collapsed,' he says. 'Liv had just come home from school and saw everything – all the panic, the paramedics, her mum being taken away to hospital. She died that night.'

'I can't even begin to imagine what that was like,' I say. 'It must have been terrible. But I guess you had to hold things together for Liv?'

'Yeah. It's good that she was there really. Good for me, I mean, to have that focus.' Fergus thrusts his hands into his jeans pockets. He's wearing a thick black polo-necked sweater, a waxed jacket and a woollen beanie, well insulated against the cool air. I've learnt to dress for the climate too. 'You need to layer up, girl!' Alice had scolded, jokingly, during those first few days when I had yet to adjust.

'Such a tough time for you though,' I add.

Fergus nods. 'We got through it, thanks to our friends. There are a lot of good people around here.'

'Yes, I can see that. So what happened with the shop at that time?' I ask, feeling privileged that he's sharing all this with me.

'Helen was still working with me then. She absolutely kept it going. It would've crumbled otherwise. Then she had the audacity to move away with her family . . .' He breaks off and smiles. 'Imagine, not wanting to spend

252

your entire life working in a second-hand bookshop—'

'There are *far* worse things,' I say, picturing Wilma's pinched face at the hotel, and my seemingly colossal trotters crammed into those heels. Already, it seems like a lifetime ago.

And now, as Fergus and I find ourselves cutting through woodland along a narrow path, I'm not thinking about Shugbury Spa Hotel at all. Instead, I realise that the winding path, softly carpeted in pine needles, is throwing up memories for me. And when we reach a single-track lane, that does too. The forest clearing in the distance is as familiar and comforting as pulling on a soft, warm sweater. Or the furry bear slippers you love so much you want to sleep in them.

When we stop, and Fergus takes my hand, that feels familiar and comforting too – even though a million sparks are shooting through me.

He squeezes it lightly and smiles. 'D'you know where we are, Kate?' His soft grey-blue eyes catch the evening sun.

I nod. It feels as if my heart has stopped. 'Yes,' I say. 'Yes, I do.'

And now I know. That connection between Fergus and me; it hasn't been my mind playing tricks.

We've met before, many years ago. When I was a child, tearing around the campsite with the local kids – and then again, a little later, when I was fifteen.

I'd begged not to come back to Scotland that summer. My friends at school in North London went to Spain and Greece. And we were going to spend a whole week in a tent?

'We'll go to the ceilidh in town,' Mum said on our last night there. 'It'll be fun. You might meet some people your own age.' A night of traditional Scottish dancing? I cringed at the thought. We'd had dance classes at my primary school back in Glasgow and I'd been awful at it. My feet just wouldn't do what they were meant to do and it had always been so embarrassing and awful. That had been another bonus of our hasty escape to London. No more Dad, obviously – and no more of those blasted Scottish reels!

However, as soon as we stepped into the hall, I was transfixed by the music and crowds and everyone dancing and laughing. And I wanted to be part of it.

Mum found a table for us, and as newcomers we were welcomed immediately into the fold. When she danced with men, I was happy for her. Because it was wonderful to see her whirling around like the young and happy woman I could see – perhaps for the first time – that she'd once been.

Eventually, I sidled off and got chatting to a bunch of teenagers installed at a table in the corner of the hall. They grabbed a vacant chair for me, and one of the boys said he remembered me from when we kids: the Glasgow family who'd come to the same campsite three years in a row. And then we'd just stopped coming. 'I missed you!' he said with a shy smile. I remember blushing and feeling delighted, but not knowing what to say. Then someone snuck me a beer and after a few sips I felt a little more emboldened. The night went on, and towards the end the shy boy and I stepped out of the hot and stuffy hall for a breath of air. He showed me the stars – stars like you never see in London.

We perched on a low stone wall and looked up at them. And then it happened. His lips on mine, just briefly. Then we kissed again, for longer this time. Long enough for my head to fill with shooting stars.

My first kiss was with this handsome, gentle boy. All those comments about George, when we were younger – that he had the face of angel while I'd 'grow into' my looks. I'd never felt pretty. I knew I wasn't. But that night I felt like a beautiful girl and I wanted the kiss to go on and on forever. Then my name was yelled, horribly close to my ear: 'Kate! Kate! I'll tell Mum!' And I sprang away from the boy, mortified, and hurried back into the hall after my maddening little brother.

And that had been that. Perhaps the boy had gone home after that, because I never saw him again.

'It was you, wasn't it?' I say now. 'All those years ago?'

Fergus nods. 'Yes, it was me.'

I look at him and laugh and shake my head, hardly able to believe it. 'When did you realise?'

'I'm not sure. The first time you came into the shop, I knew there was something about you. Something familiar about your face, your voice – everything. And then you talked about your holidays here and I kept

255

thinking, "Is Kate that girl from all those years ago?" But I didn't want to say anything,' he adds. 'I didn't know how to, without it sounding weird. So I kept it to myself.'

'It wouldn't have sounded weird.' I beam at him, my heart brimming with happiness now.

'No, I realise that now.'

I take his hands in mine and smile and say, 'But now we know for sure. And, you know, I've never forgotten that night . . .'

We start walking then, following the leaf-strewn track deeper into the woods. 'Neither have I,' he says.

CHAPTER THIRTY-FIVE

Vince

By the time Agata knocks politely at the front door, Vince has just about stopped cringing over his sexist faux pas. Of course, by now he should know that women are far better at this kind of stuff than he is. However, Kate tended to involve him. ('Can you come and hold this, Vince? If you're not *crazily* busy right now?') In contrast Agata approaches the task with calm, quiet precision, as if she were making those pastel-hued confections in her kitchen.

She'd come back with a tiny enamel box embellished with bluebells. A manicure set, he'd wondered? Then he'd caught himself. Kate's been gone for less than four months and he's turning into a neanderthal oaf. Is this what a lack of female company does to him?

Of course, there were dainty little tools in the tin. 'My flatpack kit,' Agata explained, smoothing back her choppy fair hair.

'Nifty,' he said, genuinely impressed. 'So, what can I do?'

She grinned at him. He detected a glimmer of playful humour in her hazel eyes that he'd never noticed before. 'Put the kettle on, love?' she said in a mockney accent. So off he trotted to make tea and arrange some sugary biscuits in a fan shape on a plate.

Twenty minutes in and she's expertly fitting sections together, not a bead of perspiration on her face. It's a mystery to Vince why it feels fine for Agata to build him a shelf unit, yet when Colin had muscled in with the bathroom door removal, he'd wanted to cosh him with the standard lamp. The difference is, she doesn't make him feel like an idiot for not doing the job himself. So he hangs about while she builds the thing – *without instructions*. He imagines she doesn't need a recipe for those macarons either. She just knows, instinctively, what to do.

'You really are very good at this,' he marvels.

'I'm just one of those weirdos who finds it satisfying,' Agata says, happily winding a little metal thing round to tighten something up.

'I wish I did,' Vince remarks.

'Well, you're good at lots of other things, aren't you?' She gets up from the floor, and together they lift the unit into position against his study wall and stand back and admire it.

'Looks great!' Vince announces. 'I really appreciate that, Agata. Thank you.'

'No problem. Can I help you organise it? Get your stuff out of those ratty old cardboard boxes?'

Vince hesitates, because he realises now that Agata is an extremely *precise* kind of person. He can't imagine she'll be impressed by the colossal muddle of his papers, jotters and books. 'I should probably go through it all myself,' he says with a trace of reluctance – because now he realises he'd like Agata to hang out here for a while.

Vince has felt horribly lonely, these past few months, biffing around his eerily silent house with only Jarvis for company, apart from visits from Gail next door. (Since the planning committee dinner Deborah has definitely been giving him a wide berth.) Sure, Kate went out to work – she had her hotel shifts – so he was alone then. But before he knew it she'd be home again, cooking and chatting and they'd settle down in the evenings to watch TV and have a glass of wine.

While Vince has always thought Agata to be perfectly pleasant, she's usually overshadowed by Deborah, who towers over her and seems to boss her around. Before today he'd never had a proper conversation with her. Yet there's something reassuringly calm and unflappable about her, he decides. Perhaps that comes from being married to a doctor. These days Lenny has settled into life as a small-town GP, but Vince knows he's worked in some hectic urban hospitals in his time. Maybe Agata has learnt to be a steadying influence.

'I'll let you get on then,' she says with a smile.

'Don't fancy another cuppa, do you?' he asks quickly.

'Or something stronger?'

'Oh, um . . .' She looks surprised, but not horrified, by the offer. 'Are you having a drink?'

'Yes, why not?' He's aware that his booze consumption has crept up since Kate's departure. He's found himself having lunchtime and even *breakfast* beers just to get those creative juices flowing. But this is fine, this is evening, and so he pulls a bottle of red from 'the cupboard where we keep the wine', as Kate had snapped during their party.

He pours two large glasses and hands one to Agata, trying to ignore Jarvis giving him the side-eye from his basket in the corner of the kitchen.

'Thanks.' She grins at him. 'Why not, eh?'

'Why not indeed?' he says, cringing at his choice of words. He's speaking like a louche game show host. 'Anyway,' he adds quickly, 'shall we go through?'

'Sure,' she says brightly, following him through to the living room where they settle on the sofa, clutching their wines.

'So, how's the book going?' Agata asks. There it is again; that cheeky look in her eyes that's never been apparent until today.

'It's, uh . . . coming along.' He forms a grim smile, then laughs. 'Actually, I've been having a bit of trouble with it. Deadline came and went months ago . . .'

'Really?'

'Yeah.' He shrugs. 'But, y'know, in the grand scheme of things it's no big deal. The world won't end, will it?'

260

''Course it won't,' Agata says. 'Have your publishers been hassling you?'

'No, not at all. They're pretty cool,' he says blithely.

'That's because you're their star author,' she asserts. 'They know you won't do your best work under pressure.'

Vince looks at her as if she's just said something miraculous. It's not as if she's going to write his book for him on top of constructing the shelving unit. Yet her clear-sightedness has caused a jolt of realisation in him, like someone striking a bell in his head. Of course, it's not that Zoe doesn't give a fuck about his stupid book. She said he can take all the time he likes – simply so he can produce his very best work.

'That makes sense,' Vince says, nodding.

'When's it actually coming out?'

'Next summer,' he replies.

'There'll be loads of wiggle room then,' she says confidently. Vince sips his wine, believing now that this gamine woman was beamed into his bungalow with her dainty tool set to save him. Is this what Edie means when she goes on about talking therapy? He certainly feels a lot better now.

'This is lovely wine,' she remarks.

'It's the bottle Lenny brought round for our party,' he admits. 'I gave our guests the cheap stuff.'

She laughs. 'He's always had good taste in wine. And I think the situation deserves it, don't you?'

'Does it?' he asks, a little confused.

'Well, yes! Your shelf unit's built and you've realised your publishers don't hate you because you're late . . .'

Christ, does Agata know what he's been thinking? Can she *see* his inner fears dancing around inside his head? It would seem so, because now, as they drink their wine and he refills their glasses, she's pulled off those strap-and-button shoes and curled up on the sofa with her feet tucked under her tiny bottom, and is saying, 'Vince, I hope you don't mind me bringing this up. Please say if I'm being nosy or out of order because I really don't want to pry or anything . . .' She breaks off and looks at him. Vince knows what's coming next. Curiously, he doesn't mind because he needs to get everything out there, off his chest.

'Go ahead,' he says lightly.

'Well . . .' Her mouth twists. 'That night at Deborah's dinner party. The way you turned on Colin . . .'

'I'm really ashamed of that,' he murmurs.

'Yes, but what I wanted to say is, I understand why you did it. Everyone interrogating you like that, in public. It wasn't fair. And since then it's like you've been hiding away from us all . . .'

Vince nods. 'Yeah, I s'pose I have really.'

'I realise you've been putting on a brave face all this time,' she continues, 'but it's awful what's happened to you. And I wanted to say, you can talk to me, you know. About the whole thing, I mean. Because it's not good for you to be all breezy and pretend you're okay.'

Vince is conscious of his heartbeat quickening as he

262

sips his wine. And then, because she's so kind and calm and the Pinot Noir is flowing straight to his brain, he tells her how shocking it was for Kate to leave suddenly with a Stilton and broccoli quiche burning in the oven, when he had no idea there was anything wrong. He tells her about the crazy woman at Euston, basically kidnapping his wife and warping her mind on the train with God knows what. Gin from the shop? Psychedelic drugs? She must have done *something* to make Kate spend months clearing out a dead woman's house.

Brainwashed her maybe? Is she part of a cult? She must be, to have convinced Kate that being stuck up there in the middle of nowhere was more appealing than coming home to him and enjoying a weekend at a spa with pampering treatments with her best friend. On and on he goes, admitting to Agata how hard it's been, trying to pretend he's okay when he can't work and his agent seems to have gone quiet too – does *nobody* want him anymore? Apart from his mother-in-law, who's forever calling the landline, without realising that it's connected to his central nervous system and makes him shoot out of his seat every time. He's ignored her calls and interminable messages on his parents' prehistoric answerphone: 'You've both been pretty quiet lately. Got your messages, Kate. But I think you must both be busy, you especially, Vince. I watched your whole Scottish thing again the other week. They should make another series. You were *so* funny, especially the bit about trying to fish and whacking your float into that boat's window . . .'

Blah-blah-blah ad infinitum. He's considered pulling the damn phone out of the wall.

'And then there's Gail,' Vince continues, 'showing up on the doorstep with her chickpea moussaka . . .'

Agata nods grimly. 'I've encountered the chickpea moussaka.'

Just as well I'm alone here, seeing as there's no bathroom door. Vince doesn't say this. He's grateful for Agata's company and he doesn't want to repel her.

'I'm glad you've told me all this,' she announces. 'You know, you seem kind of . . . different today.'

'Different? How?' He's genuinely curious.

She finishes her wine and he fills their glasses for a third time, finishing the bottle. He hopes he doesn't have red wine lips or stained teeth. 'Like you've let your guard down,' she explains. 'You're not being "comedian Vince", all confident and cocky—' hang on, does she think he's cocky? '—and holding court. You're just . . . being yourself.'

He shrugs, letting her observation settle. 'It's actually been really nice to have some company today,' he remarks. And that's all he means. That's it's been something of a relief to have a human to talk to instead of just the dog.

'I've enjoyed it too,' Agata says. 'And you've got a new a piece of furniture!'

'Yeah.' He chuckles. Does this mean she's planning to head home as soon as she'd finished this glass of wine? He doesn't want her to. Not yet. It startles Vince

264

to realise this, and he tries to shake off the feeling. After all, they've nearly sunk a bottle of wine and she'll want to get home and start cooking or whatever it is she does in the evenings. He imagines Lenny cooks too; he's a decent, obviously highly capable guy, if not in the flatpack-building arena. But then, Vince doesn't really know them. It was only Deborah that Vince went to school with. The Kemps moved here a few years before him and Kate.

Their glasses are empty again. 'That *was* lovely wine,' he announces, and she nods.

'Delicious!' Before he's properly considered it, Vince has gone and fetched another (inferior) bottle of red wine, plus a bottle of sparkling water and glasses for that too.

'So, whereabouts were you before you moved here?' he asks, in a 'tell me again?' kind of way. Because he probably should know that. Since Kate left him Vince has gone over and over what he might have done wrong, and 'not listening enough' strikes him as a possible contender. He's gregarious, a chatterbox. He knows this about himself. But perhaps he should pay more attention to other people. He can practise now, he decides, as Agata starts to tell him about her childhood in a sleepy Hertfordshire village, with a Polish father and an English mum, and how she went to college somewhere or other and then met Lenny and he couldn't turn down the position at the surgery here, all that.

It's not that Vince *isn't* listening. He's just not focusing on the details as her bright and pleasant voice fills his ears, and she drinks the wine, and he refills their glasses again and again and finds himself telling her about his childhood here, in this very house.

He breaks off, encouraging her to talk some more, and he tries to really listen. '. . . At that stage I was happy for a new start,' Agata is telling him. 'And it's so friendly around here. Deborah took me under her wing. She even recommended me for my job. I felt so lucky, with her living a few doors down, and then meeting you, of course. You and Kate . . .'

Agata's mention of Kate reminds Vince to keep listening and not let his attention drift, as it is prone to do. He must try harder and 'do the work' on himself, as Edie would put it. That's how he'll be a better person. A better man. He's not listening particularly well now, as he and Agata are chattering over each other and laughing, in the way people do when they really click.

We really click! he realises as she fills their water glasses from the bottle of San Pellegrino. 'Token drop of token water for you, Vince?' she teases.

'God, yes. I'd better.' He grins and they clink their glasses, tipsily.

'Can't remember the last time I did something spontaneous like this,' Agata says, cheeks flushed now, eyes a little squiffy. She looks cute, Vince decides, rashly. She's so pretty and dainty with a blush to her cheeks. She's like a little pink macaron, or a French film star, the pixie-cut one who runs around Paris in a Breton top in that movie – what was it again?

À Bout de Souffle. Breathless in English, the first French film Vince ever saw and only because Kate chose it.

That's it. She's like the actress from *Breathless* and can build a shelving unit without instructions and cycles about with her wicker basket. She should have a baguette in that—

Then Vince isn't thinking about baguettes or flatpack because his neighbour, with whom he'd never had a proper conversation before, is leaning closer towards him. And closer still. And then suddenly it's not talking therapy anymore because Agata Kemp has wrapped her pale and slender arms around him, and is snogging him on the lips.

CHAPTER THIRTY-SIX

Kate

It's not one of those fancy campsites with a shop and a bar and all that. It's just a grassy area – a glade, you'd call it – dappled in afternoon sunlight with forest all around. The red-brick building tucked away at the far end houses the loos and showers.

I know this because this is where we stayed: Mum, George and me. I know there's no office on site, or even a kiosk. The farmer comes around daily to collect money and check that everything's okay. At least he did all those years ago. It might be run differently now, although I doubt it. The site looks exactly as I remember it.

I turn to Fergus, my heart beating hard. We're holding hands. I know he hasn't brought me here by accident. There are lots of other places we could have gone for our evening walk.

'This is it,' I say, turning to look at him. 'This is where we used to stay . . .'

'Yes, I know,' he says gently.

I glance around the site. There's a couple of tents but no cars; you have to walk to get to the clearing. One of the tents has a gas stove set up on a camping table, but there's no one around as far as I can see. 'I wonder where we hid that grill?' I muse, turning towards the woods now. 'The one Mum made out of wire . . .'

The smile teases Fergus's eyes. 'Shall we look?'

'I don't think so.' I laugh, filled with happiness at being here. At being here with *him*. 'It's a needle-in-a-haystack-type thing,' I add.

He shrugs and there's something about his smile, as if he's holding a secret close. 'Let's just see, shall we?'

I shake my head at the madness of what's happening here. Not just his crazy suggestion to find the thing, but feeling his warm hand wrapped around mine. Sparks are shooting through me as we step into the cooler darkness of the woods.

Yet it's not all darkness, once we're in there. Fragments of sunlight land on the soft forest floor, shining like gems. His hand is still wrapped around mine as we find our way deeper into the forest, pushing our way through when the path becomes so narrow it's barely there at all.

In the distance I spot the path opening out into a narrow lane where there's a farm gate with a table outside, partially covered by a red and white checked awning.

I let go of Fergus's hand and run towards it, glancing backwards as I go. 'I remember this!' Boxes of eggs and jars of home-made preserves are set out on the table, along with a wooden box with a secured lid, in which there's a slot. An honesty box.

Suddenly, I find myself wondering how it was for Mum, being whisked away from her village just an hour's drive north of here, when she was just a teenager. She'd been nineteen when she'd met my dad. And then suddenly she was a housewife in Glasgow and, not too long afterwards, mum to me and then George. But she'd always loved bringing us back here.

I pull out my phone and take a photo of the stall. We'd always bought supplies here for our little camp. We were fascinated by the honesty box system and couldn't believe that no one would break it open or steal it. *People are different up here,* Mum said.

Then Fergus arrives at my side and my heart seems to turn over. I look at his kind, handsome face, overcome by a desire to kiss him. Apart from the chirp of birdsong there are no sounds at all.

'I'm really glad you turned up again, Kate,' he says. 'It's kind of funny, isn't it?'

I know what he means: it's funny how things have turned out. How the two of us have fallen into a friendship, and we're now working together – but it's not just that. It's there again – that feeling between us, glimmering like the dappled sunlight on his face. A feeling that something could happen. Of course it won't. It *can't.* It's been less than four months since I scrambled out of the bathroom window. So the very idea of even feeling *anything* for anyone is ridiculous and wrong. I'm still married to Vince, and we have so much to untangle and sort out. Yet somehow time has warped and distorted up here, and it feels as if I have known Fergus forever.

He squeezes my hand, then lets it drop and turns away from me. *Don't!* I want to cry out. *Don't turn away. Come here.* But Fergus has walked away now, and I stare at the back of him, at the broad shoulders and the expanse of his back. 'Fergus?' I call after him. 'What is it?'

It's okay, I want to tell him. *I'm feeling it too.*

He's stopped again and raised a hand to the sturdy tree trunk in front of him. He steps around it, and I catch his expression, set in concentration until he seems to find what he's looking for.

'Kate?' He beckons me over, grinning now. And *now* I get it. The local boy with scruffy light-brown hair who'd turned up at the campsite, wanting to hang out with us. Lured by sausages, Mum said. Just part of the local gang of kids. Years later, we'd kissed on that low stone wall. I know he remembers that part. But Fergus also remembers those times we cooked our supper on the grill, back when we were little kids. I hadn't expected that. But it was part of his childhood too.

'What is it?' I ask.

'Come here. Look at this.' I can hardly breathe as I step towards him, twigs crunching beneath my feet. He waits until I am right there beside him to lift the thing from the hollow in the tree, all rusted with age but definitely our makeshift cooking implement.

'That's it.' I look at him, feeling as if my heart could burst.

'Yeah.' He nods, smiling, and taking both of my hands in his. 'I thought you'd come back the next year, but I didn't see you again until that time, years later, at the ceilidh—'

'I know,' I say softly.

'And I thought I'd come and see you here after that night. But you'd already gone,' he adds. 'I wondered if you'd ever come back.'

His beautiful grey-blue eyes seem to pull me in, and then I do it. I lean forward and kiss him softly on the lips.

'Well, now I have,' I say.

CHAPTER THIRTY-SEVEN

Vince

Vince has never cheated on Kate. Not once in all these years together. There's been the odd flirtatious fan hanging around after a gig, but all comedians get those. Even gnarly-faced ones like Vince. (He doesn't consider himself to be especially attractive; he's always got by on his humour which is how the whole comedy thing started.)

He's enjoyed the attention from these fans, and occasionally flirted back. But he's never been tempted do anything – not even with Deborah, despite all those lurid fantasies. Okay, so he's never had the opportunity – and if she'd launched herself right at him, then he *might* have reciprocated. But this isn't Deborah! It's Agata Kemp with the bicycle and enamel tin of tiny tools, whose husband prescribed Vince some ointment when he had a fungal toenail infection! And now he's kissing her on his parents' sofa, which Kate had been

273

badgering him to get rid of. It seemed immoral to have it taken away to the dump when there was still plenty of wear left in it.

Immoral! He's a fine one to talk about morals as somehow they've progressed to lying side by side on the sofa and their clothes are strewn around the living room like bunting after a carnival. They're naked and kissing deeply and her cool, slender limbs are wrapped around him. How could this be? It feels like only minutes ago that Agata was cycling home with a bunch of tulips in her basket. Of course several hours have spun by, and they've sunk a good few glasses of wine in the interim. But it feels sudden and kind of shocking, as if a freak hurricane had whipped through the bungalow, taking with it their clothes plus Vince's common sense and moral code.

He kisses Agata's slender neck, her skin as pale and fine as his favourite china tea mug, and then her breasts, and her smooth, flat belly.

He wants her. He really wants her. She is breathing heavily, and they're kissing again on the mouth, and then – oh God, it's going to happen and he is powerless to stop it – she climbs on top and straddles him.

He looks up at her, thoughts crashing through his brain. Well, Kate left him and hotfooted it to Scotland without telling him and he doesn't know when she's coming back. Maybe it's all over and she'll want a divorce and why shouldn't he sleep with Agata, as they're both consenting adults? Yes, he's still married in theory and she's married in – well, she's *married*. But look at her now, so beautiful sitting on top of him and he's so horny and wants her so, so much, and never mind Dr Kemp and the fact that this is the sofa his mum chose from DFS about twenty-seven years ago. He's an adult man, he has needs and he's tremendously excited and—

Arf-arf-arf-arf-arf-arf-arf! In a cacophony of barking Jarvis runs in.

'Oh, my God,' Agata gasps.

'Jarv, out. Out!' Vince commands. Jarvis stares up at them, then turns around and plods dejectedly out of the room.

'What made him do that?' Agata asks. She's still straddling him but it feels somewhat ridiculous now.

'I don't know,' Vince starts. 'Some noise maybe. Some frequency only dogs can detect . . .'

They look at each other and, for a moment, neither of them says anything. Then Agata's expression turns to one of resigned acceptance. 'Aww,' she murmurs. Then: 'Never mind.' Is anything worse, Vince reflects, than hearing those words just as you're about to do it? As if you've scraped your knee and need a plaster on it? She bends to kiss him lightly on the lips. But it's no good. The moment has been lost and now, on top of the rude interruption, Vince is thinking that Agata's his neighbour and fucking hell – *they nearly shagged on the sofa in his house.*

Agata clambers off him as if dismounting her bicycle.

'Sorry,' he mutters. 'It was just a bit distracting, Jarvis running in like that.'

She sighs and smiles acceptingly, and reaches for her plain white knickers and bra and quickly pulls them on. Her dress and cardigan follow. She smooths down her hair with the palms of her hands. Vince gets up, retrieves his boxers from over by the TV and pulls them on, hoping to convey a *Well, that's that* kind of message. To put a full stop to that crazy little episode there.

Maybe they can both pretend it never happened.

'Don't worry, Vince,' she offers.

'It's fine. I'm not worried,' he insists, blushing madly and pulling on his jeans and T-shirt. He looks around for his socks. Where the hell are his socks?

'It happens to most guys sometimes,' she adds.

He blinks at her, aware that he's still blushing, which seems ridiculous considering he was kissing her breasts moments ago. 'I, er . . . it's never . . .'

'D'you know you don't have to go to the doctor for it anymore?'

The word 'doctor' is like a massive alarm going off in his head. 'For what?' he manages, trying to avoid her gaze.

'For . . . *you* know. Little blue pills. *Viagra*. You can get them over the counter now—'

Vince feels as if he has fallen through a hole into some alternative, terrible universe in which Agata Kemp – who he was on the brink of having sex with – is reassuring him that it won't be necessary to consult with her husband about his erectile difficulties.

He doesn't have erectile difficulties! He never has in his life! Well, not unless he's had a skinful and that happens to every bloke; it doesn't *mean* anything. But try to remain fully excited on the very sofa where he and his wife have sat drinking wine and nibbling Wotsits and devoured all four seasons of *Succession*, with a spaniel barking at them? Try being some kind of super-stud in those kind of conditions?

'I don't think I need anything,' he murmurs, 'apart from my socks.'

Agata smirks, finding them partially disappeared under the sofa, and pulls on her shoes, the Daisy Janes or whatever they're called. Vince inhales deeply to steady himself as she pecks him lightly on the cheek and says, 'That was fun. Naughty us!'

'Ha-ha, yeah,' he says without humour.

A beat's silence hangs. 'Well, I'd better get home.'

'Yes!' he says, too eagerly. She trots through to his study to fetch her dinky little toolkit. Aware of sweat beading on his forehead, Vince hovers awkwardly in the hallway, waiting for her to leave. Agata opens the front door and steps outside.

'Let me know if you need any other flatpack erecting,' she quips with a grin before sauntering off down the street.

CHAPTER THIRTY-EIGHT

Kate

October is beautiful here. Forests are dusted with copper and gold, and although visitors still come, the town has taken on a sleepier quality. Curls of woodsmoke fill the crisp, cold air and frost sparkles on the ground on our walks.

I've learnt about Fergus's childhood here, and how he went away to Edinburgh University but was pulled back to the place – and the woman – he loved. He and Jane had settled back here, both of them teaching: him in the English department of a secondary school and her at the local primary. When the bookshop had come up for sale, and Fergus had yearned to take it on, she'd been full of encouragement.

'It was a brave move,' I ventured.

'Brave, or rash?' He laughed.

We walk along the riverside holding hands. There's the occasional tentative kiss. We are more than friends;

that's obvious. But after that first kiss, in the woods by the campsite, it feels as if we're being cautious.

There's time, for one thing. Fergus's life is all about the shop and Liv and the baby. I'm filled with desire for him but I'm also scared. Does he want it too? Or is he happy with the way things are? Although I've moved into the flat above the shop, I still see Alice regularly, and share all of this with her.

'I knew there was something between you,' she says over coffee in our favourite café. 'I could sense it.' I'm glad she's decided to stay on at Osprey House while viewings are happening. There have been a few, although no offer yet.

'What d'you think I should do?' I ask. 'D'you think he's holding back, or doesn't want to get involved?'

'I can only guess,' she offers, 'that he's taking things slowly. You work together, after all.'

She's right, I decide. He doesn't want to spoil things. But late at night, in bed in the freshly painted flat, I imagine how it would be if I were to say, 'Shall we go upstairs?' after we've shut up shop for the day. Would it feel awkward? Or just weird? What if he said, 'I don't think that's a good idea, Kate,' and it was mortifying to be together the next day?

Plus, I'm still married to Vince, and he's the only man I've slept with in twenty-five years. Would it be different with Fergus? What if our wonderful closeness just didn't work when we were naked together in bed? There are so many ways in which it could be awkward or spoil what we have, which feels precious enough. It feels greedy to want more, or even play with the possibility in my mind. *Be content with the way things are*, I tell myself. But as the days go by I'm aware of every cell in my body being highly sensitised to his presence. I can't push it away. It shimmers there, just beneath the surface.

I have fallen for this calm, kind, hardworking man who adores his daughter and grandson. He makes me laugh. My heart soars every morning when I first see him and he hands me a mug of coffee in the shop. I love the way he talks enthusiastically about Celts, Picts and Romans as we sort through new consignments of books. And then one dark, cold afternoon, just as he turns the sign on the shop door to 'closed', I tell him all this. How these thoughts fill my head, and how I want him, yet I'm scared; and as we sit together on two easy chairs in the reading corner in the back room, it all pours out.

'Well,' Fergus starts, 'I feel the same, Kate. And I haven't known what to do.'

I look at him, my heart beating fast. 'I don't want to spoil things.'

'No, I don't either . . .' He shakes his head.

'I feel like I've been pushing you away a little bit,' I add, 'since that day in the forest . . .'

He smiles. 'I haven't felt that at all.'

I laugh, pushing back my hair from my face. What Vince called my 'Pam Ayres bob' has long grown out, and I haven't worn make-up since I've been here. 'I've been with the same person so long,' I start, 'I don't really know how to do this—'

'Kate,' he cuts in. 'It's fine. Honestly. I'm the same. There's been nobody since Jane, and that's been three years—'

'Really?' I ask, surprised.

He chuckles. 'Yeah. Sounds a bit sad, right? But I've lived in a weird world of dusty old books and formula milk.'

I look at him, wanting so much to hold this man close. And then I do, and we are kissing in the shop's back room. And it's not tentative at all. Quite the opposite, in fact. And all those fears and doubts seem to fly away as we hold each other and I say, 'Shall we go upstairs?'

CHAPTER THIRTY-NINE

Vince

So many thoughts are rattling through Vince's brain as the taxi follows the winding road out of town. How Kate will react is the main one, obviously – because he didn't tell her he was coming to Scotland.

He knew what she'd say. That he should stay put; that there was no point in him trekking all the way up here. However, he's clinging to the theory that once she sees him, and realises he's scrambled over hill and dale to get to her – well, taken three trains and a taxi – she'll realise she's had quite enough space or freedom or whatever it was that swept her up here with that madwoman in the first place. And now she's ready to come home.

On top of all that, it was the only option he could think of to quell the terrible guilt that's been ripping through him, since Flatpack Monday, as he's privately called it ever since, trying to convince himself it was more about furniture construction than rolling about naked with his neighbour. Hadn't he always said that self-assembly was a sure-fire route to frustration and pain?

The fact is, he and Agata hadn't actually done it. But only because biology wouldn't let him. Vince had never thought he'd see the day when he'd be grateful for such a situation – but there you go.

We were just celebrating, he's tried to reassure himself. Celebrating what? The successful building of a shelving unit? He can't imagine that would stand up in a court of law. Meanwhile, another benefit of this hastily arranged trip is the fact that it's a very long way from Sycamore Grove. So he can rest assured that he won't bump into Agata – or, worse, her devoted husband, Dr Lenny Kemp. He's been terrified that Agata might have an urge to confess, and that Lenny would set out to 'get' him. He'd even dug out the balaclava that Kate had bought him, jokily, for that televised trek across Scotland. ('Well, you keep going on about how cold it'll be.') But then, he'd reasoned, would wearing it every time he ventured out draw even *more* attention to himself?

He's disgusted with himself, actually, for getting naked with Agata when, if he's absolutely honest, he'd never even paid her much attention before. Is he really that pathetic that he was absolutely up for having sex with a woman just because she was up for it too? So, yes, it's something of a relief to be far away from all that.

'So you're going out to view the place, are you?' the taxi driver cuts into his thoughts.

'Sorry?' Vince barks.

'Osprey House. The big house out here. Lovely place, especially now they've knocked the gardens back into shape . . .'

Vince catches the man's eye in the rear view mirror. 'No, I'm actually, erm, visiting someone.'

'Oh, right. Alice? Is she still there then?'

Alice? Is that the woman who'd kidnapped Kate at Euston station? 'No, it's someone else,' he says vaguely, not wanting to get into the details with this stranger. Vince hopes that's it for their conversation as the driver takes them down a narrow lane.

'You mean Kate then?' he asks.

'Er, yes,' Vince says with a start.

'Hmm. I'm not sure if she's still there. I know she was doing agency work . . .'

Agency work? What is this man going on about? 'But she's working at the bookshop now,' he continues.

Christ, do people know everything around here?

'Really?' Vince manages, trying to sound casual.

'Yeah. And she's loving it. A natural with the customers and all those books. Made a big difference to Fergus, I reckon, running the whole show on his own . . .'

Fergus? Who's Fergus? At the mention of another man's name, Vince's blood seems to chill.

'Liv was helping out,' he goes on, 'but you know how the young 'uns are. Got their own thing going on – and there's the kiddie of course. The wee man. Rory's good with him but he needed to be with his mum really. Give

284

him the best start in life. You know how it is – are you a father yourself? – those years flash by before you know it. My three, I look at them now and think, who are these strapping adults? It's like, blink and you'll miss it—'

'So, d'you know where Kate might be right now?' he cuts in, somewhat rudely.

'Maybe here. Or at the bookshop?' the man muses as a house comes into view. The vast, grey stone building has turrets and extensive grounds, and now Vince can make out a lake and a pale blue wooden summerhouse.

'Is this it?' he asks, sitting bolt upright now.

'Yep. Here we are.' The driver pulls up at the enormous wrought-iron gates. Quickly, Vince pays and thanks him and slings his small rucksack onto his shoulder. Then, just as the driver is pulling away, he runs back to the car and waves madly.

'Can you wait? Just for a few minutes so I can see if she's there?'

The man's mouth twitches in a bemused way as he turns off the engine and drums his steering wheel, somewhat ostentatiously, with his fingers. 'Sure. You go check the house. Me, I've got all the time in the world.'

Did he mean that or not? Vince doesn't care as he turns away and virtually hurtles up the driveway towards the house.

He bangs loudly on the front door. A few moments later it's opened by an elegant older woman with a silvery bob. She's very neat and slender in black trousers

285

and a pale grey turtleneck sweater. 'Hello?' she asks in surprise.

'Hi, hi.' Vince catches his breath, hoping he doesn't look manic. 'Sorry to disturb you. I'm . . . I'm looking for someone. Kate Weaver. I think she's been here, helping you to clear out your, um . . .'

'Oh!' The woman frowns slightly. 'There was a Kate here. But it wasn't a Kate Weaver. It was Kate Harper. I booked her through an agency, and she did an *incredible* job—'

'Through an agency?' Vince exclaims. 'No. No, Kate wasn't with an agency. She said she met you at Euston, and you needed someone and that was that.'

The woman's face seems to pale, and she takes a step back. 'And . . . who are you, if you don't mind me asking?'

'I'm Vince,' he says hurriedly. 'Kate's husband. She'd just, um . . . well, we've had a few problems and she needed a little bit of time away and—' He breaks off. 'Is she here now?'

'No, she's not,' the woman says, rather curtly. 'But let me get this straight. Are you saying Kate – I mean, the Kate who's been here all the time, living with me – isn't the Kate I'd actually booked?'

'I don't know!' It comes out more forcefully than he'd intended. 'I'm sorry. I don't know anything really. Only that I need to see her and . . .' He rubs a hand over his face. 'D'you know where she is?'

'Kate Weaver or Kate Harper?' She purses her lips at

him. 'Sorry. I'm a bit confused . . .'

She's confused? These days Vince feels like his brain has been removed from his skull and put back the wrong way round. 'The Kate who was here,' he says carefully, 'working for you.'

The woman seems to study him then, and for a moment Vince thinks she's going to slam the hefty front door in his face. But instead, she says coolly, 'Are you sure she wants you to find her?'

'Yes!' he cries. Then: 'I don't know. I mean, I hope she does. I've come as a surprise.'

'I think you should warn her then,' the woman says, then she takes another step back, to signal that their exchange is over, and quietly shuts the door.

*

Of course Kate doesn't pick up the call. It just rings out, and eventually Vince gives up and stuffs his phone back into his pocket as the driver chats away. '. . . Never thought they'd manage to get the place looking so good. But Kate hired a gardening team, took charge of the whole project. Worked like blazes, they did. They've done wonders, considering the state it was in . . .'

Kate – *his* Kate – has overseen a gardening project? Back home she'd only ever plucked out the odd dandelion and very occasionally scrubbed bird crap off his dad's water feature. It was Vince's job – albeit undertaken grudgingly – to drag his dad's ancient mower up and down. As the man rants on, Vince is in awe of how much he actually knows about the comings and goings around here. He is used to his movements being observed and noted back home, in a way that they never were in London. But this seems like next-level surveillance and he's at a loss as to what to do next.

Finally the man takes a breath. 'So, where d'you want to go now?'

Where my wife is, Vince wants to shout. *I want to hold her close and say sorry for not appreciating her. I want to tell her how amazing she is, throwing buffets together and trotting off to work at that poncey hotel without a word of complaint and basically writing my books and always knowing when a semicolon is appropriate.*

I want to thank her for boosting me, that night we met – a quarter of a century ago now – at a terrible open mic comedy night and for raising my daughter with me and taking her to Brownies and all those nature places with birds and animals and loving her with every cell of her being. I want to acknowledge what she's done for me, like moving to Shugbury because I wanted to, and loving me even though I've been utterly wrapped up in myself. But he can't say this because the driver would think he's some mad southerner, rambling incoherently. He might even drive him to a police station – not that Vince imagines there's one open around here at 7.45 p.m. on a dark autumn night.

'I'm not sure,' he replies. 'Just back to town, maybe?' He places his hands over his tired, scratchy eyes and

288

groans quietly.

'You all right, mate?' The driver glances round briefly. He has a kind, ruddy face and he frowns in concern.

Vince nods. 'Yeah. Yeah, I'm fine.'

Mercifully, the man falls silent then. It's so quiet out here, Vince notices. The only sound is the hoot of something. An owl, maybe? Kate would know. Edie would too. There were owls, along with otters, at the animal sanctuary Kate had taken his daughter to all those years ago. They'd come back brimming with excitement and described each one: snowy, tawny, barn . . .

'Look, mate,' the driver says now. 'If it's Kate you're looking for then I think I know where she might be staying now.'

'Really?' Vince jolts upright. *So why the heck didn't you say?*

'Yeah. They were doing the place up the other week. Rory was helping. Borrowed a stepladder from the Coffee Spot? He's a good lad, does his best with the little man. Honestly, young people get a bad rap these days . . .'

Please don't go on about this Rory person for a hundred years, Vince wills him silently, pressing a knuckle against his own skull. *Just deliver me to where my wife is.*

'So I reckon that's it,' the driver concludes brightly. 'I think Kate's moved into that little flat above the shop.'

CHAPTER FORTY

Kate

. . . And suddenly all those tangled thoughts unravel and I know it'll happen tonight. In the living room of the tiny flat Fergus takes my hands in his, and we kiss, tentatively at first. Desire rushes through my veins.

Our kisses grow deeper, more urgent. We stop momentarily and he says, 'I don't know how to say this . . .'

'What is it?' I ask.

'I've fallen for you, Kate. I've tried to just be . . .' He grins and pushes a hand through his hair. '*You* know.'

'Professional?' I smile and touch his face, tracing his cheek, his jawline. The handsome face I've grown to know so well. 'I feel the same,' I say.

'But . . .' His gaze seems to search mine. 'Is it okay? I mean, are you absolutely sure—'

'Fergus, I'm sure. A hundred per cent.' Then we're kissing again, my head swirling with wanting him, all mixed up with relief that I can still feel this way, so heady and wild.

There's no way we're stopping now. We're going to sleep together tonight. It's not wrong, I tell myself. It just *is*. Which makes it right, doesn't it? We pull apart and, hand in hand, go through to the bedroom.

There, we kiss again, touching each other now. He presses hard against me, and I feel like I am melting as we tug off our clothes until we're naked together on the bed. His body is beautiful as I knew it would be: strong and taut, so warm against me.

'You're lovely,' he murmurs, kissing my neck, my breasts, all of me in a way that shoots me into the sky.

It's been so long since I've felt this way, I can barely remember it. To feel desirable, even beautiful – and not a lady robot with colossal feet. Not just a cook and cleaner and household fixer, handling life's tedious details rather than the more thrilling 'broad strokes'. Not a cleaner-upper of dog sick and burner of cakes and quiches and scrubber of a purple bathroom that used to make me think, every time, *What am I doing here?*

Because nothing crushes your self-esteem more surely than knowing it's partly your fault. That you agreed to this; that you're culpable. Are you weak or what? What happened to your gumption, your spine, the woman you used to be?

She's right here, I realise now. Here in this freshly painted white bedroom with sloping eaves and a gauzy curtain that wafts gently in the light breeze, and a jar of garden flowers on the windowsill that Fergus put there for me. And right now I'm remembering that intimacy is the most powerful, wonderful thing – because it makes you feel alive.

Lying side by side, we kiss deeply and trace our fingers over each other's bodies. My heart is beating hard. I wrap my legs around him, utterly unselfconscious as I close my eyes as his hands sweep over me. I feel desired and free, and my heart is pounding loudly, so loudly I can almost hear—

And then I realise that's not my heart. At least it's not *just* that. It's something else, coming from outside of me and actually, beyond this bedroom. It's coming from out there, down in the street.

I try to block out the sound but it's no good. It won't stop.

Fergus frowns, pulling away from me. 'Are you okay?' he asks softly.

'Yes.' I nod. 'I think so. But someone's outside, I think? D'you hear that?'

We lie still for a moment, wrapped up in each other's arms. Then the noise comes again. 'Yes,' Fergus says. 'I think someone's out there . . .'

'Sounds like they're knocking on the shop door.'

'At this time?' Fergus looks confused.

'Should we go and see—' I start. But before I can finish a voice calls out: 'Kate? Kate? Hello? Are you up there? It's me!'

CHAPTER FORTY-ONE

'. . . Would've told you I was coming but I was worried you'd say no, don't come. Didn't want you to pull up the drawbridge . . .' Vince laughs awkwardly. 'Or throw boiling oil at me or shoot arrows into my head—'

'Vince, *please* . . .' I hand him a mug of tea and sit beside him on the sofa as if we are on a train. Fergus is still here, perched a little awkwardly on the living room windowsill. He doesn't *want* to be here, but he knows it would have seemed odd if he'd rushed off immediately. (I realise that by now I can virtually read his mind.)

'You should've let me know,' I add firmly. 'Just a message, Vince. That would've done . . .'

'Yeah.' Vince nods slowly, going to sip his tea and scalding his lip. 'Sorry if it's an inconvenience, if I've put you out—'

'You haven't put me out,' I say quickly. *No, it was absolutely ideal! As a comedian you've always had brilliant timing!* But then, it could have been worse. We could have been actually doing it. As it was, I'd

293

scrambled into my clothes and run to the window and peered around the curtain. There was Vince, standing in the light rain with a small rucksack, looking up.

I'd waved at him as if he were a delivery man. *I'll be down in a tick!* And I'd hurtled downstairs, flattening my hair as I went and panicking that every cell of my body was screaming out, *Your wife was just about to have sex with another man.*

Could Vince tell? Could he see it shining out of my eyes, or sense all those fresh kisses all over me? Did I even have to hide it from him?

Of course I did because he is my husband and has travelled four hundred miles to see me. And now that whole incident there – already I'm thinking of it as an 'incident', like pranging the car – seems ridiculous and wrong. What were we even *thinking*?

I brought Vince upstairs to the flat. 'Vince, this is Fergus. Fergus, Vince . . .' It was stiffly polite, with handshakes and the unspoken question shimmering over us: *Are you sleeping with my wife?*

'We work together in the bookshop,' Fergus had explained calmly.

'Oh, right. I see.' Vince looked tired, confused and certainly thinner than he was four months ago. Paler too – light-starved even, as if he's been spending an awful lot of time indoors.

Now we're all here together, drinking tea, trying to pretend everything is normal. Vince turns to me. 'So, d'you like working in the shop?' he asks, like some distant uncle.

'I do. Yes.' I bite my lip and make a weird noise, sipping my tea.

'Looks like a nice town,' he adds.

'It is.' I try to muster enthusiasm. 'It really is lovely—'

'Okay, well I'd better get off home,' Fergus announces, jumping up and taking his mug to the tiny kitchen and swilling it out. 'Nice to meet you, Vince,' he adds.

'You too,' Vince says without conviction.

'See you, Kate. Bye.' And then he's gone, leaving Vince and me occupying what had felt like a normal smallish sofa, and now seems more suited to a doll's house.

'So . . .' I start.

'I just . . .' He exhales, placing his mug on the wooden floorboards. 'I just wanted to see you, Kate. But I'll leave right now if you want me to.'

'Of course I don't want that,' I say, adding quickly, 'not after you've come all this way—'

'I'm not expecting to stay here,' he adds. He leans forwards, placing his hands over his face momentarily.

'Oh, Vince. It's okay.' When he takes his hands away I see that his eyes are wet. 'Please. Don't get upset . . .'

'Are you with him?' He looks anguished now. 'With *Fergus,* I mean?'

'We're friends, Vince.' Of course it's not the whole truth, but I don't know how else to describe it.

'D'you often hang out after work? Up here, I mean?'

'Not really, no.'

'Have you slept with him, Kate? Please tell me. I

295

won't do anything—'

'Vince, please stop this! You can't do this. You can't appear suddenly and start interrogating me. It's not fair. I'm sorry if you're hurt and upset, but—'

'No, *I'm* sorry.' He rubs at his eyes with his knuckles. 'I think I must've gone a bit mad to do this. To come up here, I mean, and spring myself on you. I should go home right now—'

'Don't be crazy.' I touch his arm gently. 'You're not going home. You wouldn't be able to get back tonight anyway. How about we go down the road and have a drink? The pub's lovely and they have rooms upstairs. You could stay there. I'm sure they won't be booked up at this time of year . . .'

He nods sheepishly, picks up his mug of tepid tea and sets it down again. 'Okay. If you want to.'

'I think that might be best.' I pause. 'And we can spend some time together, okay? We can talk things through.' I muster a smile, and Vince manages one too. He takes my hand and squeezes it. 'I've really missed you, Kate,' he says simply.

I look at him, all tired and rumpled, his reddish hair long outgrown its cut. 'It's good you're here,' I tell him. 'We do need to talk. So, come on. I think we could both do with a drink.'

*

It's not the big and serious stuff we discuss, tucked away at the corner table in the pub. It's not 'Why did you leave me?', 'Are we getting divorced?' or 'How are we going to divide everything up?'

Instead Vince tells me, with a note of pride, how he'd found me. How he'd deduced that the 'big house' I'd mentioned was some way out of town, and that the owner and I were probably clearing it out in readiness for it being put up for sale. Then he'd googled estate agents and there it was: Osprey House. He'd been so thrilled to find it that he'd come off the site and booked his train tickets immediately. An open return, so he could stay as long as he wanted to. Or needed to, I suspect, in order to persuade me to go home.

'It was a mad, spontaneous thing,' he explains. 'Once I'd decided, that was that. I just had to find someone to take care of Jarv . . .'

So it's 'Jarv' now. That makes me smile. Something seems to have changed in Vince. 'It was a bit of a palaver,' he adds. 'I asked Deborah but of course she's out at work all day . . .'

'I guess the Kemps are too,' I remark.

'Um, yeah.' He colours slightly and looks down at his hands. 'Gail and Mehmet said they'd love to help, but only if he could stay in our house rather than theirs. They'd just pop in to walk and feed him, all that . . .'

'Oh no,' I exclaim.

'No, exactly. Couldn't leave him all on his own.' His mouth twists into a smile, as if he's about to divulge something. 'You won't believe it but . . . he's been sleeping on our bed. I mean *my* bed,' he adds quickly, and my heart squeezes a little.

'You've been letting him sleep with you?' I'd be no more surprised if he'd said they'd started sharing a dinner plate.

'Yeah.' Vince grins now, and relief settles over me. He's okay, I tell myself. He hasn't fallen apart.

'You used to say, "Would you take a calf from a farmyard and dump it on a human bed?"' I tease him. Vince was always disgusted when he heard about dogs sleeping with their humans.

'I said a lot of things.' He sips his beer. 'You pointed out that there's an emotional connection between people and pets, and that it's not the same as sleeping with random livestock—' He catches himself and laughs.

'No, it's definitely not.' I look at Vince, thinking how strange yet weirdly normal it seems to be sitting here with him on a wet autumn night. In our early months together we were barely out of pubs. It was a 'quick drink' here, there and everywhere, in the London neighbourhoods that were mine and his, and then became ours together. And now we're installed in a cosy, sleepy pub in a pretty little Perthshire town. There's no drama, no further interrogation over what might be going on between Fergus and me. No anger at the way I've gone about things either.

A group of elderly men are chatting quietly at the bar, sipping pints. The barman made pleasantries as he served us, and a fire crackles in the hearth. 'There was an ulterior motive,' Vince adds, 'for me deciding to let

Jarvis sleep on the bed.'

I study his face. 'Was he whining to be let in? Or scratching at the door?'

'No.' He shakes his head. 'The bed felt massive when you'd gone. It was like Russia. Or China. Far too big for me to inhabit all by myself.'

Something twists inside me. 'I'm sorry, Vince,' I say truthfully. I never wanted him to feel lonely or sad. In fact, I'd wondered if he'd even care very much that I wasn't there. It seems now that he did.

'So, anyway, Colin's looking after Vince while I'm here,' Vince goes on.

'Colin?' I gasp.

'Yeah. Amazing, huh? He's off work at the moment with a torn hamstring but he reckoned he could manage some gentle walks, that it'll help his rehabilitation.'

'That was good of him.'

Vince nods and smiles. 'He also said it'd be nice to have the company.'

'Oh.' I'm about to say, *Poor Colin*. But that would imply *Poor Vince* too.

'I know I've been a bit mean about him,' Vince adds. 'But he was happy to help. Y'know, he's actually quite a decent bloke . . .'

I want to hold him close to me then. Not in a holding-Fergus sort of way but because of all we've been through. All those years spent building a life and raising Edie and trying to get pregnant, and finally deciding it was okay as we had our wonderful, clever girl.

299

And so I do. We hug and then we have another drink, still avoiding those enormous subjects that we both know are hovering there. Instead, we chat like old friends who are happy to see each other. I ask about his work, and how his book's going, and even whether he managed to build the flatpack. 'Bit of a challenge,' he admits.

'But you conquered it?'

'Yeah.' He nods, flinching slightly. Perhaps it's triggering for him. 'I conquered it,' he says with a small laugh.

He tells me about his journey, too, and how he spent the whole train ride in a fizzle of nerves – and then went out to Osprey House to find me and met Alice there.

'How was that?' I ask, a little alarmed.

'A bit weird, to be honest. She seemed to think your name's Kate Harper? So I told her it's not. I thought that was odd, but maybe you'd been operating under a different name, undercover or something . . .' As he chuckles bewilderedly I sense the blood draining from my face.

'Oh, Jesus Christ.'

'What?' He stares at me. 'Did I do something wrong?'

'No, no. It's fine.' I pick up my wine glass and drain it.

His face is full of concern now as he grabs my hand. 'The last thing I wanted was to come all the way up here and make things difficult for you!'

'Vince, it's okay, honestly,' I say quickly. *So it's done*

now. And there's nothing I can do about that.

At nearly closing time we get up to leave. Vince has booked in here for two nights and his room key glints on the small circular table. 'So you're not angry that I came?' he asks hesitantly.

'No, of course I'm not angry,' I reply.

He smiles, jokingly mopping his brow, feigning relief. 'You're not going to throw hot oil over me?'

I laugh then, and we hug again briefly. 'I'll never throw hot oil over you! But what was that thing you said, about wanting to cover me in paraffin—'

'It's a skin-softening treatment,' he insists. 'I was just trying to be nice—'

'You're saying I'm all gnarly,' I tease him, 'like a rhinoceros?'

'You're *so* not like a rhinoceros,' he exclaims. 'You're perfect, Kate.' Then his eyes flood with tears as, quickly blinking them away, he says, 'You've always been perfect to me.'

CHAPTER FORTY-TWO

Over breakfast the next morning, in the café by the town clock, the serious stuff still doesn't come up. We spin it out, dawdling over a second coffee, and when we've finished I suggest a stroll around town and out into the hills. I know Fergus is manning the shop so I won't be needed today.

'It's actually really beautiful here,' Vince marvels, looking around as if he has never been in the countryside before. Or the north, for that matter.

'Didn't you notice, when you did that big walk?' I suppress a smile as we cross the footbridge over the river.

'Not especially. I was more focused on survival then. It was tough out there, y'know—'

'Oh, yes. You thought you were going to be charged by a ram . . .'

'Gored, more like!' He grimaces. 'They have horns, don't they? What're they for, if not to be used as weapons?'

We carry on this way, chatting and reminiscing and

even joking around as we walk. We buy a makeshift picnic from one of the town's numerous bakeries to eat by the river during a brief sunny interval, when Vince berates himself for not packing thermal layers. 'Lovely shop, that,' he remarks, munching into freshly baked rolls and cherry cake. I don't mention that it's Fergus's favourite bakery, and that he often pops in there to fetch our lunch. Later, we have an afternoon drink at the Boat Inn. And all the while we're avoiding the big issue, hanging like a barrage balloon above our heads.

Vince stays a second night at the pub, and when we meet up on a damp and chilly Thursday morning he says he wants to talk. 'Properly, I mean,' he clarifies, in a different café this time. I suspect we are deliberately avoiding being together in my flat, above the shop. We are avoiding mentioning Fergus too. It's as if he has ceased to exist, but of course he's still there in my head; a secret. And I have never had secrets from Vince.

'I thought I'd catch the eleven o'clock train today,' Vince says over coffee, which we drink steadily, and eggs on toast, which we can barely eat.

They do a lovely breakfast here. But neither of us is hungry. 'If that feels okay,' I venture.

'I s'pose it does. I'd better get back really. For Jarvis,' he adds.

I look at him across the table. 'I hope you're okay, Vince. I mean, I hope you don't feel worse, after coming here.'

He shakes his head firmly. 'No, I feel better. Honestly.

Just seeing you has helped a lot. Seeing your lovely face . . .'

My cheeks burn and guilt swirls inside me. I lift my mug and take a sip to steady myself.

'Look, Kate,' he adds, 'I don't want to pressurise you. That's not why I came here, to make you do anything you don't want to do. But I'll change, okay? I'll do anything—'

'Vince, you don't have to—' I start.

'Shall we take a couple of months off together? Do an amazing trip? We can do that!' he announces, and I catch an elderly lady glancing towards us from the window table.

'It's not as a simple as that.'

'Okay, but the offer's there,' he says, a shade too loudly.

'You don't need to offer me things . . .'

'I do, though. I need to make up for . . . *everything*. Honestly, Kate, I've had all this time to think about you – about us. And how amazing you've been all these years, with Edie, with me, running our whole lives. I'm sorry.'

Wordlessly, I place my hand over his.

'I shouldn't have made you move,' he charges on. 'It was selfish of me. I thought, if I persuaded you, then you'd grow to love it and we'd have this nice little small-town life. But it was me I was thinking about. What *I* wanted. I didn't even consider how you loved your job, and all your friends in London. I acted like it was

304

nothing and then, when we'd moved, I expected you to adapt, to fit in. Even though I knew it was never really you . . .'

'It's all done now,' I say quietly. 'And I could have refused, you know. I could've dug in my heels—'

'The worst thing is, I know I've taken you for granted,' he cuts in. 'And I only realised that when you'd gone.'

'Oh, Vince.' I don't know what else to say.

'I'm an idiot, Kate. I don't deserve you. Please, will you forgive me?'

I look at him and then the café door opens and my heart seems to freeze.

'Aw, aren't they cute!' a customer exclaims. Two little dachshunds have trotted in. Not by themselves, of course. Alice has swept in, silvery bob immaculate, in slim black trousers and her camel trench.

'Hello, Adele!' she says brightly to the girl behind the counter. She doesn't spot us at first. She peruses the goods behind the counter and then she turns and blinks at me in surprise.

Instinctively, I raise a hand and jump up from my seat. 'Alice!'

She has already turned back to the counter to ask for her favourite seeded loaf. 'Alice,' I say again, at her side now. 'I . . . I wondered if we could have a chat . . .'

She seems to appraise me with distaste. It's as if I'm a door-to-door salesperson, come to harangue her into buying something she doesn't want.

'Here you go, Alice,' the girl says, handing over her

loaf in a brown paper bag.

'Thank you.' She takes it from her and says, quickly, 'You could have told me, Kate. You could have explained. How foolish d'you think I felt, when I called the agency and they said they'd emailed me to explain that Kate Harper had had some family illness to deal with and had to pull out of the job? And they'd sent me some other CVs but had heard nothing from me?'

'I'm sorry. I really I am,' I murmur, my eyes brimming with sudden tears.

'Maybe it's my fault. Maybe I should have checked my emails more carefully,' she says tersely.

'It's not your fault! It's all mine,' I insist. 'Every bit of it. I don't know what else to tell you, Alice. Except that I loved my time with you. And I'd do it all over again, in a second—'

'Well, thankfully you won't need to,' she snaps, bidding the young woman a quick goodbye before murmuring, 'Come on, girls. We have things to do.'

And then she's gone, and I'm aware of Vince standing up, flinging his rucksack over a shoulder and quickly paying our bill at the counter. We step outside where he pulls me into his arms.

'I'm so sorry. I really landed you in it, didn't I?'

'It's not your fault,' I say quickly. 'C'mon. Let's go.'

He keeps glancing at me as we stride along the narrow street, lined with quaint cafés and gift shops, towards the station. 'Are you okay?' he asks.

I nod, wishing I could run back and find her and

explain. Instead, we sit on a bench on the platform, waiting for Vince's train home. His eyes are lowered now, his mouth set in a grim line. 'Vince,' I start, 'never mind me and the mess I've made of things. Are *you* okay?'

'Yeah. I'm fine.' He turns to me, and he's clearly *not* fine as he envelops me in a hug.

I realise my husband is crying. Properly crying, I mean. He wasn't even like this when his dad, and then his mum, died.

We hold each other tightly, no longer our middle-aged selves, worn around the edges and addled by age. We are those young people who met, and loved each other, when everything was thrilling and new.

He pulls back, wiping his face with a hand and looking at me. 'I'm sorry,' he says.

'What for?' I ask, genuinely not knowing.

'For being mean and horrible about so many things. About your vests—'

'My vests?' I exclaim.

'And for pointing out that hair growing out of your chin,' he says, trying for a joke now.

'Better than me walking around with it, poking people in the face—'

'You're my love,' Vince cuts in suddenly. 'Your vests are too! And your big old-lady pants!'

'You love my vests and old-lady pants?'

He nods wordlessly, and then we laugh. Then: 'Are you going to come back home, Kate?' he asks, his gaze searching mine. 'Or is this your home now? Are you staying here forever?'

I start to speak but the words won't come. *Nothing has to be forever if you don't want it to be.* 'I don't know, Vince . . .'

'When will you know?' His dark eyes catch the sharp winter sunlight.

'I don't know that either. There's no plan, Vince. No schedule. I'm just here at the moment, and you're down in Shugbury, and I'm glad you came here. Really, I am. Because now I know you care—'

'Of course I care! Fucking hell, Kate. Did you think I didn't? You're amazing, you know? You can do *anything*. I love you so much—'

'And these two days are the best we've had together since . . .' I break off, glancing round at the station kiosk where the bookshop used to be. 'Since I don't know when.' My voice cracks and I stop as he puts his arms around me again.

I rest my head against his chest. His heart is thumping and I know his eyes are wet. I know this man inside out: every pore, every cell of him.

We pull apart at the sound of a soft metallic rumble, growing louder now. 'Here's your train,' I murmur.

He pushes back his hair and seems to gather himself and smiles a big, confident Vince Weaver smile. 'Thanks for having me,' he jokes.

I muster a smile. 'You're very welcome.'

There's a kiss on my hot cheek as the train comes

to a halt. Then quickly – because it's easier this way – he climbs aboard and looks back, waving briefly. 'Bye, Kate.'

'Bye, Vince. Safe journey.' I smile and wave, then walk away quickly, before he sees the tears spilling down my face.

CHAPTER FORTY-THREE

Vince

Considering the way things turned out, it's weird that Vince feels better about things with Kate. But he does. At least they spent time together, and she seemed relaxed and happy to see him. Okay, not *deliriously* happy every single minute – but not sick to the teeth either. Which had to be a good sign, hadn't it?

Since he's been back home, he's had a few gigs. They've boosted his morale and helped to get him back on track. And he's gone down well, and the reviews have been decent and Gail has stopped foisting chickpea moussaka on him. Once he even had half a roast chicken sheathed in foil from Radish Sue – as if he's been sick or incapable or both. He might be alone now but he does *not* need meals on wheels.

Also, happily, he has only glimpsed Lenny Kemp from a distance and he didn't charge towards him with a knife. He hasn't seen Agata at all. She might have told

Deborah about Flatpack Day – or maybe she's kept it to herself? He hopes it's the latter but anyway, what they talk about is out of his control.

Gradually, Vince has started to relax and venture out and about in the neighbourhood again. Kate hasn't come back – that's what he's still holding out for – but he finally managed to crank out the last chapter of his book, and has sent it off to Zoe. She hasn't come back to him yet, to announce that she loves it or to tell him it's crap. She's probably busy, he's reassured himself.

Best of all, Edie will soon be by flying home from the States for the festive break.

Vince hasn't mooted the Christmas situation with Kate yet. However, he's thinking that the presence of Edie will certainly coax her down south, even just for a visit. Surely she'll want to see her mum and her brother and nieces too? He certainly hopes so. But, as he's learnt recently, merely hoping isn't always enough.

Vince needs to think of some other way to persuade Kate to come home for good. The spa thing didn't work, obviously. What else can he give his wife? He remembers her lukewarm response to the handwash last Christmas, and Edie pulling him aside later with a wild-eyed look: 'Dad! *Handwash*? What were you thinking?'

He hadn't understood what was so bad about it. Was this the lot of the modern man, he'd wondered? *I don't know what I did wrong, your honour.*

'It was expensive,' he said defensively.

'It could've cost two hundred pounds and it's still

handwash, Dad. It's basically soap—'

'Yes, in liquid form, made from the finest ingredients—'

'I wouldn't have given that as an end-of-year teacher present.'

Vince had had no involvement in teacher presents. That had been Kate's area too.

So, obviously, that level of gift simply won't do. He could call Harry for advice, but news has just come out about his oldest friend being offered a show with the BBC. *The Harry Bonomo Show* no less. Why hadn't he told him about it? Once upon a time they'd shared everything: hopes, dreams, a dented frying pan and an E.-coli-harbouring fridge.

Vince is out shopping in the old town one afternoon when he happens to glance in the estate agent's window. Shugbury is a popular town for young families and retirees. The schools are great and it's safe, with a community atmosphere. *But we're in neither of those demographics,* he reflects, scanning photos of picturesque cottages and grander detached homes. *Our girl is all grown up, but retirement's a long way off; Kate is only forty-nine.* He thinks about her fiftieth birthday coming up in March. Who will she spend it with? Fergus and her other 'friends' up there? Was she being truthful when she said he was just a friend? Maybe things have developed in the interim, now Vince is out of the way.

He remembers Mehmet from next door, going on recently that the events company he works for is faltering, and that they're on 'special measures'. That's what Vince needs: 'special measures' in order to rescue his marriage.

He stands there checking out more photos and house prices in the estate agent's window. And that's when it hits him, square between the eyes – the thing he must give her.

He's so thrilled by this that he wants to run home and put his plan into action right this minute. At long last, Vince Weaver has had a cracking idea – and it's bound to win Kate back.

*

Small pieces of the elephant, Harry advised him. And Kate said something similar when he called her for advice about the flatpack (although he prefers not to think about that): 'Just take it bit by bit.'

Vince no longer dwells on the Agata aberration, or fantasises about Deborah scooping him into her powerful arms and throwing him against her double-doored fridge freezer. Instead, he has serious work to do as he is going to sell his house.

Obviously it's not quite as simple as flogging an unwanted trumpet or a set of dumb-bells. Preparation is needed, in order to present it at its best. It's not that Vince is fixated on achieving maximum profit. After all, the bungalow was gifted to him by his beloved mum and dad. However, if and when Kate comes back, he'll want her to see the changes he's made, and how he's worked so hard to put things right. Then, when the house is sold, they'll be able to look at buying a flat in London together.

It'll be smaller than this place. He realises that. But he knows Kate won't mind, and that being there right in the heart of things is more important to her than having their own garden and being able to park outside their own front door.

They might even rent for a while. Kate isn't even that fussed about owning property – not like most people seem to be. But he'd ignored that fact. He hadn't taken her wishes into account at all.

The first piece of the elephant requires a meeting with Colin over a beer one evening, where he basically plunders Colin's contact list of every decent tradesman in the area. Some of the work Vince can do himself: repainting the kitchen and stripping off all that dated wallpaper in the living room, bedrooms and study. But he can't plaster walls and he's certainly not about to tear out the purple bathroom all by himself. Or indeed install a modern white one – the kind that Kate had asked for all along.

It all snaps into action quite quickly. 'D'you have a paint roller extension pole?' Colin announces during one of his many, many visits. He's taken to popping in almost daily while his hamstring injury heals, keen to advise on the 'upgrading'. Plus, he grew fond of Jarvis during those couple of days when Vince was in Scotland. Jarvis runs to Colin, delighted, whenever he shows up.

'I don't know,' Vince admits. 'Is that just a normal pole

or something different?' Next thing Colin's gone to fetch his. Over the next few days, with his new friend back at work now, Vince tackles the job. Painting is surprisingly easy – cathartic even. He just feels a bit guilty shutting Jarvis out of the kitchen while it's going on.

Next comes the wallpaper stripping. He's found a metal scraper thing in the shed and sets to work, starting with his study as it's the littlest room in the house. *Small pieces of the elephant.* It's laborious and thankless work. At this rate he'll be at it until summer – or until death, whichever comes soonest.

One slate-grey rainy afternoon, he tosses down the scraper, checks his emails to see if Zoe's got back to him yet, and mooches through to the kitchen. With his enthusiasm waning Vince wonders if he should have just painted over the wallpaper instead. Too late now. It's all scraped and hacked at – a complete mess.

Bizarrely, the bathroom is easier as he doesn't have to involve himself with it. The old purple fittings are taken away by two magicians named Phil and Naz, and the new white bath, loo and washbasin installed in their place. At least, it seems like magic to Vince. The job is done and dusted before he's managed to scrape off a square metre of wallpaper.

He's mulling over what to do next, while flicking through properties for sale in east London. There's a place in the next street from Tash's. Could he bear to live in a flat again? Of course he could. Who needs a garden when there are public parks, and you don't have to look after them? He could live in a bedsit – a hut, even – if Kate was with him—

At the sound of a knock on the door he goes through, thinking it'll be Colin back from work. Vince plans to ask him about the hallway, and whether he thinks he should rip up the ugly grey carpet and sand the floor—

He opens the door. 'Hi, Vince,' Lenny says. 'Got a minute?'

Vince freezes. It's as if he's been winded. Thrown belly-first onto that wooden horse. But nothing happened between him and Agata! Nothing at all! Hang on, he kissed her naked breasts. Is that 'nothing'?

Lenny gives him a steady and sympathetic look, as if he were a patient. *So, what can I help you with today?* With his heart battering in his chest, Vince tries to wrestle his expression into some semblance of normality as he croaks, "'Course I have, Lenny. D'you want to come in?'

CHAPTER FORTY-FOUR

Kate

Lately, it's seemed as if life has conspired to keep Fergus and me apart. He's been out and about, picking up book collections from as far away as Glasgow and Aberdeen. Then baby Finn had a fever, and Liv needed her dad to help out. It was all hands on deck and, for a week or so, Fergus disappeared into family life. 'Don't even think about the shop,' I reassured him. 'I can take care of everything here.'

Something else is happening too. Practicalities aside, since Vince's visit, we've stepped back from each other. No more kisses, even on the rare occasions we've been alone together. I've felt a little awkward around him – because of my deceit. And now it feels too late to come clean, to tell him the real story of how I ended up here.

Whenever Fergus says, 'Have you seen anything of Alice?' my heart seems to thud.

'No,' I've replied. 'Not for ages.'

'No news about whether there's been an offer on the house?'

'Not that I know of,' I said. And he gave me a look that said: *I thought you two were friends?* It seems all the odder to Fergus as, since he bought her mother's book collection, Alice has been a regular customer in the shop. She's helped us out too, making coffees and pottering around, straightening books on the shelves. She's even manned the shop occasionally.

And now she doesn't come at all.

I miss her, and want to call or drop round. But she made it pretty clear that day how she feels about me now.

The bells tinkle above the shop door, even though we turned the sign to 'Closed' an hour ago. I swing around to see Liv at the door. She greets us both, announcing, 'Happy birthday, Dad!'

'Thanks!' Fergus grins.

'It's your birthday?' I exclaim. 'Why didn't you say?'

'I don't make a big deal out of my birthday.' He chuckles. 'Far too long in the tooth for that.'

'Just saying, "It's my birthday today" is hardly making a big deal out of it,' I tease him.

'No one's forcing you to have a party, Dad,' Liv jibes him.

'Yeah, well . . .' He shrugs dramatically, as if he's trying to shake off the fuss. But Liv laughs disparagingly, and catches my eye in a *men, what are they like?* kind of way. I return her look with a silent: *Tell me about it!*

318

Now she's produced a parcel, which he unwraps carefully, then holds out a soft light blue sweater and a big bar of posh dark chocolate and a piece of paper liberally daubed with sunshine-yellow paint. 'Finn's first painting!' she announces. 'Just for you, Dad. He did it all by himself. Covered me and half the kitchen with it but never mind . . .'

'A masterpiece. I'll treasure it.' He's all smiles then, and she adds, 'And also you and Kate are going out to dinner tonight. Okay?'

'*Are* we?' I ask in surprise.

'Yeah.' She nods firmly. 'You are. Our treat – mine and Rory's.'

'What?' Fergus exclaims. 'No, that's way too much!'

She folds her arms and grins at us. She seems so much more self-assured since that day with the exploding jam. 'Dad, you do so much for us. We wanted to say thanks. So I've sorted it with Gianni's,' she continues, meaning the little Italian place on the high street. 'Go out for dinner and we'll sort the bill.'

'You don't need to do that,' I insist, turning to Fergus. '*I'd* like to take you out to dinner. If that's okay?'

'Of course,' he starts. 'That'd be—'

'No, it's *our* treat,' Liv says firmly, and I wonder if the 'our' suggests that she and Rory are working things out. I suspect, too, that the look she gives us suggests that she knows there's something between her dad and me. Something more than being bookshop colleagues, that is. And that, in forcing us out to Gianni's tonight, she's putting her seal of approval on it.

But can anything possibly happen now? It hits me then, as I glance at Fergus.

I can explain everything tonight.

And then all the tension inside me will fade, and we can see what happens next. He might be confused or disappointed or even decide I'm far too weird and duplicitous to be involved with. I do hope not. Because whatever happens, I want to kiss this man with clear, kind eyes, his face a little lived in, a smattering of salt and pepper stubble around the jaw. It's a strikingly handsome face, although I know he's unaware of the fact. He lives in faded jeans, roomy sweaters and sturdy walking boots.

'Looks like you've got quite a backlog to sort, Dad,' Liv remarks now, indicating the boxes of books neatly stacked by the counter.

'Hey, these have just arrived,' he says. 'Give me time!'

'I was going to stay on a bit and get started,' I tell Fergus.

'We could do an hour or so,' he suggests, looking round at Liv. 'What time's our booking, honey?'

'Eight,' she replies, peering into an open box of books. 'Looks like they're mostly nature, local guidebooks, history . . .' Fergus nods. 'Make sure you put them in the right sections,' she chides him, glancing at me now. 'Me and Dad didn't always agree where to put things. *That's* why it was a nightmare, working here . . .' She sniggers. 'Like a historical book about nature . . . like this one!'

She plucks a book from the box. '*Fern Collectors of the Victorian Era.* Where does *that* go?'

'There's a lot of crossover,' I agree.

'And we didn't always see eye to eye, did we, Liv?' Fergus raises a brow.

'No, we didn't,' she says firmly. 'But anyway – I need to get back for Finn. So, enjoy your night . . .'

'Thank you love,' Fergus says, hugging her.

I hug her too. 'Thank you Liv. It's such a lovely treat.'

She steps back and beams at us. 'Promise you'll have all the courses and loads of wine?' Her eyes are gleaming now.

'Not just a few breadsticks?' Fergus suggests, crooking a brow.

'No, Dad. *All* the courses. That's the deal.' Then she's off, and Fergus smiles.

'Well. That's us told then!'

'Yes, seems like it.' I laugh and reach for his hand and squeeze it. And then we look at each other and he leans towards me and kisses me. It feels like it's just a light peck on the lips, like the brush of a butterfly. But he doesn't move away. Instead, his mouth stays on mine and he pulls me closer, wrapping his arms around my waist.

I feel like I'm dissolving. As if I could split into millions of particles in this room full of books. It's as if we've been waiting for this moment, when it's just us, alone together – not pricing up books or tidying shelves or debating whether *The Poacher's Almanac* should

321

go under memoirs or natural history. Instead, we're standing here, kissing in the middle of Fergus's shop as if we've waited so long for this chance and now we can't stop. And somehow time spins by, until we pull apart and he smiles and looks the happiest I have ever seen him.

I glance at the clock on the wall behind the counter. 'Fergus,' I say, 'it's nearly eight!'

He looks at me in a bemused way and then turns to the clock and says, 'Where did all that time go?'

'No idea! What were we *doing*?'

He laughs and kisses me lightly on the lips. 'We'd better go, right?'

'Yes! And we're having all the courses, remember? That was the deal.'

'Can't wait,' he says. Then we turn off all the lights and lock up the shop, and he takes my hand as we step out into the cool October night.

CHAPTER FORTY-FIVE

Vince

'. . . So I hear you're doing up the house?' Lenny says. *I wouldn't bother with that because I'm going to murder you in it.*

'Yeah, that's right.' Vince is conscious of his face blazing.

'Just wondered if this might be useful?'

He's holding something, Vince notices now. A box containing some kind of device. 'What is it?' he croaks.

'A wallpaper stripper. A steam one. If you have a minute I can show you how easy it is to use?'

And that's all he came round for: to be helpful, like he was with the patio jet-washer. He demonstrates the thing, and Vince watches with intense concentration as if being shown how to administer a loved one's life-saving injections. And soon, the floral wallpaper his mother chose in something like 1987 falls away. The pinky-and-grey floral pattern has always reminded him of childhood, of birthday parties and being allowed Viennetta ice cream as a treat. He'd expected to feel sad to see it go. However, he feels nothing apart from relief as he powers through the job alone, steaming the stuff off like a manic. Relief at finally making headway and Lenny not punching him in the face.

'He doesn't know!' Vince informs Jarvis. 'Everything's going to be all right.' Not only with Lenny but with the house upgrade too. Already, with the dreary florals gone, it's so much lighter and brighter. Vince can't wait for Kate to see it. Not that he expects her to want to stay here, but because she'll see how much he's achieved, and she'll be proud of him and realise that she really does love him, despite him being a useless shit. He imagines her lovely face breaking into a huge, sunny smile: 'Vince! You've done an amazing job!'

The plasterer comes next: a swaggery guy with a soft pink belly lolling over his low-slung jeans. He brings a radio and plays Smooth FM all day long, crooning along to Barry White as he skims over where the wallpaper once hung. Now everything is beautifully smooth. It's like the bungalow has been Botoxed and Vince feels renewed and sprightly, ready with his paint roller.

He tears into the task, aided by Colin and his fantastic extension pole. 'You just need the right tools for the job, Vince,' he informs him.

Vince is aware of a sharp twang of guilt as he drops off four boxes of his parents' bric-a-brac at a charity shop in town. But then, they're just porcelain rabbits and horses and shepherdesses, and little knick-knacks his mum picked up on holidays in St Ives in the Seventies. What does he want with a macramé pot holder and a wicker-edged tray depicting a Cornish seascape? His beloved mum is gone. As if to reassure himself that she really *won't* march into the house, demanding to know what he's done with a lurid pink vase patterned with kittens, he stops off at the cemetery on the outskirts of Shugbury and visits his parents' grave.

He goes there occasionally to tidy it up and have a little chat with his mum and dad. Kate doesn't even know. 'I'm selling the house,' he murmurs, crouching down in front of the granite headstone. 'I'm sorry. I hope you don't mind.' Realising his eyes are wet, he rubs them on his sleeve. 'What'll I do about the water feature, Dad? It's kind of half finished. It doesn't really look like anything apart from . . .' A smile crosses his lips. 'Anyway, I'll always be grateful for the house, and I'll always love it. But I've decided it's time to move on.'

He leans over then and plants two quick kisses on the headstone. One for Iris, one for Walt. 'Bye, Mum and Dad,' Vince says, his voice cracking a little. Then he straightens himself up to his full height and strolls out of the cemetery, feeling lighter than he has in living memory, as if a weight has been lifted and suddenly everything feels sharper and brighter and he knows *exactly* what he must do.

*

Obviously, late October isn't the best time to put a house on the market. Sensible people wait until spring, when the garden is coming back to life. But Vince isn't a sensible person and he can't wait until spring.

Time is of the essence here if he's going to win his wife back. So, on a bitterly cold morning he calls the estate agent in town. 'Of course, yes,' says the cheerful young woman. 'We'll come over on Monday at ten if that works for you? We can take measurements and arrange a time for our photographer to visit.'

'Great,' he enthuses. That gives Vince the weekend to do a final tidy-up. Easy, he tells himself. Everything will be ready by then. But first, there's a slightly tricky job to tackle.

He knows Colin would help him, but Vince feels confident that he can do to the job himself. Lately, he's proved to himself that he can be more practical than he'd ever imagined. When Colin came round to inspect his paint job he was clearly impressed: 'Looks good, Vince! Did you prep the walls?'

'Of course,' he lied.

'Great job. Well done!'

Vince had glowed with pride then. Now he's picturing Colin's look of amazement when he sees that the bathroom door is no longer propped up against a wall, but has been rehung. Plus, Vince will be able to go to the loo without Jarvis gazing at him! It's the last step: the final piece of the elephant.

Whistling to himself like a proper tradesman, Vince

excavates the shed to find the toolbox (Kate had hid it really well) and locates a screwdriver. The night of the book festival party, Colin had popped the door's hinge pins in an envelope labelled HINGE PINS and slid them into a kitchen drawer, so they're no trouble to find. Blimey, Vince muses. Colin should be someone's back end instead of being abused by gym-shirking teenagers every day of his working life.

However, when it comes to the meaty part of the job, it's not so easy. Groaning loudly, Vince tries to manhandle the door into place. But he can do this. He's looked on YouTube and knows he has to position the door on its hinges and then insert the hinge pins and voila! Job done!

The hinge pins are in his jeans pocket and he's holding the door and fishing out a screwdriver from his other pocket. That takes one hand, and with his other two hands he tries to reposition the door as it needs to be flush with the frame and it's a bit wonky and hang on – how many hands is he supposed to have?

He only has two. Is he meant to have sprouted another one? Now he's dropped the screwdriver – 'Shit!' he shouts. He's still holding the door with both hands; no, *one* hand like some display of strength performance at a circus and he's trying to reach the screwdriver from the floor while propping up the door and twisting painfully and Jarvis is watching the fascinating spectacle with his pink tongue hanging out.

'Pass me the screwdriver!' Vince shouts. But Jarvis

merely ambles off to the kitchen.

Vince wants it to stop now – the holding and reaching and twisting. Because he's *not* a tradesman, he's a comedian, so why should he be expected to be able to do this stuff? It's like Kate with the bake sale! Why should being a woman mean you're automatically good at cakes? Then suddenly he's not holding or twisting or even thinking about Kate. He's not even standing or seeing anything because the door crashes down on him, throwing him backwards and his head cracks against the wall and Vince's world goes black.

CHAPTER FORTY-SIX

Kate

The restaurant is perfect. Small and busy and smelling delicious, with glowing lights. 'Isn't this so thoughtful of Liv?' I say.

'She's not too bad, is she?' Fergus says with a trace of pride.

'She's lovely,' I say. 'And you're a great dad.'

'I don't know about that,' he says, brushing it off with a smile. But I understand the feeling. When your child has reached adulthood and they do something, some tiny thing maybe, that makes you think: they're okay. It's all turned all right in the end. And I wonder now if it will all turn out okay in the end for us too.

We eat and chat and drink and it's lovely, even though I need to say *the thing*.

That I hadn't been booked by Alice after all, but had pretended to be the other Kate. It'll be okay, surely, I reassure myself as we drink our wine.

'Y'know, I've loved you being here,' Fergus ventures when our plates have been whisked away.

'I've loved it too.' I look at his face across the table in the candlelit glow. 'It's been . . . wonderful really.'

'D'you think you're going to settle up here?' he asks.

I pause, wondering what to say. 'I don't know, Fergus. It depends on so many things . . .'

'Like what?' he asks lightly.

I sip my wine, wondering what I'm trying to say. 'I love working in the shop – you know that.'

'I'm not really talking about the shop, Kate,' he says with a wry smile. And I know exactly what he means.

He wants to know about us. And what I'm feeling about him, and being here. 'I'm just enjoying things,' I say, 'as they are.'

He nods, taking this in, and then looks at me across the table and says, 'Whatever you're feeling, it's okay, you know? It's good!'

The smile breaks over my face like a wave. Could it really be as simple as that?

'Really?' I say.

'Of course,' he says with a small laugh. 'Why not?'

But there's something you should know. 'Fergus,' I start, 'the thing with Alice. With me working with her . . .'

'What is it?' he asks.

I pause and take the deepest breath. 'It just . . . it didn't quite happen in the way you think it did. I mean, the way I *made* you think it did. What I led you to believe . . .'

He chuckles bewilderedly, gaze fixed on mine. 'What you *led me to believe*? What is this, Kate? What's it all about?'

Fiddling with a napkin, I take in Fergus's rapt expression in the candlelight. Even if he totally goes off me after what I'm about to tell him, at least he's listening. At least I'm being *heard*.

'I just met Alice at Euston station,' I start. 'And she thought I was the woman she'd booked to help her clear out the house. And I kind of went along with that. I don't know why. I'd just walked out on Vince and I was swept along, and there we were on the train together with the dogs, and she really needed someone and . . .' I break off suddenly. Tears are filling my eyes.

'Hey, it's okay!' he exclaims.

'And I needed someone too,' I add.

His mouth twists, and he seems to digest this for a moment. Then he takes my hands in his across the table and just holds them. 'Why didn't you just say?'

'Because I'm an idiot,' I blurt out.

'But you're not, Kate. You're so not an idiot. Please don't say that. And anyway, maybe I knew something was a bit . . . off?'

I blink at him. 'Really?'

Fergus shrugs. 'I don't know. Maybe. You just didn't seem the type . . .'

'What type *did* I seem?'

'I don't know. Sort of . . . wild.'

'Me? Wild?' I say incredulously.

'Yeah! Absolutely. Wild and brave and spontaneous. Like nothing can tie you down. I know you care deeply about people, and I hope you care about me . . .'

'Of course I do!'

'. . . but you also know your own mind, Kate. You left home because you weren't happy. How many people wish they had the strength to do that?' Briefly I think of Mum, ushering George and me onto that London-bound bus. Vince isn't a bad person. He hadn't punched the wall or thrown chartreuse creams across the room. But I wasn't happy. I was lonely and sad – and now I'm not.

'You're strong and independent and nobody's pushover,' Fergus continues. 'And I love that about you.'

I smile then, and wish we were in that little white bedroom above the bookshop and I could pull him into my arms. 'I needed something different,' I say simply. 'From my old life, I mean.'

'Yeah.' He pauses. 'And maybe I needed something too. And I didn't realise that, because I've been wrapped up in my own stuff, with Liv and Finn and the shop and all that. That is, until I met you.'

I look across the flickering candle at his kind and handsome face. 'I'm so glad,' I murmur. 'I'm so glad I met you too.' His eyes seem to search mine and I want to lean over and kiss his beautiful mouth. I don't of course. We just sit here, holding hands across the table; two people enjoying his fiftieth birthday and we don't need to say a word.

Then finally, I smile and say, 'Liv said *all* the courses.'

'Oh God, yes!' He laughs and lets my hands drop as a young waitress arrives at our table with dessert menus. 'Would you like anything else?' she asks.

'We'll have a look,' I say, catching Fergus's eye. Because tonight, I know we don't really want panna cotta or tiramisu. We just want to go back to that little flat above the shop. We want to be together, and spend the night there, and I don't know if that's wrong or not.

'Erm, I think I'm all done actually.' Fergus catches my eye over his menu.

I try to keep down my smile, but it's impossible. 'Yes, I'm not sure I could manage anything else,' I say. So we thank the waitress, who assures us that the bill is all sorted, and hope we won't be in trouble with Liv for skipping dessert. Then we step outside into the cool dark night.

'So, where to now?' Fergus asks.

I look up at him and lean into the warmth of his body as he wraps a strong arm around me. Even through the layers of a jacket and sweater I can feel the thud of his heart. 'Oh,' I say lightly, smiling now, 'I think we should just go home.'

He pulls back, his eyes glinting with amusement. 'I'm glad it feels like home.'

'It really does,' I say as we start to walk, hand in hand, along the sleepy high street, past the souvenir shops and newsagent and cafés. Then my phone rings, and I stop.

Fergus frowns as I fish it from my bag. *Vince?* his

concerned look says.

But it's not Vince. It's Deborah. What does *she* want?

'Kate, hi,' she starts. 'Sorry to spring this on you . . .'

'What's wrong?' I ask, alarmed.

'I wasn't sure if you'd want to know but he told me to call you. Vince has had an accident—'

'Oh, God!' I cry out.

'It's okay. It's a head injury—'

'What? Is he going to be all right?' Immediately I start to tremble. I turn away from Fergus, suddenly not wanting to be here at all. What does she mean, she's not sure if I'd want to know?

'Yes, he is,' she says calmly.

'What happened?' I'm striding along now, and it's started to rain, suddenly and heavily, but I'm barely aware of anything else.

'Knocked himself out,' she explains. 'Doing some kind of DIY . . .'

DIY? *Vince?*

'He's conscious now,' she continues. 'They say he's going to be fine but he's broken his arm and dislocated his shoulder.'

'This sounds far from fine, Deborah!'

'It's okay! We've all been taking care of things . . .' *If you hadn't left him,* is the implication, *then this would never have happened*. And now, as I stride on ahead, leaving Fergus way behind me, she explains that Colin had found him, after hearing frantic barking from inside the house. Not a burst of postman-at-the-door barking,

334

but on and on, alerting help.

At first, Colin hadn't known what to do. But he knew Jarvis well enough to know something was wrong. And although he'd never have done this normally, he let himself into the house and found Vince unconscious on the floor.

'Colin thought I'd have your number,' Deborah added. 'Vince didn't take his phone to hospital with him.'

We finish the call. I turn back to Fergus who hurries towards me. All in a rush, I tell him what's happened, adding, 'I'm sorry. I just need to be on my own tonight. And I'm going back home tomorrow.'

He nods, understanding. 'Of course. Look, if there's anything I can do—'

'No, there's nothing,' I say quickly, wanting more than anything to be on my own now, and for the night to speed by until I can catch the first train back home, to Vince, where I belong.

CHAPTER FORTY-SEVEN

'You needn't have come,' Vince says, looking pale, bruised and more than a little shellshocked in the hospital bed. He's wearing a hospital gown, the kind that look like they're made out of paper. Although I was as gentle as I could be, he still winced when I hugged him.

'As if I wouldn't,' I exclaim, perched on the plastic chair beside his bed.

'They're probably going to release me later. They just want to make sure there are no effects from concussion or anything like that. Brain stuff,' he says in a jokey voice.

'Oh, Vince.' I look at him and place my hand over his. 'I've been messaging Colin. He said a *door* fell on you? What were you doing?'

A smile flickers, barely there. 'Just a little health and safety mishap. Don't try it at home, kids.'

'I'm just relieved you're all right.' My eyes fill with unexpected tears, and he spots this instantly.

'Hey, no need to be upset! The drugs have been

fantastic and it's all turned out pretty well.'

'Has it? Why's that?' I ask, startled by his stoicism.

'After Colin came with me in the ambulance, he went back to the house and hung the door for me *and* scrubbed the blood off the wall.'

Then we joke about crime scenes and Colin being a hero because humour is the way Vince deals with difficult things. And later, as predicted, Vince is allowed home.

It's not the home that I'd left. The floral wallpaper has gone – *and* the purple bathroom. It's all been freshly painted and vigorously decluttered, and is virtually unrecognisable as his parents' house.

'Like it?' Vince asks as he shows me, with his arm in a cast and clearly still in some discomfort, around the place.

'I do. It looks amazing, Vince. Really, I can't imagine how much work it's all been—'

'Aw, it was nothing really,' he says with a shrug. A pause hovers. I will him not to say, *So, will you move back in, now I've done all of this for you?*

Perhaps he senses my apprehension. Because instead he just smiles and says, 'I'm really happy you like it. Now, I'm sorry to be such a hopeless idiot with my arm stuck in this blasted thing, but d'you mind making us a pot of tea?'

*

Shugbury hasn't changed. Of course it hasn't. It's barely

altered in one hundred and fifty years – apart from the fact that a teeny sliver of Manchego costs something like £875 from the fancy cheesemonger's. The days – and then weeks – go by, and although Edie wanted to fly home immediately, we persuaded her that everything was okay. She might as well finish off a work project and fly home for Christmas as planned.

I drive us to meet her at Heathrow. Spotting us at arrivals, her face breaks into an enormous smile. 'Dad, are you all right?' She hugs me and kisses him, taking care not to knock against his bad arm.

'Good as new, sweetheart,' he assures her. 'Just been roughed up a bit. D'you think it makes me look tough?'

She laughs, then steps back and assesses Vince more thoroughly. 'What are we going to do with you, Dad?'

'Wait on me hand and foot?' He arches a brow.

'Business as usual then, Dad?' she teases him, catching my eye. My heart swells with love for her.

There's no awkwardness; no suggestion that things are different now, and that it will be stilted, the three of us being together. As I drive us back to Shugbury it's almost as if Alice and Perthshire and the bookshop had never happened at all.

'Why were you even doing DIY? You know you hate it,' Edie retorts as she surveys the home make-over.

'I was trying to be manly and macho,' he explains, 'to impress Kate.' I smile at him then. Christmas is going to be okay – I can feel it. And as the days go by, when we're alone together, I tell her everything that's happened.

Between her dad and me, that is. And okay, I miss out certain aspects – the Fergus aspect – but she seems to understand and takes it in her stride.

'Shugbury *is* a lovely town,' she ventures the next day. We've bought paper cartons of mulled wine from the Christmas market in front of the church.

'It is,' I agree. 'There are loads of places far worse than this ...'

She catches my eye and we laugh. She's cut her reddish-brown hair short, and it shows off her expressive brown eyes and generous mouth. In a baggy sweater, black jeans and Converse, she is a natural beauty. 'It's not for you, though, is it?' she ventures.

I hesitate. 'No, darling. I know it sounds horribly ungrateful because loads of people would kill to live in a town like this. And I have tried, honestly.'

'I know, Kate. I feel disloyal even saying this, 'cause it was always lovely to visit Gran and Granddad here ...'

'They doted on you,' I remind her with a smile.

'Yeah. They were so kind to me. But I couldn't bear it, being here permanently,' Edie continues, 'and I do understand why you left.' She looks at me. I know she means, *It's not just about Shugbury, is it? It's about Dad too.* 'Whatever you do will be the right decision,' she adds, sounding so much older than her years. I'm grateful to her for understanding, even though I don't really know what I'm doing next, and what the 'right thing' will be.

Edie seems so much more self-assured than the last

time I saw her properly, face to face. Last Christmas, it was – a whole year ago. She didn't make it over in the summer as a bunch of her new friends persuaded her to go on a road trip instead. 'Maybe you and Dad could come out here?' she'd suggested. But that hadn't happened either. Instead I'd run away from my life here, and made a new one in a little Perthshire town.

And now, it seems, that's over too.

*

Edie and I choose last-minute treats from the Christmas market. Then we stroll home and decorate the real tree I picked up from a nearby farm. Vince's parents always had an artificial silver one but I knew Edie would prefer a real pine, like we always had when she was growing up in London. 'I love the smell of it,' she enthuses.

Christmas Day is just the three of us, although Vince had invited Colin over for drinks in the evening, worried that he might be lonely. During Vince's brief hospital stay he took care of Jarvis again. He seems to have been something of a rock these past few weeks.

The four of us drink too much, and there are rowdy toasts:

To Vince for hauling this bungalow into the modern age in preparation for selling it!

To Colin for finding him knocked out cold on the floor!

To Jarvis for not eating him!

To Colin's fantastic extension pole!

To Edie for a glowing performance review before Christmas!

To me for calling up Ingrid, my old manager at the museum, just as she'd found out that one of our old colleagues was leaving!

To Vince for finishing his book!

To bought Christmas puddings!

To Colin for making the jump to go part-time at school as he actually enjoyed the hamstring recovery period, hanging out with Vince and going on gentle walks with the dog!

'Time for a better life balance,' he announces, draining his glass. 'Since Angie left me I've been obsessed with my job. But the kids are little sods. They'll be the death of me.'

'I'm sure you're a very good teacher,' Vince assures him, tipsily.

On and on we go, toasting Gail's terrible chickpea moussaka for 'flushing out' Vince's digestive tract, and my mother for calling the landline, which he reckons was good for his nervous system and reflexes.

It's a different sort of Christmas. But weirdly, it's also one of the best.

As Edie is installed in the spare room, I sleep with Vince. I mean that in the actual *sleep* sense; merely sharing a bed. 'I could kip on the sofa,' he offered, but after his accident I wouldn't hear of it. And Edie would have found it weird, discovering either of us cocooned in a sleeping bag in the living room. It would hardly have announced, 'Look how well we're functioning as a family!' As it is, we climb into our respective sides and lie there, aware of the closeness of each other.

Occasionally, when we talk late into the night, I think he's going to kiss me. Touch me, even. All those things I yearned for, before I left, so I'd know he still loved me. But he holds back and I'm glad because I don't know how I'd respond. If it would all come surging back: those feelings I had for him, when we could barely keep our hands off each other.

As it is, it's not just the two of us here anyway. Jarvis is here every night, snoring throatily between us, at the foot end of the bed.

Then one night, at some point in the early hours, I realise Vince's hand has folded loosely around mine. I don't take mine away. Gradually, I just drift back to sleep, feeling warm and safe and believing that, somehow, everything will be okay.

CHAPTER FORTY-EIGHT

On Boxing Day my brother George arrives with Mum, his wife Malena and their two little girls, Lois and Sophia. It's relaxed and fun, the only tricky moment being when I take Mum aside in the kitchen and tell her that Vince and I had had a break, and that I've actually been in Scotland and I'm not sure what's going to happen now.

'I knew something was going on,' she exclaims. 'You walked out on him? Don't you realise how much he loves you and how lucky you are?'

Of course, any man who doesn't smash a hole in the living room wall is a hero. 'I'm not getting into his now,' I tell her firmly.

'At least you're back now,' she mutters.

I press a large glass of wine into her hands and exchange a knowing glance with my brother, who's appeared in the kitchen and delves into the fridge for drinks for the girls. Then I reach for my phone and pull up a photo. 'Recognise this, Mum?'

Reluctantly, she takes it from me and peers at it. It takes her a moment to figure it out. Then: 'Is that the honesty stall near the campsite? Where we bought eggs and jam?'

'Yes! It's just the same, isn't it?'

'Looks like it. Amazing! Here, George, come and see this!'

'I have already,' he says lightly.

Mum blinks at it, seeming quite choked up now. 'Funny, isn't it, to think that that little part of the world hasn't changed at all in all those years?'

I nod. 'Yes, it is. D'you remember that bookshop on the station platform?'

'Oh, yes. Of course I do. You nagged to go there all the time. Is it still there?'

'Not where it was,' I reply, 'but it's still in the town, yes. I worked there for a little while.'

She stares at me. 'You worked in a bookshop?'

'Yes, just to help out . . .' But she's already plonked my phone on the table and turned towards the kitchen door.

'Poor Vince with that broken arm,' she announces. 'Well, at least you've come back to your senses now. At least you're back where you belong.'

I watch her leave the room. 'Just ignore her,' George says quietly.

I smile, grateful that he's here. I hadn't seen him since spring. He's almost impossible to pin down, and even when he's around, Malena has to virtually force him

344

to socialise. 'Oh, it's fine. It's just Mum being Mum,' I remark. 'You know how mothers often think no one's good enough for their kid?'

George grins. 'Yeah. I guess that's pretty common.'

'In our mum's case no one's good enough for Vince.' We chuckle conspiratorially, then go through to the crowded living room where Mum is holding court, telling everyone about those camping holidays she took us on all those years ago and making me show everyone the honesty stall photo.

Everyone's heard it all before. But no one minds – certainly not George and me because Mum is incredible really. She masterminded our escape from Dad. She worked three jobs so she could provide us with whatever we needed, and bought George his first piano.

And now we're all together again over an immense Boxing Day feast. Everyone pitches in to help – even Vince with his arm in a cast. We've moved the kitchen table to the living room and extended it so everyone can fit around it. Dishes are passed back and forth amidst chatter and laughter, glasses constantly refilled. Edie remembers that George doesn't like gravy or greens; just lamb and potatoes for him. She loves her quiet, shy Uncle George, who performs all over the world and doesn't say an awful lot. But he's happy, I can tell, with his family around him.

'Tell them about your trip to Tokyo, George!' Mum commands him.

'Maybe later.' He smiles.

'He's so modest.' She tuts loudly, badgering him some more, and I'm relieved that her attention is focused on him for now.

When everyone's gone, and it's just Vince, Edie and me, we settle into cosy days of watching films and perpetually snacking – a little world of our own. Then one day, having checked that Vince really will be okay on his own, Edie and I head to London for a visit. 'It's time you two got out from under my feet,' he joked, virtually shoving us out of the door.

While Edie catches up with university friends, I meet a gang including Tash and Ingrid, my old boss at the museum. She urges me to apply for the vacancy straight after New Year, but tonight's not the night for work talk.

'You're interested, though, aren't you?' she asks, eyes shining.

'I could be. We'll see.'

'Imagine, being back with all your friends! It's where you belong, Kate.'

I *can* imagine. But I'm not quite the person I was, when I scrambled out of the bathroom window six months ago. Later, Tash and I talk into the night, considering all my choices. 'You'll get a gut feeling of what do to,' she says.

And I think she's right.

CHAPTER FORTY-NINE

The next day I cross town to meet up with Alice, who jumps up from the restaurant table when she sees me. She's as chic as ever in slim black trousers and a cream roll-neck sweater, her silvery bob expertly blow-dried. 'Kate! So good to see you. How was your Christmas?' She grimaces as if to add, *Was it terrible?*

'It was actually fine,' I tell her. 'Far better than I'd even dared to hope.'

'And what about Vince?' She knows about his accident. When I messaged her I wasn't sure if she'd respond. She was right to be angry of course. But apparently, that soon dissipated. *I'd have found out if I'd checked my emails,* she messaged, as if it had been her fault really. *But I've always been terrible at that. Max despairs of me. And if I had found out, then maybe we wouldn't have had all that wonderful time together and I wouldn't have you in my life.*

Even so, I'm relieved to know that the agency fully refunded the real Kate's fee, albeit somewhat belatedly.

Alice even wanted to pay it to me – but there was no question of that.

'Vince has been great, actually,' I tell her now. 'And it's been lovely to spend so much time with Edie.'

'And your mum?' Alice arches a brow.

I smile as the waiter glides over. 'My brother was there, and she adores him, you know. So between him and Vince there wasn't an awful lot of focus on me . . .'

'And that was okay?'

'Definitely,' I say truthfully.

We order lunch in the delightful old-fashioned bistro she chose for today. ('My treat,' she insisted, 'and no arguments!') She tells me that Osprey House has a potential buyer: 'A couple in their thirties from down here. Full of energy and ideas. They want to turn it into a proper little boutique hotel.'

'That's great,' I enthuse, sensing a lightness about her that wasn't apparent in Scotland. 'It must be a weight off your mind,' I add.

'I suppose it is. Anyway, the estate agent said they're planning to put in an offer any day now. So let's see.'

'Great! I'm so happy for you.'

Her eyes sparkle under the chandelier. 'Thank you, Kate – for everything. I can't tell you how much it helped to have you there with me, with Ruthie gone.'

'Oh, Alice. It was a pleasure, really.'

'You know, it was never a happy place for me.'

'I gathered that,' I say cautiously.

'It never felt like a proper home,' she continues. 'It

was all about the B&B – the paying guests. I don't want to sound self-pitying but I always fended for myself.'

'You're the least self-pitying person I've ever met.' I catch her gaze and she shrugs. 'Is that why you had the tiniest room when you were a child? Because all the others were guest rooms?'

'Yes and, crazy as it sounds, they still felt that way when you and I were there together. As if I didn't belong in them and would *sully* them just by going in. My father argued with Mum about it, saying I deserved a nicer room as a child, and not that gloomy little cave, as he put it. But she wouldn't back down and I loved that little room, actually. It was the only part of that big old house that felt truly mine.'

Our lunch arrives, and although we fall into chatting about her son, and my family, I sense she is holding something back. 'Can I ask you something?' she asks finally, when our table has been cleared.

'Yes, of course.'

'You're a gut-instinct person, aren't you, Kate?'

'I never thought I was,' I reply. 'I'd always wanted to feel secure and steady, and that's probably why I jumped straight into life with Vince. But lately . . .' I think of my bathroom window escape, and the fact that I didn't hop off that Glasgow-bound train before it pulled out of Euston. 'I think maybe I am,' I add.

'So, I have dilemma here,' Alice explains. 'The couple who want to buy Osprey House are lovely. I know they'd make a great job of it . . .'

'But . . . ?' I prompt her.

'But I don't want to sell it, Kate. It's insane, I know. But since Ruthie died our place here just hasn't felt the same, and I miss her *too* much—' She cuts off, catching my surprise. 'Did I mention that we lived together?'

'No, you didn't,' I say.

'Platonically, I mean. But actually . . .' Alice smiles, her face filled with sunshine and memories '. . . she was my wife. My platonic wife. We were just this perfect pair, and it worked beautifully, and we always said we'd share a cutlery drawer until one of us died.' She stops and tilts her head, checking my reaction. 'Does that sound strange?'

'Living with the woman you love?' I smile too. 'It sounds perfect.'

Alice chuckles. 'Well, you know, I think about her all the time but time's passing. I can't stay in that flat, keeping it as some sort of shrine. Ruthie wouldn't want that. She was the adventurous one who planned our trips to India and South America. If it hadn't been for her, I'd have been sitting with a cocktail by a pool.'

'So . . . what are you going to do?' I ask.

'I want to take Osprey House off the market, Kate. I want to sell my flat and move up there and run the place myself.'

'Are you sure?' I try to picture her alone up there, in her mid-seventies, rattling around in all those empty rooms. 'But I thought you weren't happy there?'

'It's different now,' she asserts. 'It feels as if it's

filled with possibilities. And I was thinking, I loved my students when I was still lecturing. Young people make me feel alive and vital and I've missed that so much. So I was thinking I could have groups of students staying. Young people on geography field trips or art students who want to immerse themselves in the landscape. Or urban teenagers who don't have the chance to get out to the countryside.' Her face is flushed, her eyes shining brightly. 'I don't need to make money from it. I just want to do this, and bring the old house back to life.'

'I think it sounds wonderful,' I say.

'Morag is in on the idea,' she goes on, 'so we could manage it together. I mean, I'm no spring chicken.' She laughs lightly. 'But we'd run it so the young people all pitch in and help, and it's a community thing.'

'Alice, I think you should do it.'

She beams at me and squeezes my arm. 'Darling, that's exactly what I wanted to hear. You're so smart. You always know the right thing to do.'

After lunch we stroll to her flat. She'd described it as a shoebox but in fact it's quite beautiful. On the second floor of a mansion block, it has gleaming parquet floors, tasteful mid-century furniture and a balcony overlooking leafy communal gardens. The dogs race towards me, a blur of ears and tongues and tiny feet. I spot a window box housing shrivelled plants. Presumably these were once tended by Ruthie.

Alice makes tea and we step out onto the balcony. 'So you'd really feel okay selling this place?' I ask.

'Oh, yes. I'm way too young to retire, Kate.' She catches my eye and laughs. When it's time for me to leave she insists on clipping on the dogs' leads and walking me to the tube station. Christmas decorations sparkle the whole way along her local high street.

'I just wanted to say,' I venture as we reach the station, 'I really am sorry that I lied to you and made you believe I was the real Kate . . .'

She stops and glances briefly down at the dogs. 'Kate, listen,' she starts. 'I don't know how to say this. I was quite deranged at the time, still so bereaved and grieving . . .' She stops, sweeping a hand over her face. My heart is beating hard. 'I saw you standing there,' she continues, 'looking as if you didn't know where you were going. You looked lost. And when I heard you shout, "I'm Kate!" on the phone I thought, gosh, is that really her in that funny outfit with no luggage? We're really going to be spending three weeks together?' She laughs then.

'You must've been pretty horrified,' I say, laughing too.

'You just . . . weren't what I expected. But you were wonderful and I realised I should never make judgements like that,' she continues. 'And you *are* the real Kate. You'll always be the real Kate to me.'

We stand there for a moment with people milling around us, in and out of the tube station. And then I hug her tightly.

'Alice, I *was* lost that day,' I say as we pull apart. 'And

352

you helped me to find myself again.'

She beams. 'So what now? I mean, what's next for you?'

Alice knows my options. I went through them with her over lunch, just as I did with Tash last night.

'I promise I'll keep you posted,' I say.

'I'm sure you'll make the right decision.'

I smile at that, filled with warmth and happiness. 'I'm just making it all up as I go along, Alice. Just like Mum did, when we ran away to London.'

'That's what we all do really,' she says. 'And I think that's a perfectly fine way to live our lives.'

'I do too. And, Alice . . .' I pause. 'You rescued me. Thank you so much.'

'Nonsense,' she says, stepping back and looking at me, her eyes wet with tears. 'I didn't rescue you, Kate. You rescued yourself.'

CHAPTER FIFTY

Vince

Kate was a better driver than he was really, although Vince always drove when they were out and about together. Not today, though. Today, Kate is at the wheel because Vince's arm is still in a cast. It's annoying and painful sometimes but he's getting better. And actually, being the passenger is okay.

This whole period, with Kate and Edie being home, hasn't quite turned out as he'd hoped. He'd wanted it to be just like it used to be. And of course that was impossible. Edie is a grown woman now, and Kate has changed, and he probably has too (for the better, he hopes). Yet it's still been a wonderful, special time, the three of them being together again.

'I'm going to really miss you two,' Edie says as Kate turns off for the airport.

'C'mon, you're desperate to get us out of your hair.' Vince grins, glancing back at her from the passenger seat. He's determined not to be tearful or maudlin as they see her off for her flight.

'I'm not!' she says, laughing. 'How can you say that, Dad?' He's about to fire back some retort, but his phone rings, and when he sees the name displayed his heart seems to thump against his ribs.

'Hi,' he says, all bright and perky. 'Yeah, we did thanks. Hope you had a good one too . . .' He catches Kate giving him a quick look. 'Right,' he goes on. 'Oh . . . *right*. I see. That makes sense. I did wonder, yeah. It's been quite a while. Yep, I understand that. Well, I'm glad. I'm glad . . . for him.' There's a flurry of pleasantries and he finishes the call and blows out a lungful of air.

'What was that?' Kate asks.

His face is flushed and he's raking back his hair, not knowing what to do with himself, trapped in the passenger seat with his arm encased in plaster. 'That was Zoe. My editor—'

'I know who Zoe is, Vince.' She frowns. 'So, any news about your book?'

'They're, um . . . pausing it,' he mutters.

'What does that mean, Dad?' Edie asks.

'I think it means . . . they're putting it on hold.'

'Oh, Dad,' Edie exclaims.

'They can't do that, surely?' Kate sounds outraged.

'Well, yes, they can. They've just taken on Harry Bonomo—'

'No, really?' Kate glances at him again as they near the airport.

'Yeah. He has a TV show, you know.'

'Yes, I heard.' Kate indicates, coming off the roundabout.

'And they want to get his book out as quickly as they can. Strike while the iron's hot, sort of thing. So they want to put all their energies into that . . .' He pauses, clearing his throat. 'Maybe my iron's not quite as hot at the moment. Maybe it's a . . . *lukewarm* iron.'

'But you're doing okay,' Kate assures him. 'You've got all those gigs. There's so much good stuff coming up—'

'Those postponed gigs, yeah,' he says huffily.

'Your cast'll be off soon and you'll be fit in no time,' she adds firmly. No one says much more as they arrive at the short-stay car park and then make their way to the terminal. The hanging around is always the hardest part; all the waiting, time ticking away.

'Maybe you'd better go through now, love,' Kate says with a catch to her voice.

'Yeah. I guess.' Edie rubs at her eyes. 'Will you two be okay?'

Vince glances at Kate, and she starts to answer but he jumps in, which probably annoys her. She's often said he interrupts.

'We will, won't we, Kate?'

She smiles then. 'Yes, Edie. I promise you we'll be okay.'

Then she's heading through departures, and they're waving until she disappears from view, their wonderful girl with her carry-on luggage, heading back to where she belongs.

Vince looks at Kate and both of their faces are wet with tears. 'Look at the pair of us,' he says. 'What a state to be in.'

'It's awful isn't it? These goodbyes?'

'Just the fucking worst.' He laughs and squeezes her hand and already he feels better.

'But I'm proud of her, aren't you?' Kate says.

He nods. '*So* proud. And so much of it is thanks to you.'

Kate's face breaks into the most beautiful smile. 'And you, Vince. It's thanks to you too.' She pauses, and he doesn't know what else to say.

'C'mon then,' Kate adds lightly, linking his good arm with hers. 'Let's get you home.'

CHAPTER FIFTY-ONE

Kate

I stay until Vince's cast is off and he's well on the road to recovery. He is still intent on selling the house, and keeps reminding me that half of it is mine. 'We don't have to talk about that now,' I tell him.

'I'm just saying,' he says.

'Well, we can sort that out later. There's no rush. So, what d'you think about this job?'

As well as the opening where I used to work, Ingrid has tipped me off about a role at another museum, in Glasgow. 'I know the team and they're really keen on you,' she said. 'I think you'd love it, Kate.'

'Go for it if you think it's right for you,' Vince says. 'It's a promotion, isn't it? It's what you always wanted.' He's right; it's the curator's role. 'Not ass-cure, but actual *cure*,' he adds lightly. 'You're in demand these days.'

I smile, brushing off his compliment.

'It'd be a long way from Mum,' I add.

'George is near her,' Vince reminds me, 'and I could get to her if there was some disaster.'

'And so could I,' I add quickly, grateful for his support. We'll always be close, Vince and I. If I accept this Glasgow job, I'll be far away from him too, and my London friends, but now I think I'm pretty good at making new ones. And the thought of an adventure, in the city I knew only as a little girl, is thrilling to me.

'Anyway,' he says now, 'are you all packed and ready?' I can tell he's putting on a brave face, being brisk and businesslike.

'I think so,' I say. 'Just the basics really, if that's okay with you. I can pick up the rest of my things when I'm more settled.'

''Course it's okay,' Vince says. I'd looked into taking a short-term let in London, but as soon as Tash found out, she wasn't having any of it. So, just until I make a decision, I'll be living in her little spare room.

'It'll be just like old times,' she enthused, meaning our flat-sharing days.

Now Vince is helping me to carry two large cases out to the waiting taxi. As the driver loads them into the boot, Vince and I hug, standing there together for what feels like a very long time.

The hug might have felt awkward, especially with his arm in its cast – not to mention the fact that I am leaving. But somehow, it doesn't. It feels like a hug between two close, old friends who love each other.

It's only when we pull apart that I see that his face is

wet, and realise mine is too. It's a relief when Jarvis runs out, tail wagging, tongue out. 'Hey,' I say, bobbing down to fuss over him, 'I'll miss you, Jarv. Look after Vince for me, won't you?'

I straighten up and smile and Vince has mustered a smile too. 'Never mind that. I can look after myself, y'know!'

'I know that,' I say.

We stand there for a moment, then he nods towards the driver who's back in his seat, waiting to leave. 'So this is it then,' Vince says.

'Yep. This is it.' I clear my throat.

'Hope you can manage these cases on the train . . .'

'I'll be fine,' I say quickly, spotting Deborah and Agata as they appear around the corner, both wearing tracksuits. Looks like Agata has got Deborah into running. 'I'd better go,' I add, 'or it'll be all round the estate.'

'Probably too late to stop it,' Vince says with a wry smile as I climb into the taxi. I wave as we pull away, catching Deborah and Agata's looks of rapt interest as we drive past.

'Catching the London train, are you?' the driver asks.

'Yes, that's right.'

'Holiday, is it?'

What can I say? *No, I've just left my husband for a second time?* Only this time, it wasn't done on a wild impulse, but because really, it was the right thing to do. I think Vince knows that too. 'I'm actually moving there,' I say.

'I wouldn't want to live there,' he remarks. 'So busy and noisy and no one knows their neighbours.'

'Oh, I've never felt like that,' I tell him as I look out onto the bright winter's morning. 'It's always felt like home to me.'

EPILOGUE

A month later

Tash was right. It was like old times, us living together again. But when Alice calls, asking if I'd like to flat-sit for her, I jump at the chance and transport my belongings across town to West Hampstead. We have dinner together, and next morning she waits for the taxi that'll take her to Euston for her train north. She is spending a couple of months in Scotland, figuring out the logistics of how she'll host groups of young people at Osprey House. I can imagine many long evenings spent with Morag, as they hatch plans.

'Thanks for letting me stay here,' I say as she is about to leave.

'Oh, you're doing me a favour,' she insists. 'I'm not crazy about this place lying empty, and of course Max is too busy to pop over more than once a week.'

'I'm looking forward to meeting this elusive son of yours,' I tease her.

'You will, I promise. We'll do something when I get back.' There are hugs then, and off she goes with her two little dogs, leaving a cloud of her distinctive perfume in her wake.

I feel instantly at home in her flat overlooking the communal gardens. Unlike Osprey House, it's small and cosy and everything has its place. I can see now that Alice leads a very orderly life. Meanwhile, I commute across town to the museum where I'm working on a freelance basis for now. The Glasgow job would start in April, if I choose to take it. *You'll make the right decision,* Alice said. It could have seemed like a platitude but somehow, coming from her, I believe it.

I believe it too when, one cool February afternoon I take the tube to Euston. Checking the boards, I spot a train to Shugbury. But I'm not looking for that one. I turn instead towards the arrivals board and see that the train I'm waiting for is arriving on time.

I wait in the allotted spot, where Alice found me and decided I was the right Kate. My heart quickens as all around me people are rushing for trains, or staring at the board, and next to me someone is chomping an enormous baguette.

I wait and wait, aware of my heart racing until I spot him, and he waves, his face literally lighting up at the sight of me. He weaves his way towards me, as I do towards him until here's right there, folding his arms around me. 'So, here you are!' he says, kissing me.

'Here I am.' I beam at him, pulling back and taking

in his lovely face. A whole week, Fergus has managed to take off from the shop. He might even stay longer. There aren't many customers at a second-hand bookshop at this time of year.

He takes my hand and we cross the station concourse together. 'So what shall we do?' he asks eagerly.

London has everything, I told my little brother all those years ago. 'I'm not sure,' I say now. 'I haven't made plans.' He smiles and kisses me gently and a million sparks seem to shoot through me.

'We could just . . . see what happens?' he suggests.

Then we head to the tube together, and a whole future that we can't even begin to imagine. 'Yes, let's do that,' I say. 'Let's just see.'

The End

ACKNOWLEDGEMENTS

Thank you to my fantastic agent, Caroline Sheldon - over a decade together and what a wonder you've been. Thank you to Sarah Bauer, Rachel Hart, Raphaella Demetris, copy editor Helena Newton and the whole fabulous Avon team. Special thanks to Tania for reading in her ever-perceptive way, and to Amanda - that night you suggested that 'you don't just *knock up* a buffet' triggered something in me! Thank you to my wonderful friends, Jen, Kath, Riggsy, Susan, Michelle, Fliss, Cathy, Liam, Jackie B, Maggie, Ellie, Marie, Jennifer, Mickey, and the Currie clan for all the laughs and inspiration. Thank you, Elise Allen, for leading our coaching group - and to Christobel, Mif, Annie and Anne. You're so boosting. Thank you to Lisa, Fraser, and our Bracken group - it's about art rather than writing but it refreshes my brain! Thanks to Simon for the cheeky Quality Street. Finally, thank you to Jimmy, Sam, Dexter, Erin and my dad, Keith, for everything. With all the love in the world.

Here's an exclusive extract from Fiona Gibson's next hilarious and heart-warming read, *The Full Nest*!

January. Currently living at Sandybank Cottage: Carly, Frank, Eddie

We're not nagging. We're just his mum and dad, and we care about our son, and are *worried*.

That's the way I frame it, when dealing with Eddie. 'So, love,' I start, 'I saw this job advertised—'

'I'm-not-qualified-for-it,' he announces.

I look down at my son. He's lying on his back on the sofa, gripping his phone. The open Quality Street tin sits on his stomach.

'How d'you know?' I start. 'It's not head of ICI, Eddie. It's not Secretary-General of the United Nations. It's just an admin assistant role with the council—'

'Ugh,' he groans – as if I'd said, *And you'll be extracting worms out of cod, with your teeth.*

'But it wouldn't be forever,' I go on, casting a quick look round at his dad.

'Yeah, it'd just be a start, Ed,' Frank offers.

'To get something on your CV,' I add, to which Eddie shakes his head. He clearly thinks it's a blatantly ridiculous suggestion – that he should get off his arse and find a job – as he dunks a hand into the tin.

'My CV's-fine-thanks!'

Is it though? I reflect as he selects a chocolate, seemingly at random – as if making a conscious decision would require way too much effort.

I frown as he unwraps it. 'I though you didn't like those ones.'

'Now you're deciding which Quality Street I like?' he bleats.

'Eddie, for God's sake,' Frank exclaims.

'You always said the Orange Creams are the devil's work,' I remind him, finding this far more significant than I should. But he did say this. Back when he was still my sweet and lovely boy, before he took to lying around, dirtying all the mugs, while his dad and I are out working all day, earning money to keep him.

Eddie suddenly liking Orange Creams somehow signifies that things have taken an even darker turn.

'Hey, pick that up!' Frank says as Eddie tosses the gleaming wrapper onto the floor.

'Can you both stop looming over me like this?' he snaps. 'It's freaking me out.'

'We're not looming,' I insist. 'We're just *standing*.

Aren't we allowed to do that in our own house?' As he mutters something under his breath, I exchange a look with Frank, wondering how we ended up like this; with our smart and perfectly capable twenty two-year old son opting to do nothing with his life.

Eddie is our eldest child by two years. His two sisters left home the minute they could, bolting like horses from the trap. Yes, we miss them very much, but we were happy to see them getting out there, finding their place in the world. Because there's not much for young people in our once thriving, but nowadays pretty beleaguered little Ayrshire coastal town. Here the guest houses are peeling, shedding their fading paint, the crazy golf course is smothered in weeds and the Italian cafes have shut down one by one.

Perching on the arm of a chair now – God forbid I should loom! – I try again, once Frank has left the room. 'Eddie,' I start, 'that council job, you could just do it until—'

'I don't need you to plan my life for me, *Mum*.'

He's so cutting sometimes, and mostly it bounces right off the mental armour I've constructed. But not today. 'I'm not,' I protest. 'I'm just trying to help. How about going back to college, then? Maybe you could look at—'

'College wasn't my thing,' he states, shuddering.

'So, what *is* your thing?'

He shrugs. 'I'm not sure yet.'

'But love, everyone needs a *thing*…'

368

'Well, I don't!' he announces. 'I'm not like you, happy to trundle off to the library every day for years on end.'

'Eddie,' I cry. It's a stab of hurt, like a fork being jabbed in my gut. He locks gaze with me and then scrambles up, stomps across the room and out of the house, leaving Quality Street wrappers gleaming like jewels on our worn-out rug.

Frank reappears, grimacing, then pulls me close. My darling, handsome Frank. It's clear to me where our son's more exasperating traits come from. From Frank Silva, the Portuguese barman I met on the Algarve thirty years ago, when we were just twenty years old. Maddening Frank, who I still love so very much.

'What are we going to do with him?' I ask.

My husband shrugs and smiles in a *what-do-I-know?* kind of way. Then, he kisses me briefly on the lips and, with a wry chuckle, he says, 'I take it he's not interested in that council job?'

*

I'm still pretty hurt the next morning as I *trundle* to the library with snow landing softly on my face. I do love my job, but I've been there a very long time; seventeen years now. And I can't help thinking about Eddie's comment.

I'm not like you, he'd said. Meaning he's not prepared to settle for any old job (as I have, apparently!) just to earn money and pay bills and buy food and keep the family together while his father's crazy entrepreneurial schemes – risky, but at least more exciting than being a librarian – consistently go tits up.

Where have we gone wrong? I wonder. Am I that hard, round toffee in the Quality Street tin? The one that's nobody's favourite and is really just there to fill space? A twist of annoyance snags at me as I arrive at the library and unlock the hefty main door.

Immediately, a sense of calm starts to settle as I make coffee and tidy the main desk. Cool winter light filters in through the arched windows. As one of the key holders I try to make a point of arriving first, just to revel in the calm and stillness of the place. The gleaming tables are bare, the smell of books mingling with a tinge of furniture polish and something else that's impossible to pinpoint; the smell of learning and study and history and a place just to *be*. Then the library wakes up like a sleepy old giant as our lenders start to arrive. There's Bill, who's researching his family tree, and Jemma with her toddler, who always comes in on Tuesdays for Story Corner. There's Laura who likes to read, quietly, on the sofa in the sci-fi section. Then more parents and children arrive for the story, read by Prish, my friend and colleague, who's fantastic with the kids. As soon as that's over the book group arrives; a gang of forceful ladies in their sixties who immediately commandeer the big table by the stained-glass window, which they regard as theirs. We moved it once, to maximise space.

Carly, we're really not sure about the repositioning! You'd think we'd covered it in custard or something for all the furore it caused. We ended up moving the darned thing back because those ladies are not to be messed with.

'Everything okay, Carly?' asks Prish. Story Corner is over and now we're sorting through a pile of new acquisitions on a table by the kitchen hatch.

'Yeah, all good,' I reply, and then it all spills out, about Eddie and how his outburst rattled me. Prish is a little older than me and immensely kind, with a huge extended family (I bet they don't accuse her of trundling!).

'He'll find something,' she assures me. 'Some people just take a bit longer to find their feet.'

'But how long, Prish?'

She shrugs and smiles. 'Piece of string?'

I chuckle. 'I thought me and Frank would be empty nesters by now.'

'You'll miss Eddie madly when he's gone. You'll sit there crying in his bedroom,' she teases.

'Oh, yeah,' I say, with a wry laugh. 'The carpet'll be *sodden* with my tears.'

'Seriously, though, you've done a great job with those kids.'

Have I though? I think later, on the brisk walk home along the almost deserted seafront, back to the cottage where we've raised our family. Or have I just muddled along?

When I met Frank, on that girls' holiday, the last thing I wanted was to peel off from the group and be utterly consumed by a fling with a Portuguese bar tender. But I couldn't stop myself. Frank's beautiful deep brown eyes and huge, warm smile melted the very core of me. After the holiday we kept things going long distance through impassioned letters, and the occasional visit when we could rake together the cash.

It was madness, both of us knew that. But neither of us could let go. Finally, five years after we'd met, Frank joined me in my home city of Glasgow. But he'd grown up near the wild, windswept south-western Portuguese coast, on his family's sweet potato farm, and he wasn't a city person at all. And that, coupled with the arrival of our son, propelled us to the west coast of Scotland, where we found this little red sandstone cottage and fell in love with it instantly.

It was battered by salt winds and in need of extensive repairs, but had glorious views of the Isle of Arran and, on clear days, the island of Jura beyond it. It was perfect for us. Then along came Sofia, and then Ana, amidst the backdrop of Frank's hare-brained business schemes. He took over a failing ice cream shop with malfunctioning fridges that he couldn't afford to replace. It wound up after six months (imagine not being able to keep ice cream cold!). Next came a tiny bakery, tucked away down an alleyway, where he planned to wow our small town with Portuguese custard tarts. Frank's not a baker, but he was adamant that he'd hire the right people. However the pastel de nata craze had yet to sweep the UK – or certainly our little corner of Scotland. And even when he'd managed to hire a baker who didn't spend all his time out the back, smoking, no one wanted the tarts anyway.

Of course I felt terrible for Frank, to see his dreams shattered. But I was furious, too, at how he blundered in without giving these plans proper thought – it wasn't just him after all! We were a family, and these ventures nearly ruined us, my steady job barely enough to keep us all. We've lived on yellow stickered supermarket food and watched our kids head off to start the new school year with the same scruffy old trainers and rucksacks. It's infuriated me, how much Frank's wild schemes have actually cost us. Whilst I've always loved him, I also hated him sometimes too. These days he works as a mechanic at his mate's garage, and somehow we've scrambled through.

Nearly home now, I try to prepare myself for Eddie's ill humour. *Don't rise to it*, I tell myself as I let myself into the house. However, it's immediately apparent that something is different. Eddie isn't lying prone on the sofa or shut away in his room. No, my son is upright – and actually in motion! Most bizarrely of all Eddie is *smiling* as he bounds into the hallway to greet me.

Greeting me, as if I am actual human being, with feelings!

'Hey, Mum,' he says brightly.

Startled, I gawp at him. Has he broken something? Is this cheery display a way of buttering me up before imparting bad news? Or maybe he feels bad about yesterday?

'Hey, love,' I say, hanging my jacket on the hook. 'Everything all right?'

'Great, yeah. I'll just put the kettle on, shall I?' And off he goes.

Suspicion wells up in me as I follow him through and take in the sight of my son doing something more useful in the kitchen than flinging open the fridge, and staring into it, and announcing that there's 'no food'.

'Here you go,' he says now, handing me my tea in my favourite mug. My eldest kid is strikingly handsome; tall and brown eyed, like his dad, all cheekbones and angles, his hair thick and dark and glossy, rarely cut or washed – or even combed – but somehow still the hair any young man would want.

'Thanks,' My entire body is tense, fizzling with tension. What is going on?

He leans against the sink and sips his tea. 'Dad back soon?'

'Just the normal time,' I reply, unable to quell my unease. 'You seem very… *perky* today.'

'Perky?' He laughs.

'Well, yes.' And your deathly pallor has gone, I notice, and you're more like the old Eddie. The younger Eddie, I mean, who would hug me for no reason at all, before this interminable malaise set in, like a mould, that no amount of forced jollity, or trying my damnedest to be kind and patient and understanding could shift.

'It's nice to see,' I add, 'but you seem, I don't know—'

'Well, I have news,' he announces, smiling.

374

'What is it?'

'I'm leaving home.'

I stare at him. 'You're *what*?'

He laughs. 'Leaving home! It's what people do when they're adults, Mum. They break free of parental constraints. They fly the nest and forge their own independent lives. They grab opportunities...' *No, other people do that. Eddie Silva lies on his back, scratching his bum and leaving takeaway cartons of half-eaten samosas and pointless salad garnish sitting on his bed.*

I don't say this. Instead, as I must be in shock, I sip my tea and scald my lip.

'There's a room going,' Eddie is explaining, 'in Edinburgh. Raj and Calum said I could have it, so I said yeah...'

'But what'll you do?' I cut in. Surely he doesn't think we can afford to pay his rent?

'Work,' he says simply.

'But what kind of work?'

'There's a job going in a restaurant.'

'Waiting tables?' I ask.

'No. Kitchen work.'

Oh my God. Last time Eddie made toast he set the smoke alarm shrieking and we had to open all the downstairs windows and doors. 'Will that you be okay, doing that?' I ask cautiously.

'God, Mum, yeah.' He laughs in disbelief. ''Course I will. D'you think I'm incapable or what?'

'Of course I don't, love,' I say quickly. Still reeling, I clear my throat. 'So when is this happening?'

He grins and sips his tea, flushed with excitement. 'I start tomorrow.'

'Tomorrow?' I gasp.

'Yeah! Don't look so shocked. You're getting rid of me at last. You're meant to be happy for me, Mum.'

'Oh, Eddie, I am happy,' I exclaim, my eyes smarting with unexpected tears. 'I'm really happy for you.'

He beams and then, totally unexpectedly, he sets his mug on the counter and throws his arms around me; my big, tall, handsome boy, and my heart seems to crack as he says, 'Sorry I've been... y'know, like I've been. It's just, Sofia and Ana are so clever and amazing and they're getting on with their lives and doing so well. And you and Dad are always going on about that. About how proud you are.'

'Eddie, we're not! We've *never* compared you...' Have we, though, unwittingly? Guilt twangs at me, deep in my gut.

'...And I've felt left behind,' he continues, 'like I'm this failure, this massive disappointment to you both—'

'Darling, you're not! Please don't say that. You're not at all.' Tears escape now, trickling down my cheeks. As Eddie steps back I see that his face is wet too. 'Honestly,' I add, 'you're not a failure. Never think that. You have so much going for you. You're clever and popular and kind and—'

'I love you, Mum,' he blurts out, quickly wiping his cheek with a hand.

'I love you too Eddie.' I grab a less-than-fragrant tea towel to blot my own face. 'And I'm so pleased for you.'

'So can you or Dad give me a lift over to Edinburgh tomorrow?'

'Yes, of course. After work, if that's all right?'

'Yeah, great.' He's smiling now, flushed and happy, his dark eyes sparkling. 'So you can stop worrying about me now, okay? 'Cause everything's gonna be all right.'

I look at my son, hardly able to believe this is happening. No more dropped, wet towels and samosa cartons left in his wake! Of course he'll be all right. And we will be too, as empty nesters. It's what we've yearned for, Frank and I.

What could possibly go wrong?

Is he just a summer fling?
Or the one she's been waiting for . . .

A hilarious and heart-warming tale of second
chance love, perfect for fans of Sophie Kinsella
and Kristen Bailey.